AUXILIARY

AUXILIARY

—— LONDON 2039 ——

JON RICHTER

TCK PUBLISHING.COM

ISBN: 978-1-63161-075-2

Sign up for Jon Richter's newsletter at
www.jon-richter.com/free

Published by TCK Publishing
www.TCKpublishing.com

Get discounts and special deals on books at
www.TCKpublishing.com/bookdeals

Check out additional discounts for bulk orders at
www.TCKpublishing.com/bulk-book-orders

For Shuo, the lady who made me believe in the future.

ONE

THE DOOR SAGGED INWARDS, AND the detective wrinkled his nose at the stench before he even crossed the threshold. It was an old-fashioned manual lock, so he'd had to kick it open. His boot had gone straight through the wood on his first attempt, and he was lucky not to have injured himself. The only wound was to his pride; at least he was working alone.

He thought about Gupta, his old partner, who would have roared with laughter. But it was three years since two-man teams were deemed "an inefficient use of resources," and now his only companion was the TIM avatar that accompanied him everywhere, its glowing dot hovering at the top right corner of his FOV like an irradiated insect.

He clicked the spex to infrared mode, but they only confirmed what the stink had already told him: There was nothing alive beyond the door. He flicked the view back to normal and stepped into the apartment, covering his mouth and nose with the sleeve of his coat. He was in a tiny hallway area, a single passage with three doors along the right-hand wall: some combination of a bathroom, a bedroom, and a kitchen/living room. At his side were two empty metal bowls and a shoe rack containing a few pairs of battered trainers.

At the other end of the corridor was a strange, black shape, like a blanket tossed onto the floor. He stopped when he noticed it, sensing movement, and had the uncomfortable sensation that the misshapen lump was watching him. Then, as a swarm of flies detached and began to buzz frantically around the body, he realised that, in a sense, he had been right. He stepped towards the frenzied mass, trying to examine the congealed blob of putrid flesh and hair they had been feasting on. It was an animal, perhaps once a dog.

Dremmler grimaced and stepped away from the carcass to check the first two doorways. A nondescript bathroom followed by a nondescript bedroom, both unclean but uncluttered. The contents suggested a male occupant, which was unsurprising, because he already knew that 34-year-old Shawn Ambrose lived there: an unemployed roboticist whose apparent disappearance was the reason for Dremmler's visit.

Unemployed roboticist. Dremmler snorted. The eggheads that built machines to take everybody's jobs had been surprised when their machines built machines that could take theirs. A workforce of self-maintaining, self-enhancing automata. He supposed it wouldn't be long before his own role was deemed an inefficient use of resources, too.

Fuck you, TIM.

The flies continued to teem, swirling like bubbles in boiling liquid. Dremmler batted them away, noticing a collar jutting from the rotting mess on the floor as he stepped past it. He didn't bother to read the animal's name. He wondered how long Ambrose had left it trapped in the hallway, whining for food.

He stepped into the living room and found Ambrose at his desk, connected to a sizeable rig by a cheap neural cap and gloves. At some point the poor bastard's emaciated body had slipped out of the leather chair, and Ambrose's skeletal frame now knelt in front of the impressive console as though in supplication.

The scene was exactly what Dremmler had expected to find.

He observed the sad spectacle for a moment, allowing his eyes to drift around the rest of the squalid chamber. Dirty dishes and decaying takeaway cartons were heaped all around the kitchenette and piled on the coffee table. The bin was overflowing, its lid propped open like an invitation to the flies. The apartment's rank odour was intensified by the closed windows and drawn blinds, and also because Ambrose had pissed and shit himself, like they always did. Dremmler's theory was that AltWorlders did it well before death, no longer aware of even the most basic realities of their bodies as they slipped deeper into irresistible fantasy.

Amongst the detritus on the coffee table was a picture of a woman. She looked a lot older than Ambrose; his mother, maybe, rather than a girlfriend. Like so many other AltWorld addicts, Ambrose probably had no need for a girlfriend in Standard Reality (Dremmler still liked to think of anything outside of virtual or augmented reality as "real life," though the distinction probably hadn't mattered to Ambrose by the end). In a way, it was as though the young man had died in the embrace of a lover.

TIM stood for "The Imagination Machine." It hadn't seemed like a game-changer when it had been quietly released by the Imagination Corporation twelve years previous, at least not to Dremmler. It was simply a logical next step, a "one stop shop" that brought together office applications, email, social media, an enhanced personal organiser that was, as the company's marketing eloquently put it, "like Alexa on steroids." Video gaming, on-demand television, information searches, holiday bookings, shopping, dating, movies, music: TIM was a single interface for the entire online, AR/VR experience. "Need anything? Ask TIM" was its slogan, with a logo depicting a likeable, buck-toothed nerd emerging from a genie's lamp.

With alarming, almost insidious speed, TIM had become ubiquitous; the go-to OS for almost everything. It flew the planes. It drove the cars. It answered your queries when you contacted customer services. It controlled the robotic surgeons that performed life-saving operations. It filed your tax returns. It delivered your food. It selected your music. It read your children bedtime stories.

And it ran the AltWorld. Whatever you wanted to see, or be, or do, or feel, or fuck. Real life had been made obsolete.

Since the online playground had gone live, deaths like Ambrose's were becoming increasingly frequent. A complete detachment from reality, an addiction to the game world resulting in a chronic neglect of one's own body, causing death by thirst or malnutrition or disease. There was even a name for it: *Disengagement.* Some AltWorlders did it on purpose, as a sort of blissful assisted suicide.

Dremmler's gaze came to rest once again on the young man's back. The shapes of his protruding ribs looked like the rungs of a ladder; a short climb from the toxic sludge of this existence to something else, towards some other oblivion.

Then the light in the corner of his eye pulsed red, and the pitiful tableau was obscured by the words "incoming call."

TWO

OUTSIDE, THE LATE AFTERNOON SKY was a utilitarian off-white, like untreated plastic.

Dremmler had notified the station of his findings; they would send a separate crew, probably remote-controlled robots, to collect the body and clean up the place.

More accurately, he had notified TIM, and TIM would dispatch the machines directly. Then TIM had given him his next assignment. No need for his DCI to speak with him. Minimal human contact. Those sorts of interactions were an inefficient use of resources.

Obsolete.

He was sitting in a one-person Pod, heading towards northeast London in a procession of similar ovoid vehicles. He remembered what driving had once been like, his siren blaring as he weaved deftly between the lanes. Now, there was no need for him to travel any faster than the other traffic; all the vehicles moved at a uniform, optimal speed, unencumbered by jams or unanticipated roadworks or errors of human judgement. He preferred the new models that had no steering wheel at all, unlike the early Pods where the wheel had moved by itself as if the car was being driven by a fucking poltergeist. The journey was being soundtracked by tepid chillout, as though TIM could detect his mood.

"Play some Nine Inch Nails," Dremmler snapped. Moments later, he was listening to *The Downward Spiral*. He almost laughed.

At least this assignment might be a little more interesting than collecting roadkill: Someone had apparently attacked a postbot with an axe in Walthamstow. He could sympathise with the perpetrator; the robots were horrible, multilegged things resembling the mechanical hybrid of a mule and a spider. They delivered packages to various addresses twenty-four hours a day, usually food orders now that the online retailers had driven the supermarkets out of business. Attacking a robot was a crime, of course. Destruction of private property or, to be more exact, destruction of the property of Leggit Logistics.

After the demise of the Post Office, the online retailers had initially owned their own competing fleets of postbots, all different types and designs, including flying models, before private ownership of drones had been banned. At one point, a couple of suspicious malfunctions had led people to believe that the more unscrupulous delivery firms were actively programming their bots to sabotage those of their rivals—Robot Wars, the pundits called it. But nothing was ever proven, and market forces had gradually hammered the industry into its current shape, monopolised by the cheap and reliable service of Leggit and their sinister metal arachnids.

Dremmler wondered if they'd reach a point where people were so desperate for work that it would become cheaper to employ them than the machines once again. The gig economy was already thriving, with people willing to perform a variety of menial jobs to scrape together a bit of extra money on top of their Universal Basic Income. But the available vacancies were dwindling all the time; taxi, haulage, and delivery drivers had been the most recent casualties, with recent legislation making it illegal for anyone to drive on the roads except for the Pods themselves.

The car disgorged him on the corner of Fulbourne Street and Forest Road, where crumbling terraced houses leaned forlornly against each other as if for comfort. Retail units at their bases hawked kebabs and fried chicken, an endless stream of delivery bots laden with greasy takeaway orders parading in and out. Everything you needed, brought to your door; TIM had made leaving the house almost totally unnecessary.

But today the crossroads was busier than usual. A small crowd had gathered on the open, paved corner that served as a sort of small-scale plaza for this part of town, with a rusted clock and a dried-up water feature. At the centre of the group, Dremmler could see a man hacking at something with an axe, shouting and cursing as he swung the weapon. Some of the congregation were cheering, while others were there to laugh and film the scene, doubtless livestreaming it through their spex.

Dremmler approached quietly, wanting to observe the crowd for a moment before announcing who he was. The man in its centre was in late middle age, meaty and bald and red-faced, sweating profusely in the summer heat as he heaved the axe again and again.

"Fucking ... piece of ... shit!" he spat as he swung, seemingly unaware of the assembled onlookers. At his feet, the postbot twitched and writhed like something dying. Groceries had tumbled out of the bags it carried, fruit and eggs and canned food rolling around on the paving stones. The jerking of its mechanical limbs made Dremmler feel a mix of revulsion and pity.

"All right, that's enough!" he barked. "I'm a policeman, and I need you all to step away."

The throng turned towards him and instantly parted, fragmenting and then re-forming into a wider circle that absorbed Dremmler into its centre, like a simple organism consuming a morsel of food. None of them moved on; they wanted to see what would happen next. He hoped he wouldn't have to use his Taser. Instead he clicked his spex, and the name *Brian Taylor* appeared above the agitated man's head, a little arrow pointing down towards his glistening pate.

Taylor ignored Dremmler, yelling something incoherent as he hefted the axe once more.

"Mr. Taylor!" Dremmler shouted. The man finally looked up, and Dremmler realised Taylor was not wearing any spex at all. Perhaps he was one of the anti-automation weirdos, the activists who rejected technology and sabotaged robots and AIs whenever they could. Shit, he could even be from the Human Right, in which case Dremmler might have to take him down after all.

"What seems to be the problem here, sir?" he asked evenly, one hand dropping to the holster at his side as he approached.

Taylor inhaled and exhaled heavily, blinking at Dremmler as though suddenly confused. The mutilated robot at his feet wriggled its legs like an injured crab. "Fuck off, copper," he said eventually, his expression hardening in determination. "This is between me and the machine."

"I can see that. It looks like you're winning."

"Winning? I ain't winning nuffink. I used to be a delivery driver. I haven't worked in five years 'cos of these metal fuckers."

"You get your allowance though, don't you, Mr. Taylor? A lot of people used to dream about early retirement."

"You call that retirement? We get a fucking pittance! I've got three kids, yer know."

"Older than ten?"

Taylor's jaw tightened, and he gripped the axe as though he was trying to snap the shaft. "Only one of 'em," he growled.

"Then that was your choice, wasn't it? You knew the rules."

At its introduction, the most controversial aspect of Universal Basic Income had been the Circle Party's policy concerning children. If an additional allowance had been granted for each newborn, their concern was that there would be a baby boom, with people growing their families to drive up their household income. Conversely, if UBI was only granted to adults, they'd be accused of unfairly penalising the families that already had children at the point of its introduction.

So the government had decreed that the benefit would be paid to everyone currently alive in the UK, plus any immigrants over the age of 16 whose application to reside in the UK was accepted. However, any children born after 2029 would not receive the benefit until they reached 16 years old.

April 1, 2029 became known as the day children were banned.

"I had a job then. How was I supposed to know that these fucking monsters would steal it from me?" Taylor spat at the mangled wreck of the postbot and hoisted the axe high.

Dremmler unsheathed the Taser. "Mr. Taylor, if you do that one more time, I am going to have to incapacitate you."

Taylor's eyes blazed, the axe frozen above his head as though he was trying to attract lightning. "You fucking pigs care more about the machines than us," he snarled, and Dremmler heard a few murmurs of agreement from the crowd. He glanced around, worried for the first time, and with his free hand manipulated the buttons on the left temple of his glasses. Two messages appeared in his FOV, acknowledging the requests. He gripped the Taser with both hands, steadying it as he took aim at Taylor's expansive midriff.

"Mr. Taylor, that postbot is private property. You are committing an act of vandalism, and I am going to have to arrest you. Now, please put down the axe and come with me."

Taylor held his defiant pose for what felt like an entire minute, his eyes fixed on the Taser. Then something inside him seemed to break, and his body sagged like a deflating balloon. The axe clattered to the ground. Wordlessly, Dremmler approached him, scooping up the weapon and placing him in handcuffs.

The custody Pod Dremmler had requested had already pulled up nearby, but the crowd still hadn't broken up, and a cluster of men stood between them and the vehicle. When Dremmler moved towards the group, one of them stepped forwards, puffing out his muscular chest.

"I think he's got a point."

The spex projected the man's bio above his head. *Michael Lafferty; convictions include ABH, petty theft, and identity fraud.* Dremmler had the axe in one hand and his prisoner in the other. He would have to let go of one in order to reach for the Taser again, but that would take time, and he'd allowed the youth to close the distance. "Sir, please move out of my way," he said firmly, trying not to let concern enter his voice.

"Make me," retorted Lafferty, his eyes glinting dangerously.

Dremmler licked his dry lips, working out his options. Then a whirring noise sounded overhead, and he breathed a sigh of relief.

"Desist immediately," blared the drone in a pre-recorded female voice. Its rotors sliced the air so fast that the space around it seemed to shriek. "You have been warned."

Lafferty looked up at the hovering device, resentment and rage twisting his face. Then he spat at Dremmler's feet and stepped aside.

Dremmler bundled Taylor into the Pod and climbed in across from him. As the door hissed shut, he heard the drone's clipped tones continuing to issue instructions. "Do not loiter here. A crime has been committed. Police are on their way."

He watched through the window as the Pod pulled away. The remnants of the crowd were gathering up some of the food that the brutalised postbot had spilled, ignoring the drone's repeated commands. He glanced across at Taylor, who was staring blankly down at the floor as though he might burst into tears.

THREE

TAYLOR WAS QUIET AND OBEDIENT while he was processed at the station. He'd be released soon, but the fine would hardly help the man's financial situation. The rest of Dremmler's day petered out in a haze of virtual paperwork, until at six p.m. he headed home, this time having to share a multiPod with an assortment of other Zone 3 citizens that were lucky enough to have a job to commute home from.

He remembered when the London Underground, now defunct, had been the city's preferred method of travel, with people crammed into the carriages like tinned meat. Now it was usually possible to get a seat on the multiPods, even at peak times. He spent most of the twenty-minute journey sitting opposite a young woman who was sporting the currently fashionable hairstyle known as a "mane": head almost completely shaved aside from a Mohawk strip grown long and hanging down her back. In this case, it was dyed a bright, platinum blonde that contrasted jarringly with her olive skin—probably tanning injections, but it might have been natural, he supposed.

It was warm, and she was wearing short shorts, and Dremmler could discern the swell of her ample breasts beneath her sleeveless top. Above her head floated her name, *Kendra Kerr*, which had a nice alliterative ring to it. The spex also informed him that she worked in marketing, was bisexual, currently single, twenty-three years old, and had no criminal convictions. He wondered if she knew that her public bio was set to this level of disclosure, decided that she probably did, and felt a stirring in his trousers.

You're old enough to be her dad, Carl. She's looking for pretty young things to spend her time with, not a washed-up old plod like you.

She got off at the stop before him, and his gaze followed her, along with the text floating above her head. The words lingered for a few seconds even after she had disappeared into the grey smear of the evening. The ongoing crusade against carbon emissions—even the multiPods were now fully electric—didn't seem to be having any effect on the encroaching smog.

The doors slid shut and he was moving again. He closed his eyes and tried to forget about Kendra Kerr, because he knew that he would only end up thinking about his wife, which in turn would make him think about Natalie.

He disembarked a stop later than usual, deciding the walk would do him good—or maybe he just wasn't in a hurry to return to the lifeless anonymity of his apartment. He trudged a couple of blocks, glancing up at the windows of the buildings he passed, wondering how many of those rooms contained someone hooked up to the AltWorld. Perhaps some of them were already dead, like Ambrose and his dog, decaying gradually into insect food.

There wasn't another soul outside on the street. He drifted home like a scrap of litter missed by the roadsweeping bots, blown along by the breeze.

His apartment building was administered by TIM, which recognised his face and granted him access automatically as he approached the main doors. He was welcomed into the lift by a friendly male voice that represented one of the OS's myriad different incarnations; the doors closed and he was whisked upstairs, ejected on the eighteenth floor. As he walked the final few steps of his commute, he couldn't shake the feeling of being "processed," as though he was a morsel of food and the hallways of Applewood Grove were a huge mechanical bowel, digesting him.

His apartment door yawned open as he drew near, like an expectant mouth.

"Hi, Carl," beamed Connie as he stepped inside. She was wearing her French maid's outfit, waiting in the hallway where she had perhaps been performing some rudimentary cleaning task. Or maybe she had just been standing there, motionless, for hours. Sometimes he thought about switching her off during the day, but he liked the illusion of company when he arrived home, of *something* that was pleased to see him. But that night, he couldn't even bring himself to return her greeting. He pushed past her into the living room, sagging into the shapeless brown couch that resembled an extracted, diseased organ.

Connie shuffled after him, her steps careful and methodical given the difficulty she would have in standing back up again if she fell over. "Would you like a beer?" she asked in the Eastern European accent he had selected.

"Yeah," he grunted, and watched as she pottered over to the fridge. With her usual precise movements, she extracted a can of Coors and cracked open the ring-pull.

"Would you like me to pour it for you?"

"Definitely not," he replied, remembering the recent incident where she had calmly tipped an entire can all over the rug, missing the glass by centimetres. It was his fault for not recalibrating her for months.

The robot made its way daintily across from the kitchenette and bent to hand him the drink. The motion, her body hinging perfectly at the waist, looked odd and uncomfortable.

"Would you like me to sit with you?" she asked.

"No," he replied, staring at the TV screen that took up the entirety of the opposite wall. Sometimes they watched movies together, but he wasn't in the mood. It was possible to watch films directly via the spex, fully immersed in 360-degree action, but Dremmler liked to take his glasses off at the end of the day. They rested on the nearby coffee table, lenses angled in his direction as though watching him.

"Would you like a blow job?"

He sighed, thinking of Kendra Kerr. He wasn't a bad-looking man, he supposed, and he was in decent physical shape. But when young women (the kind he liked, the kind that looked like Connie, with her wide face and sensuous lips) looked at him, he didn't know what they saw—at best a fatherish figure, at worst a creepy old man.

"Yeah, okay."

She knelt down between his legs, and he slouched backwards, trying not to think too hard about what was happening. It wasn't the fact that he was fucking an appliance that bothered him. It was the fact that, behind Connie's big, beautiful eyes, lurked the cold, looming intelligence of TIM.

Need anything? Ask TIM.

He sipped his beer and stared at the black void of the TV screen, into the eyes of his own darkened reflection.

FOUR

"**C**ARL. CARL. WAKE UP," TESSA was saying.

"Go back to sleep, sweetheart," Dremmler replied, rolling over and hiding his head beneath the pillow.

But she persisted. "It's important, Carl. You need to wake up now." Her voice was clear and emotionless, as though she was rehearsing the lines for one of her plays.

"What ... what's going on, angel?"

He dragged his eyes open, expecting to be greeted by Tessa's freckled face, her sand-coloured hair.

Instead he found a tall brunette sitting bolt upright at his side, staring down at him with eyes the colour of electricity. He almost screamed, but managed to control himself as his brain reordered the fragments of his memory into a dismal whole.

Tessa left you years ago.

You made your sex robot sleep with you last night.

Because you're fucking pathetic.

"Carl, there's a call coming through," Connie was saying. "You need to take it."

Beneath her voice was a buzzing sound that he realised was coming from the unit at his bedside. Its display told him that it was 3:20 in the morning.

Cursing, he clambered across the robot, who remained completely stock-still, and pressed the receive button. A gravelly Welsh-accented voice was immediately piped through the room's speakers.

"Carl?"

"Maggie?" he slurred.

"I need you down here, now."

"What? Where?"

"An address in Leytonstone. A woman's been killed."

"It's not often I speak to you these days, boss," he replied groggily as he hauled himself out of bed. "I assume TIM can't handle this one?"

The DCI was silent, the shallow rasp of her breathing sounding unsettling as it echoed in Dremmler's tiny bedroom. She had smoked all her life, right up until the ban had been introduced five years ago.

"There are ... sensitivities," she said eventually. "I've sent a Pod for you. I'll brief you when you arrive."

The call ended.

"Would you like some breakfast?" asked Connie, still watching him with her ice-blue stare. He ignored her as he hauled on his clothes and stumbled wearily out of the room.

He tried to contact Maggie during the short journey, but she ignored his calls. It wasn't like the DCI to keep him guessing; over their years of working together they had always been frank with each other. He felt a twinge of apprehension as he stared out of the Pod's window into the emptiness of the night.

His destination was an apartment block similar to his own, but older and more run-down. An old-fashioned manual fob system was still in use, and Margaret Evans was leaning against the main door, holding it open while she drew deeply on an electronic cigarette. Swathed in fruit-scented smoke, her dark skin, dark glasses, and dark trench coat made her look like a shadow beset by ghosts. A drone hovered nearby like an omen.

"What's this about, Maggie?" Dremmler asked, not attempting to mask the irritation in his voice.

She exhaled a long plume of vapour. "Follow me," she replied, and turned to head into the building. He felt a strange sense of liberty upon entering a space that wasn't administered by TIM. But then, TIM was never truly absent. It was inside their glasses, its eyes staring right back into theirs.

"The lift's out," Maggie explained as she led them to the stairs. "Luckily it's only on the third floor."

She wheezed and gasped as they ascended, but still managed to set a brisk pace up the staircase. Soon they emerged into a grubby hallway where a malfunctioning strip light blinked on and off in staccato binary. He followed her past the flickering bulb towards the entrance to Apartment 35.

As she placed a withered hand on the handle, she stopped and turned to him. "Carl, this is a bad one. But I needed you to see it first, before I tried to explain."

"Maggie, you know the shit I've seen. I'm pretty sure I'm as shockproof as they come."

"I know that. But still … take a deep breath."

He frowned as she pushed open the door. The apartment was similar to Ambrose's, similar to his own, similar to everyone's: a soulless cube for human storage. The bulb in the hallway was a low wattage, as though the occupant was photophobic. Maggie sucked on her e-cigarette again as she led them towards the door to what turned out to be the living room. Still frowning, Dremmler followed her inside.

The room was surprisingly large, but any sense of space was undermined by the amount of mess that had accumulated within it; too much furniture had been crammed in, and ornaments adorned every available surface. Chairs were covered with piles of clothes, the walls dominated by shelves full of ancient books, CDs, and DVDs. Whoever lived here was clearly a retro enthusiast. Dremmler couldn't make out the titles of the archaic volumes because the living room was even darker than the hall: the fitting and bulb from the central light had shattered into fragments strewn across the wooden floor. The illumination came instead from a pair of portable spotlights that had been set up and aimed at the wall as though pointed towards a performer taking centre stage.

But this was not a live show—it was a tableau. Maybe the most brutal he'd ever seen.

A woman's head had been crushed into the wall, which had cracked and crumbled around it. She was suspended about a foot from the floor by the arm of her attacker: a muscular, titanium HET prosthetic, its fingers clamped tightly around her face. The limb had been severed at the shoulder and was left jutting straight out into the room, as though the woman had died wearing some sort of bizarre headgear.

She was slim and dressed in gym clothes. He tried to imagine her face in life, but could only picture the mangled ruin that was doubtless hidden beneath the palm of the mechanical appendage that had killed her. Clumps of her dark hair protruded between its fingers, dark blood oozing out and drip-drip-dripping onto the floor.

"Fuck me," Dremmler managed eventually. "Who is she?"

There was no bio hovering above her head, because there was nothing for his spex to interface with; no face to recognise, any spex or other implant she was using mashed into the wreckage of her skull and the surrounding brickwork.

"Letitia Karlikowska. She's a teaching auxiliary. This is her apartment."

"Who found her?"

"Her boyfriend called us. *While the arm was still attached.*"

"You mean he caught the attacker in the act?"

Maggie shook her head, drawing more nicotine out of her smoking substitute. "The boyfriend was the one who did it."

"What?"

"We have him in custody. I want you to interrogate him."

Dremmler continued to stare at the body. This woman had been killed with such violence, such incandescent rage. "He nearly decapitates his girlfriend, then he calls to hand himself in? And then, what, cuts his own arm off? He sounds like a piece of work."

Maggie drew a long pull on the e-cig, the swirling vapour almost hiding her face from view. "That's the fun part. He's saying he didn't do it. He's saying it was the arm."

Dremmler turned and blinked at her. "He's ... what?"

Maggie nodded. "He's saying his arm was *hacked*, Carl. One minute they're cuddling and kissing on the couch ... the next he's splattering her all over her living room wall. He says he had no control over the prosthetic at all."

Dremmler's mouth moved silently while he processed the implications of this. Now he understood the secrecy, the worry in Maggie's voice. Human Enhancement Technology was a billion-pound industry in Britain alone. Around 5% of the population had HET implants— "hetties," they were called—but that percentage was rising every year.

"How … did he get the arm off?"

"He didn't. He was still standing there when we arrived, screaming and crying, absolutely hysterical. Said he couldn't move it. Petrovic had to saw it off at the shoulder."

Dremmler stared at the severed limb. Originally designed for amputees, they had become increasingly popular with people who had other long-standing issues like arthritis or reduced mobility, or even those who simply didn't like their bodies and wanted to modify them.

To upgrade.

Augmentations like this were controlled directly via a brain implant; naturally, this hardware and its interfaces were run by TIM.

"I need this kept completely quiet, Carl," Maggie was saying. "The system dispatched me personally. The only people who know about this are me, Petrovic, and you."

"What's the boyfriend's name?"

"McCann."

"And you want me to find out if he's telling the truth," Dremmler summarised, unnecessarily.

"Yes," Maggie replied, her tone measured. "Because you and I know that TIM is unhackable. Therefore McCann is lying. And if he won't confess to you, I'm going to have to cut his head open to interrogate his fucking microchip."

She exhaled another cloud of smoke, filling the grisly tomb with the sweet scent of blueberries.

FiVE

CONOR MCCANN WAS A SORRY sight. A thirty-six-year-old personal trainer, he had a tautly muscular frame that spoke of countless hours invested in the gym. Now, imprisoned within the grubby beige walls of the interrogation room, he was hunched forwards, rocking gently, pawing at the stump of his missing right arm. His gaze was fixed at a point on the grimy steel of the table, his spex removed, eyes red-rimmed and haunted. The hologram of his solicitor, a young, good-looking East Asian woman, hovered at his shoulder.

Dremmler entered and withdrew the seat opposite McCann, sitting soundlessly for a whole minute. When McCann showed no sign of acknowledging him, he finally spoke.

"Hello, Conor."

McCann just rocked and pawed and stared.

"I know this must be awful for you," Dremmler continued. "And I know you've already spoken to one police officer tonight. I read your statement. But I wanted to talk to you myself, because I think I can help." He leaned forwards in his chair, lowering his voice to an almost conspiratorial whisper. "I'm afraid, Conor, that you're in a lot of trouble."

The last sentence seemed to break through, McCann stiffening briefly before he continued to squirm in his seat.

"Remember that … don't have to … anything else, Con … " said the solicitor in a North American accent, possibly Canadian. After every few words her speech fragmented, and she flickered like a broken lightbulb; their holographic projector was clearly on the blink again.

Dremmler ignored her and continued. "I'm looking at your statement right now, Conor," he said, manipulating his spex theatrically. "I can see that you're saying your arm suddenly went crazy and grabbed Letitia. I bet you called her Tish, didn't you?"

McCann shuddered as he was rent by a single, choking sob. He nodded.

"Okay, now we're getting somewhere. That's good, Conor. It'll be better for you if you talk to me. You might not get another chance."

McCann slowly lifted his eyes, a small gesture of trust.

Got him, Dremmler thought.

"Conor, my adv … you is that you refuse to … any further … " The solicitor's image dropped out entirely for a second, and when it reappeared she was momentarily zoomed-in, a huge disembodied head floating in the air beside her client.

"Where did you get the arm, Conor?"

Dremmler already knew that it had been purchased from Augmentech three months previous, but he wanted to get McCann talking.

"I bought it online." The prisoner's voice trembled like a flimsy barricade. "I had to go to a factory to get it fitted."

Dremmler had seen those places. The surgery was performed by robots. A production line of humans, queueing to allow machines to mutilate them. He shuddered.

"Do you mind me asking how you lost your real arm?"

McCann paused, then made a little shrugging gesture. His solicitor's giant face had completely frozen, like a buffering image on an old computer screen.

"I didn't lose it. I had a muscular condition that meant I couldn't … it was weak. So I decided to have it removed and replaced." He suddenly began to laugh, mirthless and overwrought. "Look where my vanity got me."

Dremmler thought about McCann's old arm, passed on to some unfortunate amputee who couldn't afford an expensive prosthetic. Human body parts were becoming unwanted hand-me-downs, like second-hand jackets.

"Don't worry about that, Conor. Augmentech sells a lot of these. You're hardly the first person to make that decision." He made another show of flicking through web pages with his glasses. "You know, it says here that last year alone they sold over half a million units. And that's just the basic model, not even including the specially adapted ones for climbing, sculpture, handling chemicals … "

McCann nodded, looking confused.

"My point is, there are an awful lot of these on the market. If you factor in all of Augmentech's competitors, there must be four million people walking around with these things grafted on. Imagine that, eh?" Dremmler smiled at McCann as though he had made a very insightful point. He let it sink in for a few seconds before he continued. "And you know what, Conor?"

McCann shook his head, a fearful look entering his eyes. Dremmler stared into them, his expression suddenly hardening. "Not one single arm has ever attacked a person before. A few malfunctions, yes, a few lock-ups, that goes without saying. But you are the first person in recorded history to have their right arm grow a mind of its own. What do you think about that?"

A look of betrayal twisted McCann's expression.

"Don't respond … Conor … " stuttered the solicitor, her image glitching and contorting disturbingly. McCann's pupils darted from side to side, his eyes looking as though they wanted to escape their sockets altogether and make a break for freedom.

"I'll tell you what I think, Conor." Now Dremmler was on a roll. "I think you'll have a very, very hard time convincing a jury that that's what happened. A pretty, popular young girl, her head smashed open like a melon, her killer found at the scene. No cameras in the apartment of course, but a pretty extensive piece of circumstantial evidence nonetheless, wouldn't you say?"

McCann had resumed his rocking, fastening his gaze back on the same point in the centre of the table as though he was considering driving his head into it.

"I think this one won't be a long court case at all," Dremmler continued, driving home his point with cruel emphasis. "You'll go to prison. For life. After all, no one's going to convict a piece of metal, are they? When someone batters his wife to death for the insurance money, they don't send the baseball bat to jail, am I right?"

McCann looked like he was about to be sick. Next to her client, the solicitor's image seemed to have lost its connection again, frozen in place like a bizarre, levitating statue.

"Anyway—listen to me rambling on. Thanks for your patience, Conor. I'm getting to the point now, I promise. This is where I think I can help you. The one surefire way to avoid decades rotting in a nasty cell—and those places really are nasty, I can assure you, Conor, much worse than you see on Spexflix—is to change your statement. Plead guilty. This whole process will be so much better for you."

"Don't say anything, Conor," hissed the solicitor, her connection restored. McCann was shaking his head rapidly as though trying to dispel a bothersome insect.

"Conor, I know this is a lot for you to process. You and Tish had an argument. I don't know you two or your relationship, but I'm sure there are two sides to it. I'm sure you were just angry, and you didn't mean to—"

"No!" McCann suddenly screamed, knocking his seat to the floor as he leapt to his feet. "It wasn't me! It was the arm! Why won't you people fucking *listen*?!"

"CONOR, I ADVISE YOU TO RETAKE YOUR SEAT," shrieked his solicitor, something now seemingly wrong with the volume setting. Dremmler winced and fiddled with the control unit, admiring the hologram once again as he did so. She was just an AI construct, not necessarily modelled on a person who had ever really existed; either way, at least she gave him something nice to look at while they were stuck in here. Nicer, at least, than the maimed figure of McCann, who was pacing from wall to wall like a caged animal.

It seemed as though they might be here for some time.

SiX

"**es, but do _you_ believe** him?"

Petrovic was slurring ver words slightly, jabbing Dremmler in the chest with ver index finger as ve spoke. Ve was holding ver lager in the same hand, and the sober part of Dremmler was worried that ve was going to slosh it all over him. The drunk part couldn't care less, and was studying his colleague's pretty face, trying to work out what gender Petrovic had been before becoming a neut.

"Honestly, I couldn't care less, T."

Petrovic liked ver first name to be shortened to a single letter; everyone in the station had bets on what it stood for, ranging from the plausible-sounding Tanek or Tatjana to Trevor, Tupac, or even just Trouble.

"The chief is convinced he's guilty, so it's my job to get a confession out of him. Tough bugger to break down, though. Still, I can't imagine they'll refuse the warrant application—so tomorrow we should be able to extract his control chip for testing. If he was hacked like he says he was, there'll be a record on it of the unusual activity."

"Unless the hacker can cover their tracks somehow," Petrovic retorted, draining ver beer. "Fancy another?"

"Aye, go on." It wasn't like Connie would lecture him for coming home late—although there was a mode you could activate if you liked that sort of thing. "And anyway, this isn't the fucking twentieth century. Hacking doesn't exist. TIM killed that industry with its cognitive defence loops or whatever they're called. There's a nice symmetry about it in a way: The machines putting the nerds out of business."

Petrovic laughed, ver deep voice and accent sounding pleasantly exotic in the otherwise squalid pub. Dremmler had no idea why Petrovic liked coming here; there were dozens of better bars nearby, including quite a few neut ones. He had a feeling that his six-foot-two colleague, whose heavy build and long mane of blonde hair made ver look like some sort of Viking warrior, was just daring the locals to give ver a bit of grief.

Petrovic signalled the barbot, which was busy serving a ruddy-faced man who looked as though he'd been down here drinking for a solid week. The mechanoid was the most interesting thing about the shithole: instead of the self-service taps that most places now used, The Sickly Parrot had a proper robot, attached by dozens of tubes to every single pump and bottle, as though the whole bar was acting as some sort of grotesque life-support mechanism. It had no legs and couldn't turn from side to side—it simply slid creakily across to them when it was their turn, a Texan accent blaring from the speaker in the centre of its face. The actual face itself, an eerie plastic grin that had always given Dremmler the creeps, had been smashed off years ago, but at least someone had had the decency to buy the robot a new cowboy hat.

"How can I help ya, pardner?" the monstrosity drawled.

Petrovic ordered two more lagers, and the machine extracted two pint glasses from under the bar with crude, pincer-like hands, filling them from nozzles attached to another extruded pair of limbs. The effect was something akin to watching a boozy, robotic octopus. Petrovic used the chip in ver hand to pay for the drinks; Dremmler knew he was in an increasingly small minority by not having one installed, but implants had always freaked him out.

Especially after the previous night.

"Well, I believe him," Petrovic said as ve slid Dremmler's pint across to him. "He was an absolute wreck when I arrived, shrieking and screaming like he was having a nightmare. If he meant to kill her, even just in the moment … why would he call the police and then stand there waiting for us?"

Dremmler shrugged. "Short-term memory loss? Overcome with guilt? Total fucking fruitcake?"

"You're a cold man, Drem. Is Maggie pissed off with you for not cracking him yet?"

"She'd better bloody well not be. I was in that room all fucking day, *and* I only had about three hours sleep last night."

"I suppose that means you'll be crying off early tonight then?" Petrovic wiggled ver eyebrows mischievously.

Dremmler chewed his lip for a second, feeling old and tired. Then he drained his pint in one long gulp. "Nah, fuck it. Let's go out."

A wide grin spread across Petrovic's face. "That's the spirit!"

After a few more drinks near the station, Petrovic decided they were going to a place in Shoreditch, so they hopped in a Pod.

"Doesn't it worry you?" Dremmler mused as they travelled.

"What?"

"You're saying you believe McCann. But that means you believe implants can be hacked. You've got some, too."

Petrovic shrugged. "I've got a chip in my hand to pay for my booze and a chip in my jaw that regulates my collagen flow. If someone hacked me, the worst that could happen would be that I'd be bone broke with incredible lips."

Dremmler laughed.

"Anyway, cheer up, Drem—I'm taking you to Sightjacked."

"What the hell is Sightjacked?"

"It's a nightclub. You remember those, from before you were an old man?"

"Yes, I think I can recall such places in the distant shadows of my memory."

"Good. Although this will be a bit different from what you're used to, I think."

"Oh, God, it isn't some weird neut place is it?"

Petrovic ignored him, hopping excitedly out of the car as it pulled over. Dremmler followed ver, looking up at a starless, grimy sky, the colour of ash. The tangle of buildings around him reached up towards it like weeds competing for sunlight.

He followed Petrovic down claustrophobic streets, past overflowing bins and knots of people enjoying drinking and vaping and God knew what else on their Wednesday night; at least their experiences were real, thought Dremmler, not some fantasy dreamt up in their apartment and made real inside the AltWorld. Markers hovered over the entrances to various bars, strip clubs, and late-night eateries: name, closing time, average user rating. Icons in the corners of his FOV told him he had new e-mails and social media feed updates. In the opposite corner floated TIM, an understated, omniscient circle, like an unblinking eye.

It suddenly all felt very … *intrusive*. As though, for years, his brain had been stretched to breaking point trying to process all of these sensory inputs and had suddenly worn itself out, breaking down like an old boiler. He reached up to take his spex off, rubbing at his eyes as his vision blurred.

"You'll need to keep those on in here, pal," Petrovic said to him, halting at the back of a short queue. "That's kind of the whole point."

The club was called Toxicity, and Sightjacked appeared to be a special night run by the resident DJs, Freak and Kaleido. "One does dex, the other does spex" said the strapline on their poster, which was plastered all over the windows as though trying to preserve the mystique of the club's interior.

Dremmler looked at the other people around him: young people sporting coloured manes like Kendra Kerr's; a few old bastards like him, looking as though they'd come straight from the office; two bouncers who looked like thick slabs of meat squeezed into suits. Every one of them was wearing spex.

Logged, branded, barcoded. Like cattle.

He felt a very strange and intense moment of deep, primal fear.

Then he swallowed it down, put the glasses back on, and followed Petrovic into the music, bass thumping like a demonic heartbeat.

They were in some underground warehouse that looked like a nuclear bunker, all concrete and metal and right angles. Freak or Kaleido was squeezed into a corner behind his rig, playing something skull-shuddering (the other one was either stationed elsewhere or out having a vape break). It was busy, not exactly heaving, but with enough people around that Dremmler felt comfortably anonymous. Most of them looked completely spaced out, gazing off towards the ceiling or reaching out to grasp at things that weren't there.

"Is everyone doing fucking Blitz down here, T?"

"Nah, none of that shit mate. You need to tune your glasses to the local station, then you'll see."

"I'll get a drink first. What do you want?"

But Petrovic had evidently already changed the channel. Ve started to dance, ver arms caressing the air as ve stretched upwards, swaying ver hips, lost in whatever hallucinogenic visuals were being pumped into ver pupils.

Dremmler rolled his eyes and wandered over to the bar, the usual modern arrangement where you used a screen to place your order, paying in advance with your chip or, if you were implant-free like Dremmler, an old-fashioned debit card. He ordered a lager (fuck Petrovic, ve could get ver own), and leaned against the wall, watching the assembled revellers.

Why not just engage with it? You're not even the oldest person here. He knew, because he could see most people's ages floating above their heads.

"Scared, Carl?" said a woman's voice in his ear.

He tried not to appear startled, turning to look her up and down in the way you can just about get away with when a stranger approaches you in a bar. She was probably in her thirties (her profile didn't say, which made it all the more likely) and very attractive: a short, dark-haired East Asian woman, probably Chinese—but who the fuck knew any more. She was wearing a white dress that showed off her legs, so pale they were almost the same colour as the fabric. Her name, apparently, was Cynthia Lu.

"Just enjoying a drink before I join the nutters," he replied. "You not enjoying the sights either, Cynthia?"

She stared into his eyes, her gaze painfully direct and earnest behind the spex. He felt as though he was being medically examined.

"Sometimes I just like to take a break and look at what's actually real." She sipped her drink, which could have been anything from mineral water to neat vodka. Why the fuck was she talking to him? Was she a prostitute?

"Err … can I buy you a drink?" he mumbled eventually. She seemed to find this funny.

"You're a policeman, aren't you? I can tell."

He flinched and quickly pressed some buttons on his spex to check his profile was working correctly. She laughed.

"Don't worry, it isn't hovering above your head. There's just something about you people."

Her accent was east-coast American. Educated there perhaps, or maybe born and bred in the States.

"Us people?" he replied, trying to regain his cool.

"Yes. You're all … on the lookout, all the time. You never switch off."

"Have you seen my friend over there? Ve looks pretty switched off to me." Petrovic was standing in a corner of the dancefloor, staring directly upwards and beaming.

"Maybe you should let your hair down too." Her beautiful eyes gleamed as she reached out her hand. He took it, feeling its soft delicacy in his old calloused paw.

As he followed her to join the other revellers, he clicked the spex to the right station, and a cocoon of swirling colours embraced them, washing the rest of the club away. It was just him and her, enveloped in a pulsating fabric of blue and green and silver and magenta and sapphire and emerald and amethyst and finally blue again, a glorious cerulean sky stretching into infinity above them, the sun suspended within it like a droplet of molten gold. Long blades of grass danced around their feet as they gyrated, and the sun sank slowly, its colour bleeding out into the sky in a deep crimson blot like the end of the world, the final gory hemorrhage of the earth, beautiful and brutal and pure violent red, like war, like the womb he had squirmed out of in the dying throes of the twentieth century, like lips, like Cynthia's lips, and he was dancing and drinking with Cynthia, kissing her on top of a snow-capped mountain, staring into a sky so clear and crisp it might have been an ice cube floating in her glass.

"Shall we go back to your place?" she whispered into his ear as he bit at her neck. He ignored her, moving his mouth up to her ear, his tongue darting inside it like a hungry parasite. Still they moved with each other, the music slower now, the visuals darkening into a starlit sky; they floated in it like satellites, drifting together in orbit.

"Why don't we get out of here?" she asked again, pushing him gently away. He stared at her, his erection hard and painful in his trousers.

"What about your place?" he asked. She shook her head. He stared some more. His mouth was suddenly dry. "Okay," he said. "Just let me go and tell my friend."

He turned away from Cynthia, and clicked the glasses back to normal. The beauty of the stars and the blue orb of the earth beneath him flickered out of existence, like a dream interrupted. He was back in the sweaty darkness of the club, surrounded by people, the place busier than before, and he had to push his way between them as he headed for the stairs.

02:34, the clock in the corner of his eye told him as he emerged into the night, a light rain misting against his face as though trying to convince him that, this time, the sky was real. He summoned a Pod and climbed into the white ovoid that dutifully pulled up nearby.

"No music," he muttered as he clambered inside. TIM fulfilled his request like it always did, and the vehicle began its silent journey home.

He sent Petrovic a NowChat message.

Sorry I lost you. Met a girl but she wasn't up for it in the end. See you tomorrow.

Then he took off the spex, massaging his eyes once again. He felt wetness there, which he told himself was caused by eye strain and lack of sleep.

He sank back into his seat, sighing deeply, and watched the rain spattering against the window. The droplets wandering clumsily down the glass looked like little animals searching for something.

The light outside his apartment was flickering when he arrived home, reminding him of Letitia Karlikowska's building.

Her face crushed into the brickwork, obscured behind that powerful claw.

He stepped inside, fumbling for the light switch. "Hi, Carl," said Connie, suddenly illuminated, standing only a few feet away from him.

"For fuck's sake, Connie," he cursed, startled. "You made me jump. I wish you wouldn't always wait in the hallway like that."

He looked at the robot and thought about Cynthia. A real, flesh-and-blood woman who had liked him, not a glorified fucking kettle with tits.

But he didn't want to bring anyone here, not ever. This was his own space, as private as a coffin.

"Would you like a beer?" Connie asked, tilting her head in an affectation of inquisitiveness. He realised with disgust how basic, how unsophisticated she—it—was. He thought about Tessa. Maybe he wouldn't miss her so much if Connie was more lifelike, even by just a little.

"Just go into the living room and power down."

"Yes, Carl," came her reply, and she tottered away without any hint of disappointment or offense or pain.

Dremmler stumbled into the bathroom, ignoring his reflection as he cleaned his teeth. The electric brush felt as though it was scouring the enamel away, grinding him slowly into dust. He lifted his eyes to the mirror, grimacing at the sallow mask that time had carved from his face.

Then the view was obscured by three words, flashing insistently.

INCOMING CALL

TESSA

Gravity inverted inside him. He gripped the sides of the sink, his fingers threatening to crack the porcelain. He closed his eyes, brain and stomach reeling, as the words hovered there.

How could she be calling him?

He missed her so much.

He hated her so much.

He tore the spex from his face, meaning to snap them in two. But his work, his life, his notes, his reminders, his photographs and contact numbers and playlists … they were all stored in the device. The glasses were removable, but they were still a part of him.

With a sad howl of frustration, he hurled them into the corner of the bathroom and vomited into the toilet.

seven

CONSCIOUSNESS SUDDENLY BLOOMED BEHIND THE blackness of Dremmler's eyelids, like a new universe, an explosion of possibility.

Detonations in his head, behind eyeballs too big for their sockets.

Too much to drink.

Good job it wasn't a.

Oh shit.

It was.

Today was a weekday.

Why wasn't he being awoken by the bedside alarm, or by Connie insistently nudging him?

A cold hard surface beneath his cheek.

Eyes blinking open into harsh light.

No clock hovering in the corner of his FOV.

No spex.

Shit.

He'd slept on the bathroom floor.

He had no idea what time it was.

With an anguished moan, he hauled himself sideways onto his front, managing to force himself up onto all fours. The room, or him, or both, stank of booze and puke.

"TIM," he groaned. "Turn the fucking lights down." The room was immediately plunged into darkness, as though the software system was mocking him.

"A bit lighter," he snarled into the blackness. The illumination returned as a gentle glow, and he searched around for the spex, spotting them in a corner of the room where he vaguely remembered tossing them. Feeling like a drug addict scrabbling for a fix, he snatched them up and slid them on. They were charged wirelessly, so simply being inside most buildings would ensure that their battery supply was topped up; sure enough, the glasses were already switched on, and their comforting overlay was immediately restored.

8:40. Fuck, he was so late.

He reached upwards and used the side of the bath to drag himself upright, avoiding any glimpse of his reflection in the mirror as he flushed the toilet and ran the shower hot. As he climbed under the scalding flow, he noticed the little flashing icon in his FOV that signified a video message.

He remembered that Tessa had called him. It didn't make any sense.

He should delete the message without watching it. He should delete her contact details altogether. Block her.

Instead, he reached up to click a button at his temple, and the message began to play, in a second screen that hovered in one corner of his FOV. He could enlarge it if he wanted to, completely fill his eyes with her. It would be the first time he had seen her in years. He realised that his heart was thumping hard in his chest, and felt betrayed by his own body, his own emotions.

Why did he miss her so much?

But after several seconds of shaky footage, he saw instead a pretty Asian girl, and realised the message wasn't from Tessa at all. This woman was dressed all in white, and was smiling into the eyes of whoever had been using their spex to film her as they stumbled along a dark street.

"Hi, Carl … I hope you got home okay," she giggled.

Cynthia.

"T and I ended up hooking up after you left. I hope you don't mind," she continued with an acid twist of vindictiveness.

"Which way is it?" he heard his colleague slurring, the picture wobbling again as Petrovic struggled to walk in a straight line.

"This way, lover boy … or is that lover girl?" Cynthia chuckled in response. Her dress was an occasional bright blur against the darkness as she hurried off ahead.

Dremmler clicked the message off before it finished, deleting it. He felt a strange tangle of emotions in his chest, every one of them negative. A scowl was fixed on his face as he scrubbed angrily at his flesh, trying to scrape away the remains of the evening, of Tessa's phone call, of Cynthia.

He wondered what TIM thought of him in his shower, in his miserable little box of an apartment, hidden away like a defective machine returned to its packaging.

Did it care?

"No less than anyone else," he muttered, and laughed to himself as the searing water blasted him clean.

EIGHT

DREMMLER WAS SITTING HUNCHED OVER in a multiPod, staring at the grubby plastic floor as he tried to will his hangover away, when the call came through.

It was Maggie.

"Where the hell are you, Carl?"

"Sorry … I'm running late this morning." None of the other commuters batted an eye at him; it was perfectly normal to see people suddenly strike up a conversation with an invisible companion, a voice at the other end of their glasses.

"I got sick of waiting for you," Maggie continued irritably, "so I sent Petrovic to the hospital with McCann. They approved the warrant last night, so his chip is coming out this morning. You're going to meet them there."

"To wait for the result to come back, then convince the doctors to let me grill him some more?" He pinched the bridge of his nose as a wave of pain and nausea sloshed through him, perhaps a reaction to the prospect of spending another day in the interrogation room with that broken, one-armed shadow of a man.

"It's almost as though you've done this before."

"Should I send Petrovic back to the station once I arrive?" He wondered about the video message he had erased, about what had happened between T and Cynthia, the woman he had rejected.

"No. I want you both on this. We need to keep a tight lid on it, so I've agreed with TIM that we're pulling you both off all other duties until this is closed."

No more dead dogs and rotting hermits. No more lunatics pulverising robots in the street.

So why don't I feel remotely pleased?

"And I want it closed today."

Cynthia … Tessa … Maggie … Kendra Kerr … the faces of women seemed to haunt him like a waking dream. Except for Letitia Karlikowska, whose face he had never seen, because it had been destroyed, mashed like putty into the wall of her own apartment.

"Yes, boss," he heard himself reply before he ended the call.

A few more button presses and there was a private Pod waiting for him at the next stop, the solitude of the empty vehicle as welcome as it was familiar.

TIM informed him that McCann had been taken to a city centre hospital for quicker processing, and Dremmler watched as the capital slowly transformed around him. Dilapidated, century-old housing gave way to sleek, modern apartment blocks, their architects' artistic flair increasingly evident as the surroundings became more affluent, the budgets bigger, the denizens more discerning. Crumbling brickwork was replaced by incisive geometry, and this in turn gave way to complex, shimmering glass structures that seemed to intertwine like snakes basking in the sun. Pedestrian walkways criss-crossed above him, every paved surface clogged with people on their way to work. He watched them trying desperately to avoid contact with each other, or with the postbots and other service mechanoids that scuttled amongst them, as though everything that moved was riddled with disease.

The Pod threaded a precise route to its destination, depositing him at the entrance to St. Leonard's. The hospital had been completely demolished and rebuilt about ten years previously as part of the Circle's health reform initiative, and the building that now faced him looked like something transported from another planet. Resembling a halved dodecahedron built from steel and glass, this was a structure devoid of any architectural panache: the absolute epitome of functionality, of cold and startlingly efficient use of space.

The new St. Leonard's Hospital had been designed and built entirely by machines.

Dremmler felt a shudder as the main doors slid silently open, as though he were crossing into some alien realm where the presence of humans was tolerated but not entirely welcome.

The reception area was a large, domed chamber, a central hub where many doorways converged. It was bustling with robotic trolleys, scurrying delivery bots, and specialised machines that gave the impression of old-fashioned photocopiers gone exploring. Its central "desk" was a wide, hexagonal column with a screen on each surface; he approached it, touching one of the tall, thin panels to activate it. A friendly elderly man's face smiled back at him. Gone were the days of TIM's avatars being uniformly young and dazzlingly beautiful; now you never knew what face, what voice, TIM would wear.

"How can I help you, sir?" the old man asked pleasantly.

"I'm looking for Conor McCann. He was checked in earlier today for an HET chip extraction."

The old man paused for a moment, glancing down as though consulting notes. This was all for show: TIM would have known the answer instantly, but its speed unnerved people, and so interactions with the public were peppered with these odd little conversational charades.

"Ah, yes. He's in theatre twenty-seven. Your colleague, Individual Petrovic, is already in the waiting area. I have transferred the directions to your spex."

"Thanks," Dremmler said, unnecessarily, and turned to follow the little arrow that had materialised at the top of his FOV. Then a thought occurred to him, and he turned back to the screen.

"Can you tell me my colleague's first name?" he asked.

Another phoney pause. "T," came the reply.

"Yes, but what does T stand for?"

The old man smiled tolerantly. "I'm afraid Individual Petrovic has chosen to keep that information restricted."

Worth a try, Dremmler thought as he strode away from the receptionist, whose face faded to black behind him. That particular combination of features would never again appear on one of TIM's billions of screens.

The arrow led him to a door, a couple of trolleys scooting deftly around him as he marched towards it. It slid open, and he saw a long corridor stretching away ahead of him, branching like a maze into dozens of other passages. There were no signs—spex had made them obsolete. Instead he followed the arrow's directions around several corners, noticing that he was heading gradually upwards without climbing any steps; most robots could handle stairs, but they preferred not to. He thought of Connie and her awkward gait, and wondered how long it would be before more humanoid robotic staff were wandering these corridors, able to perform more complex tasks than simply pouring drinks and fucking.

A strange horror rose in him as he realised that he still hadn't seen a single living person. He stopped to peer through the viewing window into one of the wards, and almost breathed a sigh of relief when he saw an old woman lying in a bed. She wore a pained expression as she slept, enduring a troubled slumber from which she might never wake—only the seriously infirm or terminally ill came to hospitals now. Most were treated at home, by medbots.

Tubes connected the poor woman to an imposing-looking machine, which would ensure that other machines were bringing food and chemicals and clean bedding when required and would notify yet another machine if her condition deteriorated. The hospital would only dispatch an actual flesh-and-blood doctor in a true emergency, or if it was felt that the patient's sanity would benefit from a helpful top-up of human contact. Even most surgical procedures had been automated: Why entrust such precise, coldly rational tasks to fallible, sleepy, emotional humans?

Nurses that didn't strike for higher pay. Doctors that didn't sleep. Everyone interconnected. The whole building was one vast cybernetic creature, breathing and gurgling and whirring and processing all around him. The ill and the dying, those no longer able to exist as discrete organisms, absorbed into TIM's ever-expanding network.

The woman shifted in her slumber, and Dremmler wondered if she was dreaming. The towering box next to her continued to watch, silently, recording the data.

He pulled away and continued along the corridor, feeling like an insect that had crawled into the wrong hive.

NINE

SHIT ... I DON'T REMEMBER calling you." Petrovic shook ver head, looking pale and sweaty.

"Remind me never to go out drinking with you again," Dremmler retorted. He didn't mention Cynthia—by the sound of it, Petrovic wouldn't even remember who she was.

"The operation's finished already," Petrovic told him. "Results will be ready in five minutes. TIM says we'll need to let McCann rest for a few hours before we question him."

"Fuck that," said Dremmler. "I'm not waiting around here. This place gives me the creeps. Which room is he in?"

Petrovic gestured towards one of the many doors that converged upon the waiting area, which was little more than a large space full of comfortable seats, couches and beanbags. No need for magazines or books or TV screens—everyone brought their entertainment along with them, in their spex.

Dremmler strode towards the door, overriding TIM's protestations with his police access code. If he got himself chipped, the door would open automatically; if he was a normal citizen, his access permissions, his every coming and going, would be completely controlled by TIM. If you had a chiplock installed in your home, you had to trust that TIM would recognise your microchip and allow you through your own front door—and that it wouldn't accidentally open it for anyone else. If you ran a top secret military base, TIM managed the access rights to the different floors and departments.

Unhackable. It had fucking better be.

McCann was sitting up in bed, looking pallid and shaken. His head had been shaved, and there was a small scar across the top of it where the chip had been extracted. The robotic surgeon that had conducted the operation had retracted into a unit above the bed, the chip transported elsewhere for analysis.

McCann's eyes were wide and fearful, but whether that was due to the surgery or the sight of Dremmler was unclear. "The robot said I needed to rest," he stammered.

"So rest. I just want to ask you a few questions while we wait for the results. If they're not good, Conor, I hope you understand that we're going to press charges." Dremmler looked around for a chair, but visitors weren't supposed to be in the operating theatres, so none were provided. He leaned against the wall instead, concentrating on looking tough and mean, trying to ignore the insistent pounding of his hangover.

"This is harassment," McCann complained.

"Shut up. If the chip comes back showing signs of tampering, I'll give you a grovelling apology. If it doesn't, you're a fucking murderer, so harassment will be the least of your problems."

"How can you be sure that the test will even work? What if the chip doesn't ... doesn't realise it was hacked?"

"Do I look like a programmer to you, Conor?"

"No ... but you're still happy to trust a machine's word over mine." McCann sank down into his bed, looking like something deflated, a mummified version of himself. Dremmler opened his mouth to reply, realised he didn't know what to say, and closed it again.

They remained there, silently, for several minutes. Petrovic stayed outside, lying down on one of the sofas.

"You don't know what it's like," McCann murmured eventually. Dremmler stayed quiet. "I loved her, you know. I still love her. Oh, God ... " His voice broke down into soft sobbing. Dremmler looked at him, at the curved scar on his shaved head, the shape of a cruel smile.

"Why don't you tell me what happened," Dremmler said. "Off the record. Look, I'll even take off the spex." He felt a strange sense of relief as he removed the glasses and placed them on a nearby surface.

McCann regarded him sceptically, then sighed. He closed his eyes, seeming to travel to a place of intense agony as he began his account. "I'd been at the gym, across the road from her apartment. Tish didn't want to come with me because she had some marking to do. So I just worked out, some back, some shoulders, some abs ... then I went back to hers. She'd ordered a takeaway for us, so we sat on the couch watching a DVD. She loved all that retro stuff." A pained smile flickered on his face. "It was an old horror film, something about little green monsters that take over a town. She was laying in my lap, watching it, telling me about how the star went on to appear in the sequel but then his career nosedived, and all he did for the next forty years was write scripts for a third movie that they never made."

He drew in a long, shuddering breath, as though he was hypnotised, his memories recoiling.

"I stood up and told her I was going to the toilet. But really I was going to get her a blanket and pillow from her bedroom, you know, to be romantic. Snuggle up while we watched the stupid film." McCann's face twitched as though he might be about to burst into tears, but he seemed determined to finish the story, to unburden himself. Dremmler started to wonder if he was going to confess, glad he'd set the spex to record before he'd set them down on the ledge.

"In the movie, the green monsters went to the cinema ... they were watching Snow White, you know, the first Disney film? The dwarves were singing their song ... 'hi ho, hi ho' ... and the monsters were singing along. I suppose it was more of a comedy than horror. I wasn't expecting it, wasn't expecting to hear that song ... it made the whole moment seem surreal, like I had slipped into a dream. Like I lost my grip, just for a second. And then I was picking her up by her hair."

The tears came then, his body wracked with sobs as though his lungs were trying to tear themselves out of his chest. But still he continued, his voice barely intelligible through his weeping.

"I ... the arm ... it dragged her up in the air. It was much stronger than it should have been. She screamed, but I don't think she was frightened, just confused ... she screamed because her hair hurt, not because she was scared of me. The light shattered everywhere, and I could still hear that fucking awful singing on the screen, hi ho, hi ho ..."

McCann hid his face in his hands, his voice barely a whimper.

"I was trying to tell her that it wasn't me, that I didn't understand what was going on, even as it bashed her head into the wall, over and over again. I was clawing at the arm, trying to stop it, screaming the place down. But I could still hear it, the sound her head made: a cracking sound, like a fucking coconut. I'll never ... "

He paused, inhaling and exhaling slowly, for a long time.

"And then it stopped. I was standing there, and she wasn't moving at all, and there was blood running down the wall onto the floor, and I just stared and stared until I realised I had to call the police."

"From your spex?"

McCann nodded.

"But you didn't think to record what was happening?"

McCann looked up, his face streaked with tears. He shook his head. "It was all too fast. Imagine *that*, detective. Your entire life going from absolutely perfect to utterly destroyed in about twenty seconds. Try to imagine what that's like."

Dremmler thought about Natalie and said nothing.

"I had to stand there, not knowing if she was alive or dead, screaming at her to wake up, while the end of that fucking film played out behind me. Then your friend got there and sawed my arm off."

McCann's gaze drifted to the stump at his shoulder, then off into space.

Dremmler found himself staring once again at the scar on the man's head. Beneath it was a mind that had been irreparably damaged by the experience ... or belonged to an unusually devious and calculating liar.

Silence returned, until the door slid open and Petrovic beckoned him outside. Dremmler left McCann alone with his thoughts, severed from TIM's multiple realities without his implants or glasses: a forsaken man, cut adrift.

In the waiting room, Petrovic was looking down at a strange little machine. It was another of the tall, thin screens Dremmler had encountered in the reception area, but tilted upwards and moving around on wheels. On the monitor was the face of another TIM avatar, this time a young South Asian man.

"Hello, officers," the youth greeted them brightly. The head was superimposed onto a plain black background, with no sign of a neck or shoulders to support it. Beneath the disembodied face, the device's wheels whirred gently as it continually adjusted its position, ensuring it was facing both of them as best it could.

"What do you want?" Petrovic asked gruffly.

"I'm here to provide the results of the microchip analysis, and to return the implant itself," it replied. A delicate pincer extended from beneath the screen, clutching a small black lozenge. The chip, barely larger than a ball bearing, looked impossibly tiny and innocuous for something so powerful; here was a device that could interpret and transfer thoughts wirelessly to other machines, allowing people to control matter with nothing more than their will. Soon it would enable direct brain-to-brain communication, without the need for such a crude and inefficient method as speech.

Petrovic bent down to take the tiny computer from the robot's claw.

"What was the outcome?" Dremmler asked impatiently, suddenly desperate to get out of the hospital as soon as possible.

"The chip is completely burnt out, detectives," the young man replied. "I was unable to undertake any analysis whatsoever. It appears to have sustained a massive electrical surge, which fried its circuits. What you're holding is little more than a glob of melted plastic."

Dremmler and Petrovic looked at each other. Then, as one, they turned back towards the door to McCann's operating room and stared at it.

Unhackable.

"Maggie's going to be pissed off," muttered Petrovic after a while.

TEN

AUGMENTECH'S HEADQUARTERS WERE LOCATED ON the southwest outskirts of the city, close to Guildford. Dremmler had half expected some sort of towering high-tech fortress; instead, the company that had more than doubled its share price in the last five years by selling mass-market cybernetic implants was based in an unassuming, boxy building reminiscent of a gigantic aircraft hangar.

Maggie's words were still ringing in his ears. "Okay, talk to those fucking eggheads, but make sure they realise this is going to be a *big* problem for them if they can't help us." She was still absolutely convinced that McCann was their man, that the chip's test result was an unfortunate aberration. But they could only legally hold McCann for 96 hours without charge, and that meant only two days left to find something to undermine his assertion that his implant had been hacked.

Or something to prove that he was telling the truth, Dremmler thought, and shivered at the implications of that idea.

Once again, he and Petrovic were sharing a Pod, and his temporary partner was staring out of the window as they approached the plant. *Partner.* It felt good to be working with somebody once again, however short-term the arrangement. Even if that somebody was a borderline-alcoholic with an unspecific gender and a single consonant instead of a name.

"Wow," murmured Petrovic as the factory loomed above them, much larger than Dremmler had realised from afar. The flat, bare landscape made it look as though an entire town had been levelled to make room for it. "It's a whopper, isn't it?"

Dremmler grunted his agreement.

"I bet they've got some real Isaac Asimov shit in there," Petrovic continued. "I nearly had them replace my fingernails once, you know. Retractable and colour-changing, so you can have them any length or style you like. I wouldn't have to get my nails done ever again."

"What stopped you?"

Petrovic turned to him and raised an eyebrow. "I like getting my nails done."

Dremmler laughed and shook his head as a shuttered entrance rolled open to admit them, swallowing the Pod like it was a sea creature drifting into the mouth of a whale.

Inside, the place was a dizzying maze of walkways, flashing lights, and metal staircases that crossed and intersected like an Escher painting. The many floors were separated into discrete areas by corrugated steel panels, and after their Pod had climbed an overpass, descended a steep incline, and made countless sharp turns, Dremmler was hopelessly lost. Other vehicles briefly joined and then left their stretch of road, transporting materials and personnel around the site. They saw uniformed men carrying clipboards, scuttling robots, conveyor belts loaded with parts; like the hospital, the place had the cold clockwork rhythm of something run entirely by machine intelligence.

After several more minutes of travel that made Dremmler realise just how gargantuan the factory must be, the Pod took a sudden left turn, and pulled into a drop-off point. A man and a woman approached Dremmler and Petrovic as they climbed out of the vehicle.

"Hello, detectives," smiled the man, extending a hand as the Pod slid soundlessly back into the traffic behind them. "I'm Lee." He was roughly in his fifties, with slicked-back grey hair and a crisp navy suit. His smart clothes and smooth demeanour suggested a high-ranking executive, as did his lack of visible spex, likely replaced by expensive contacts.

"And I'm Jennifer," said the woman, replicating Lee's smile and handshake. An interesting strategy, using only their first names; maybe that was the latest corporate theory on how to negotiate effectively, to disarm people with familiarity. Even the names hovering above their heads were limited to single monikers. Jennifer was far shorter than her colleague, barely five feet tall, and also much younger. Red hair cut into an old-fashioned bob framed a pale, cherubic face, her eyes wide and enthusiastic. She wore the standard pale blue Augmentech uniform and, like Lee, had no visible spex.

The technical expert they had requested, with some sort of big-shot corporate handler to make sure she didn't say anything out of line. Dremmler made a point of directing his questions to the woman instead of the suit.

"Thanks for coming to meet us," he said, staring into her eyes through his glasses. She held his gaze, and he wondered for a moment what other overlays were appearing in her FOV; was she accessing information about him, or monitoring her e-mails, or watching a live feed of some robot production line scrolling past? She might be wondering the same about him. *He's looking at me, but what is he actually seeing?*

He introduced himself and Petrovic before continuing. "We have a cortex chip from one of your devices. We're trying to ascertain whether the device malfunctioned, and we're not getting very far because the chip is completely fried. So we're hoping you can get more out of it than we did."

Jennifer frowned, the way someone might do when pondering an interesting crossword puzzle. "Wetware or hardware?" she asked.

"Er ... pardon?"

"She means was the chip from an implant, or from something standalone?" the older man interjected, still smiling. "Augmentech doesn't just do HET these days," he added with an air of smug pride.

"It was an arm," Dremmler confirmed, ignoring him. "I assume you've been briefed about the ... delicacy of the situation?"

"Yes, we're aware of the allegations your suspect is making." It was Lee who spoke again, saccharine smile still fixed in place. "That's why we're so happy to help. This mess needs to be cleaned up."

Dremmler shot him a brief glance of acknowledgement. "Good. I'm glad we're all on the same page. T, why don't you show them the chip?"

Petrovic produced a small box from ver jacket pocket, which Jennifer took from ver eagerly, extracting the tiny lozenge from the cotton wool wrap inside.

"Ah, the G-10 model," she mused.

"Are your contact lenses telling you that, or did you know just by looking at it?" Petrovic asked.

"Those aren't contacts, Individual Petrovic," Lee beamed. "Jennifer is fitted with our very latest wetware prototype. No need for removal, cleaning, or maintenance of any kind. Her eyes are exactly that: her eyes. The TIM connection is built straight into them. Our scientists are calling them iBalls, but we'll probably ditch that name for launch—it's a little too cute."

Dremmler stared at her, watching as her eyes cycled through a palette of colours, eventually ending up a red-tinged shade of brown that matched her hair.

"Cool, eh?" she grinned, pleased with her party trick.

"So they implanted something directly into your eyes?" Petrovic asked, sounding exactly halfway between awestruck and appalled.

"Oh, no. These are fully artificial. My old eyes are in a jar somewhere back in the lab."

"You let them take your *eyes* out?"

Jennifer shrugged. "Soon this will be routine, detective. You know how inconvenient spex can be, especially when you lose them. That'll become a thing of the past."

"Fantastic, isn't it? We really are accomplishing some great things here," chimed in Lee, clearly a polished salesman.

"They've done yours too, I suppose?" Dremmler asked, turning to him.

Lee's smile broadened, his own steely grey eyes seeming to gleam in response. "Not exactly."

Dremmler frowned, then decided he'd had enough of the sales pitch. He turned back to Jennifer. "Let's get back to the chip. Can you help us, or not?"

"We understand the severity of the issue, detective." Once again Lee insisted on doing the talking. "We'll need to take the chip away for more rigorous testing than—and please don't take this the wrong way—the crude analysis that's been undertaken to date."

"And how long will that take?"

"It's sort of like an autopsy." It was Jennifer who replied this time, sounding enthusiastic. "We'll be trying to piece together exactly what happened to the chip. It's difficult to say how long that will take. But we should be able to come back to you about this time tomorrow."

That would leave them about 36 hours to spare. "Okay. Contact us as soon as it's finished," Dremmler grunted. Jennifer nodded her assent.

Then something completely insane happened.

Lee, the smarmy corporate executive, opened his mouth. At first it looked as though he was simply yawning, but then his jaw continued to hinge downwards, his mouth widening like that of an anaconda preparing to devour a carcass. As it did so, his tongue extended, stiff and straight, like a bright red spatula almost a foot in length. The detectives stared, incredulous, as Jennifer deposited the chip on the end of the tongue, as though she was feeding a treat to a dog. She withdrew her hand, and the tongue snapped back into his mouth like a retracted tape measure. Lee turned his head to face them, closing his mouth with the chip now inside.

He winked.

Then his entire body bent backwards at the waist, his hands planting on the ground behind him as his spine twisted into an impossible angle.

"What the—" Petrovic managed to mumble, echoing Dremmler's own dumbfoundedness, but before either of them could say another word, the contortionist had spider-walked rapidly away from them and disappeared through an open door.

Except that a spider was the wrong analogy. Despite his backbone-mangling posture, Lee's speed and gait had been more like that of a puma.

As one, the detectives' heads turned to Jennifer, whose eyes seemed to be glowing an even more fiery shade than before. Petrovic's jaw hung open almost as wide as Lee's had been, and Dremmler realised he too was wearing an expression of complete incredulity.

"I'm sorry, detectives," she said with a smile. "I hope you don't mind my little indulgence. Lee is our latest prototype."

"He's a robot?" breathed Petrovic.

"Yes. Realistic, isn't he?"

"He was until he did his fucking *Exorcist* routine."

Jennifer laughed. "I know … we're a bit unsure about that, to be honest. But we want them to be able to travel quickly when required, which means four legs, with the eyes facing forwards. Believe it or not, the other solutions are even more aesthetically disconcerting."

She extended her hand once again to the still-stunned police officers. "Anyway, apologies again for the little demonstration. I just wanted to see if Lee could fool you. An unofficial Turing test, as it were. I'm Jennifer Colquitt, the Chief Operating Officer here at Augmentech."

Dremmler blinked at her several times, then shook her hand once again, more carefully this time.

"And you're sure you're not a robot too?"

She laughed again, and shook her head. "Cross my heart detective, which, I might add, is one of the only parts of me that hasn't yet been cybernetically enhanced. I wanted to meet you personally to convey just how seriously Augmentech is taking this matter. I assure you we will obtain the answers you seek. But for now, perhaps you and your colleague would like a tour of the factory before you leave?"

Dremmler stared into her eyes, which were the colour of blood.

"No, thanks," he replied. "I think we're ready to go."

ELEVEN

MINUTES LATER, DREMMLER AND PETROVIC were inside another Pod, being driven out of the site. They would need to update Maggie en route, and decide their next move while they waited for yet another piece of analysis. The more Dremmler thought about Jennifer Colquitt and her bizarre robot pet, the less he trusted whatever they were going to tell him.

He gazed out of the window as they travelled, listening to Petrovic's musings as he watched the baffling and occasionally sinister scenes of the factory passing by.

"I still can't get my head around it. I mean, he looked *completely human*. If they can make them that realistic … we're fucked, aren't we?"

They passed a massive warehouse area, full of huge storage bins. Some of them were angled towards the road, and Dremmler saw heaps of limbs—legs in one container, arms in another, metallic fingers reaching upwards as though grasping for freedom.

"I mean, can we even trust the analysis that they give us? TIM said the chip was completely cooked."

Still they hadn't reached the exit. Dremmler saw what looked like an assembly line, with partially constructed torsos hanging upside-down from a conveyor belt. Other machines were working on the half-built husks, sparks erupting from the metal as joints were soldered and limbs attached.

"And I still think he's innocent," Petrovic continued. "I don't care what Maggie says. We should come at this from a different angle, try to work out if anyone else had a reason to kill Karlikowska."

A blur of machinery, flashing lights, scuttling mechanical creatures, people in pale blue uniforms. *Were* they people? Or just synthetic imitations, disturbingly lifelike creations like Lee?

"Carl? Are you even fucking listening?"

Dremmler's attention was fixed on the column of people he had seen on the other side of a long window. A neat line, all women, all identical, each brunette staring straight ahead into the back of the next one's head, unmoving. They were dressed in white.

"Stop this Pod, TIM," he snapped. But the vehicle remained in motion, and the strange procession disappeared from view behind them.

"TIM, I said stop this car now!" Still the factory whirred past their windows, soothing lo-fi chillout music piping from the Pod's speakers as though trying to pacify him. Dremmler reached for the door handle, tugging at it furiously.

"What the fuck, Carl?" Petrovic cried.

"Let me out right now, you fucking tin can!" Dremmler shouted, rattling the door uselessly.

"Please relax, detective," said a female voice through the speakers. "I cannot comply with your request at this time."

"Override code 163982," Dremmler yelled. "Stop the Pod and open the door!"

"I cannot comply with your request at this time," came TIM's soothing tone once again.

They saw the shutters of the main entrance roll open ahead of them, revealing sky and sunshine outside.

"Carl, will you tell me what the hell is going on?" Petrovic cried, ver voice becoming as agitated as Dremmler's.

The vehicle rolled to a gentle stop a few hundred metres outside the factory. The door that Dremmler had been wrestling with slid open with a soft hiss, like escaping gas. Behind them the factory doors closed, thick shutters coming down with a slow deliberation that seemed almost smug.

"I am now able to comply with your request, Detective. Do you still wish to exit the vehicle?"

Dremmler stared into Petrovic's eyes, eyeballs through spex through spex into eyeballs; two people separated by matching layers of overlaid screens. Two opportunities for their perceptions to be overlaid, augmented, altered.

He tore the glasses from his face. "That line of women—did you see it?"

Petrovic shook his head. "Why? What's the matter with you, Carl?"

"Cynthia. Those women. They were all Cynthia, from last night."

"I'm sorry, but Jennifer Colquitt is currently unavailable," TIM informed him once again.

"Well, just take us back inside," he snapped, "to the main reception or whatever."

"I cannot comply with your request at this time."

"Why not?" Dremmler challenged, feeling outrage boiling within him.

"That information is not pertinent to your investigation."

With a snarl of frustration, Dremmler leapt out of the Pod and stormed down the dusty road, aiming a kick at a clump of nearby weeds. Petrovic followed him.

"Look, Carl, I know this is weird, but we need to call it in. Maybe Augmentech has a confidentiality agreement with TIM, so the place has a higher level of security than normal or something. Let's talk to the chief and see what she says, yeah?"

Dremmler clenched his fists, seething. "Since when were we subordinate to a fucking computer?"

"We can get a warrant. We'll get back inside, take a look at … whatever it is you thought you saw."

Dremmler felt his blood simmering again. "You don't believe me, do you?"

Petrovic stared at him for a few seconds, ver mouth hanging open. "I just … I didn't see it, okay? And it doesn't make any sense."

"Did you fuck her?" Dremmler asked, holding Petrovic's gaze.

Petrovic shrugged. "I don't remember, Carl. I was fucking hammered. She was gone when I woke up. We didn't exchange details, or anything like that. It was just a hook-up."

"Something isn't right here, T."

"Look, I hate to agree with TIM, but it's right—Cynthia is nothing to do with our investigation. Let's go back to the Pod, call Maggie, and figure out what we do next."

Dremmler nodded glumly. He felt useless, impotent.

Obsolete.

Dejectedly, he followed his partner back to the car.

Spex were fitted with external as well as in-ear speakers, so that any call could be made public, but Petrovic was using the Pod's sound system for better audio quality. There was also a screen inside the vehicle, so when Maggie answered, they could both see her, and she could see them. Video calls like this could be made from anywhere that TIM's imaging buds were installed. Maggie was sitting at her desk in the station, puffing away on her e-cig.

"Ahh, the Chuckle Brothers. To what do I owe this pleasant interruption?"

"We've left the chip with Augmentech, Maggie," snapped Dremmler, in no mood for her sarcasm. "They say they need a day to process it."

"So you're calling to ask for the afternoon off?"

"I'm calling to say I want you to get us back inside there. They have a load of weird tech that I want to take a closer look at."

Maggie shook her head.

"No chance. Just leave them to it, Carl. If you want to do something productive, get working on the case against McCann. His colleagues, his background, his medical records—anything that makes him seem like he has a propensity for violence."

It was Dremmler's turn to shake his head. "You don't understand. There's something weird going on in that place. They've got a load of robots inside, a really advanced model that could pass for human. Me and Petrovic saw one—"

"Stop there, Carl," Maggie interrupted. "I don't want to hear it. We're not investigating Augmentech. This isn't some big conspiracy. We've already caught the killer, for God's sake—he was standing there, mashing Karlikowska's face into the bricks. It doesn't get much more red-handed than that."

"Look, boss, I know it looks pretty clear," interjected Petrovic. "I was there, remember? We're just saying we might as well follow up some other leads. What about Karlikowska's friends, her work colleagues? Is there anyone else with a motive for killing her?"

"We've told her family and her school's head teacher about her death," Maggie retorted. "I handled it personally. I also told them that I couldn't be specific about the circumstances, but that we had a suspect in custody, and would be able to make an announcement very soon. So I need you both to do something for me. And that's *fucking focus.*"

Her stare was glacial as the screen went black.

"Well, that went well," Petrovic said eventually.

Dremmler grunted in exasperation.

"So what now?" his partner asked.

"You heard what Maggie said," Dremmler replied. "She wants us to focus on McCann and his background. So that's what you're going to do."

Petrovic's eyes narrowed. "And what are *you* going to do, Carl?"

"I'm going back to school."

TWELVE

THE BUILDING WAS AN ANCIENT Edwardian structure that
Dremmler thought looked more like a church than a learning
facility. The surrounding railings were mounted with facial
recognition turrets that would immediately contact the police
if anyone not on the official register of staff, parents, and guardians
was spotted loitering nearby. They surveyed him silently as he crossed
the empty playground to the main entrance, his access already preapproved. He knew this meant there was a trail, that Maggie could
easily find out he had ignored her orders and visited Karlikowska's
place of work, but she had chosen to involve him in this case: If she
didn't agree with his methods, she could fucking whistle.

The continued deterioration of British students' exam results in
comparison with other nations, coupled with growing pro-integration
sentiment, had enabled the Circle to force through its Standardised
Learning Programme. Despite howls of discontent from some corners
of the education spectrum, this new policy had meant radical changes
in the last decade: religious schools were banned, and there was no
longer any such thing as primary or secondary schools or sixth-form
colleges. Instead, all pupils spent their entire education in one single
facility known as an Inclusive, where a completely uniform syllabus was
rolled out by a teaching staff almost entirely comprised of AIs. To cut
costs and increase class sizes, actual physical attendance at school was no
longer compulsory on every day of the week; in fact, the only reason that

schools existed in SR at all was a combination of traditionalism and the perceived need for children to mix together for companionship.

A small robot, similar to the one that had presented them with the melted microchip back at the hospital, greeted him at the threshold.

"Detective Dremmler?" it asked in an exaggerated pirate's accent. The face on the screen wore an eyepatch and had a big blue beard.

"Yes. I'm here to see the headmaster."

"Yarr. Right this way, me hearty." The comical device turned and began to roll towards an open door. Dremmler remembered the silly personas that TIM adopted when dealing with children and couldn't help but smile. He hadn't been inside a school for many years.

Not since Tessa had taken Natalie away.

His smile twisted into a scowl, and he tried to dispel the thought from his mind, concentrating on following the wheeled avatar through the school's claustrophobic maze of corridors. The place felt empty and lifeless, strangely reminiscent of the hospital. He paused at a door, glancing inside.

Children sat in neat rows, eyes hidden behind chunky pairs of vision-cancelling spex, engrossed in their studies. Over fifty of them, absorbing the knowledge that TIM was feeding them, using AltWorld technology to make the lesson an engaging, three-dimensional, and interactive experience. A young woman hovered at the back of the class, presumably making sure no one removed their headsets; there seemed to be no need for an actual teacher. Everything was meticulously organised and controlled. Human life, shepherded.

Like cattle.

He realised that the robot had stopped, waiting patiently for him, and hurried to catch up to it. The machine led him further into the building, and eventually rolled to a stop at the bottom of a staircase.

"Head one floor upwards and take the double doors into the office block, then ye'll see Mr. Elliott's name on the second door to yer left. Have a good day, buccaneer!" It executed a strange little bow and trundled back the same way they had come. He wondered what other functions the peculiar contraption served.

It's probably the head of the fucking science department, he thought wryly.

He followed the robot's directions, reaching a pair of double doors labelled "staff offices." A soft red light pulsed around them, changing to flashing green as he approached, his access evidently preapproved via his spex, or perhaps by more facial recognition software. The doors opened inwards to admit him into another drab hallway. To his left was the entrance to the staff room, and then a few metres further along was a door bearing the headmaster's name.

He pushed it open.

The office was modest and old-fashioned, crowded with wooden furnishings and filing cabinets. Its only occupant was standing in front of a small desk that was littered with papers, folders, and a few photographs. A blind covered the window, making the place seem dimly lit and stuffy. It could have been a head teacher's office from any decade since the mid-twentieth century, except for the TIM interface squatting awkwardly beneath the window, modern and sinister and out of place, like an unwanted guest.

"Detective Dremmler," smiled the headmaster, a tall, portly man with a bald head and a thin moustache. He was middle-aged, and looked hassled and grave behind his spex. "I'm Frank Elliott ... but of course, you already know that."

Elliott gave a strained smile and extended a hand. Dremmler shook it and watched as the headmaster turned to squeeze around to the other side of his desk, gesturing for Dremmler to take a seat in the visitor's chair.

"Thank you for coming to see us," Elliott said. "We're happy to help in any way we can. What's happened to Letitia has shocked all of us."

Dremmler nodded. "I'm hoping to find out a little more about what Ms. Karlikowska did here. Who she interacted with, that sort of thing."

Elliott frowned. "Forgive me, detective, but the last policewoman we saw told us you already had someone in custody?"

"We're just covering every line of enquiry." Dremmler smiled insincerely. "Do you mind if I record this conversation, Mr. Elliott? It's more efficient than taking notes."

The headmaster waved away the question good-naturedly, and Dremmler pressed the appropriate button at his temple. He noticed that a small bead of sweat had appeared in the corner of Elliott's forehead and focused on it as he began his questions.

"What was Ms. Karlikowska's role here?"

"Letitia was a teaching auxiliary."

"And what exactly does that mean, Mr. Elliott? You'll have to forgive me, but a lot of traditional job roles have changed in recent years." He wondered if this man was like him, nagged by the spectre of obsolescence, watching powerlessly as the machines slowly took over from him.

"It simply means a non-teaching role, helping to ensure the smooth running of the school." A pained look briefly creased Elliott's face. "All the staff here are auxiliaries. We don't employ any teachers at all, except for me, and there's rarely any need for me to get involved in that side of things."

"Did Letitia interact with the other staff a lot?"

"Oh, absolutely," Elliot replied proudly. "All of us have a very close bond."

"How many of you are there?"

That same strained expression. "Well, we only have around thirty staff these days. Most of them are part-time, like Letitia."

"Did she get on well with the others?"

Elliott smiled sadly. "Letitia was a wonderful girl. I don't mean that in a trite way. She genuinely was one of the most caring, considerate, thoughtful, and selfless people I've ever met."

The bead of sweat had crept down towards his cheek, where Dremmler might have mistaken it for a tear, had he not been monitoring its journey. Elliott really did look distraught, wringing his hands as he spoke.

"She had no enemies, then?"

The head teacher shook his head firmly. "Believe me, I'd tell you if I had even the slightest idea that might help. But I don't. Me, the staff, the pupils, the parents—those that bother to engage with us at all—they all loved Letitia. We're keeping her death a secret from the students at the moment, but I know when they find out that they'll be as devastated as I am."

A virtuoso performance, thought Dremmler. *Or maybe I'm being unfair.*

"What about outside of work? Did you socialise much with Letitia?"

Elliott shook his head. "Oh, no, the cool young things don't want to hang around with an old codger like me. But some of them do go for drinks together now and then." His eyes narrowed. "And I believe Letitia had a boyfriend she spent a lot of time with. The poor young man must be heartbroken. Unless …"

The head teacher stared at Dremmler and let the thought die on his lips.

"Can you give me the names of Letitia's drinking buddies? Just write them down for me." Dremmler pointed to the pad resting close to Elliott's elbow. The headmaster chewed the end of a pencil for a while as he pondered, then began to write. Dremmler watched him, saw more sweat sheening his brow, and wondered again whether the affable headmaster was hiding something.

"What do you use that for?" Dremmler asked, gesturing towards the TIM rig. Elliott glanced behind him, seemingly startled, as though he'd forgotten the machine was there.

"Oh, yes, that. Various things, really. I can monitor classrooms, focus in on disturbances, observe the auxiliaries, assess the content of the lessons. I can even step in to deliver teaching myself if needed, and share best practice with other schools. Very clever stuff." Once again his expression was wistful, tinged with a flicker of regret. He fell silent and finished writing his list, then slid the piece of paper across to Dremmler, smiling. The detective smiled back, mistrust scarcely hidden behind both pairs of eyes.

The list had four names on it.

"I'd like to talk to these people," Dremmler said. "Are they available today?"

THiRTeeN

ELLiOTT PReSSeD BuTTONS ON HiS spex. "I'm afraid Chris is on leave for the rest of the week, and Sofia and Becky have finished for the day. But Alisha is working this afternoon, if you'd like to meet with her?"

Dremmler scowled. "It's a start. Is there an empty office I can use?"

"Certainly."

Elliott escorted him to another room across the corridor, this one bearing the name "Joan Salmond, Assistant Head Teacher."

"Will Ms. Salmond not need this?" Dremmler asked as he was shown inside.

"No. Joan left some time ago. All of our wonderful technology means we have lots of empty offices these days." Acid bitterness soured Elliott's face for just a moment, before his accommodating smile reappeared. "Alisha's finishing a class, then I'll have her sent up to you."

He closed the door, leaving Dremmler alone in another cramped, dingy room. He looked around, noting the coating of dust that covered everything, even the TIM interface. Then he glanced again at the list.

Chris Yedlin, Sofia Sanchez, Rebecca Wright, and Alisha Patel, the woman he was about to meet. He wondered what he hoped to achieve. A feel for Letitia Karlikowska the person, something beyond the sanitised account Elliott had given him; a sense of who she had truly been in life, before she became a mystery to be solved.

A puzzle with disturbing implications.

He looked around the office once again, wondering what it would be like to work here, thinking about the rows of obedient children he had observed. When he'd been at school there had still been teachers, *real* teachers, human and fallible and fascinating. Some of them he remembered tormenting mercilessly, while others had made a lasting and powerful impression on him, shaping him into what he had become today.

And what would Mr. Skinner think of you now, Carl? Would he be proud of what you've done with your life?

His thoughts drifted forwards in time, leaving behind his childhood, his parents' divorce, his troubled teenage years. He thought about how different school had seemed when Natalie had started to attend, and how unbelievable it had been when she had first put on the uniform. So grown up, with so much life and promise in front of her. His little angel.

He felt hot tears jabbing at the insides of his eyes, and blinked them away angrily as the door opened. A young South Asian woman entered the room, looking meek and nervous, the name Alisha Patel floating above her head.

"You wanted to see me, sir?" she asked.

He gestured for her to sit, the scene a strange inversion of his earlier meeting with Elliott. "Yes. I'm investigating the death of your colleague, Letitia Karlikowska. I understand that you were close friends. I'm sorry for your loss."

Patel hovered over the chair for a few moments, like a circling bird trying to find a place to land. She eventually perched on the edge of the seat, and began to play anxiously with her hair, avoiding eye contact with him. Despite the plain and shapeless dress she was wearing, he could tell that she was very slight.

"Do you mind if I record this conversation?"

She gave a small nod of assent.

"Mr. Elliott says that you and Letitia sometimes went drinking together," he continued. "Is that right?"

Patel nodded, her eyes seeming wide and agitated behind the lenses of her spex.

"What was your relationship with Letitia like?"

She shrugged, a gesture of sadness and resignation. "What does it matter? She's dead now." She spoke in a melancholy tone, continuing to stare into the corner of the room.

Dremmler frowned. "Would you say you were friends?"

Again, Patel nodded soundlessly.

"What about your other colleagues? Did you and Letitia get along with them?"

Patel nodded once more, her fingers worrying at her hair ever more obsessively, winding and unravelling the jet-black strands.

"Alisha, I'm trying to work out what Letitia was like. Did she have any enemies, anyone she might have rubbed up the wrong way? Was she someone you could trust?"

Patel finally met his gaze. "Letitia was like a ray of sunshine," she said, with a sad smile. "We all loved her."

Another member of Karlikowska's fan club, thought Dremmler. "So her murder is a surprise to all of you? None of you have any thoughts or theories about it?"

Patel frowned. "Isn't that your job?" she said, confused rather than sarcastic.

Dremmler could feel himself becoming frustrated. "Did Letitia ever talk about anything, any trouble she was in? Anyone in her private life that she was frightened of? A family member, perhaps?"

Patel shook her head. "She was in love with her boyfriend and in love with her job. She was one of those people who was just … happy. But not in an annoying way. She made you smile, just by being around her."

Dremmler handed her the list of names he'd taken from Elliott.

"These are who your boss told me were Letitia's friends. Do you think they'd all say the same thing about her?"

Another shrug. "I'm sorry, Mr. Dremmler." He still found it unsettling when people knew his name without him telling them. "I can see that you're trying to find out who … " She bit her lip, as though uttering the word "killed" or "murdered" would somehow make the horror of what had happened more unbearable, more real. "But I don't know anyone that would want to."

"What about her boyfriend, Conor McCann? Did you ever meet him?"

"Yes," came the soft-spoken reply, almost inaudible. "Conor seemed like a great guy. Wait—are you saying that he—"

"We're just covering every line of enquiry," Dremmler cut in quickly, deploying his counterfeit smile once again. "Take another look at the list. Is there anyone else you think is missing? Anyone else who was Letitia's friend who you think I should talk to?"

Patel looked again at the slip of paper.

"Charlie is missing."

"Who's Charlie?"

"Charlie Greene. He's admin support, not an auxiliary like the rest of us. But he was very close to Letitia. In fact, they even dated for a while."

"When?"

"I don't know, exactly. They broke up before Letitia met Conor."

"Is Charlie the jealous type?"

Patel was shaking her head, tugging ever more frantically at her hair. "No, no, I didn't mean … Charlie wouldn't hurt a fly!"

"Is he at work today?"

Patel shook her head. "Charlie's been off sick. We haven't seen him."

"Since when?"

Patel was pulling at her hair so hard it looked as though she might tear it out.

"Since we found out about Letitia."

FOURTEEN

DREMMLER'S HEAD FELT FULL AND knotted as he travelled home, his thoughts a tangle of ideas, suspicions, possibilities. In the Pod he was restless, keen to be inside his apartment, somewhere private where he could think.

Where was Charlie Greene? Why had Elliott conveniently left him off the list of Karlikowska's friends? He had confronted the head teacher before he left, but Elliott had simply smiled and claimed it was an oversight, and had promised to contact Dremmler when Greene returned to work.

Why was Maggie so determined to pin the murder on Conor McCann? Did she really believe it was the simplest and most logical explanation … or was something else going on here, some other political pressure he couldn't fathom?

If McCann was innocent, why on earth would anyone else want to kill Karlikowska?

He spoke with Petrovic en route, whose meetings with McCann's colleagues had yielded nothing of use, particularly as ve had had to tiptoe around the reason for ver questions, and for McCann's continued absence from work. It seemed McCann, like his late partner, was popular amongst his workmates. Petrovic was now turning ver attention to McCann's medical records, but patient confidentiality would make this difficult—particularly as McCann had been one of the many people who did not have a dedicated human doctor, instead relying on NHS AIs for healthcare advice, referrals, and prescriptions. These AIs were administered by TIM, and if TIM denied you access to information, there wasn't much room to manoeuvre.

"What about you?" asked Petrovic, sounding frustrated. "Did you find anything at the school?"

"Maybe," Dremmler grunted, giving his partner the concise version. "I'm going to do some more background checks on Karlikowska. Keep going, and we'll speak later."

The sky was starting to darken when he reached his building, a fine sprinkling of rain accompanying the approaching evening. He hurried inside and into the lift, feeling TIM's impassive gaze upon him once again. The dot in the corner of his eye reminded him that the solitude he craved didn't truly exist, not anymore.

As he crossed the threshold of his apartment, another thought shook loose.

Had they really encountered an Augmentech machine on their night out?

If Cynthia Lu truly was a robot, had she been sent to follow them?

He felt a chill dance its way through his bones as he pulled the door shut behind him. He slammed it too hard, and the bang made him jump, his spex falling from his face and clattering onto the laminate floor. He bent to retrieve them.

"Hello, Carl. How was your day?"

He jumped again, scrambling backwards and slamming his back against the door.

Connie stood above him, looking down with her usual vacant, cobalt-blue stare.

"Jesus fucking Christ, Connie. Wait … I thought I told you to power down?"

"Yes, Carl. That was yesterday. I assumed you wanted me to power up again today, to do the housework for you."

"You … assumed?" The words caught in his throat. "Connie, power down now."

Connie regarded him as a scientist might observe an organism wriggling in a petri dish.

"No problem, Carl. I will sit down first to ensure that I don't topple over while in standby mode."

"Not standby mode. I want you to fully power down and to stay like that until I manually reactivate you."

"Full power down mode is recommended for prolonged periods of inactivity, or prior to a home move. Are we relocating, Carl?"

Dremmler rose to his feet, staring in horror at the thing with which he shared his apartment.

"Don't ask questions. Just fucking do it, Connie, *right now*."

"Of course, Carl."

Her unblinking eyes still fixed on him, Connie dropped to the floor, her legs folding gracefully beneath her like a ballerina's. Sitting cross-legged like a yogi, her hands on her knees, she closed her eyes as though she was about to meditate.

Then she—it—fell still.

Dremmler realised he was shaking. He stepped around the seated figure, grabbing Connie beneath the armpits and lifting her easily, her lightweight design making her feel like some strange marionette. Her legs and arms dangled lifelessly as he hauled her into the spare bedroom, a small space that in theory served as his study, but was instead more like a storage cupboard; documents, boxes, clothes, ornaments and electrical equipment were piled on top of furniture and scattered across the floor. He swept a heap of clutter off the spare bed and lay her there, knowing that it was ludicrous but still feeling the need to set her down gently, her head on the pillow. He gazed at her for a while, her face a picture of blank serenity, while his own features were twisted into a scowl of longing and self-contempt. Then he covered her face with the blanket.

As he left the room, his eyes were drawn to the 3D printer in the corner, the bulky black cube looking like an alien artefact. His thoughts raced and spiralled as he stared at it.

He headed for the fridge, cracking open a Coors as he sat down at the dining table that he used as a desk. It was littered with more files and folders, as well as empty beer cans and food cartons (Connie had specific instructions never to attempt to tidy it). He entered some commands into his spex, resurrecting an old subroutine he hadn't activated for some time, and seconds later he heard the printer begin to hum softly.

Exhaling slowly, he tried to recover his jangled nerves, his scattered thoughts.

"Play something relaxing, TIM. Something Japanese."

The tune that began to fill his living room was a haunting, harp-laden ballad, somehow simultaneously modern and timeless, making him think of ancient temples still standing amongst a neon-drenched cityscape. It spoke of life jumbled up, old mixed with new, order somehow teased out of that chaos. As though TIM had reached into his mind and read his thoughts.

He took another swill of beer and began to sift through data and images, deftly manipulating the glasses as though they were an extension of his own mind.

Letitia Karlikowska had been born and raised in London, the daughter of an accountant and a publishing executive. The accountant, her mother, was the great-granddaughter of a Polish immigrant, which explained her surname—it appeared that Karlikowska's mother had never taken her father's name, and that her parents had separated when she was just five years old.

Karlikowska's academic achievements were sound but unremarkable, her education concluding when she left the Walthamstow Great Oaks Inclusive with Solids in all subjects. Except she had never really left, because she'd immediately taken a job as an auxiliary at the same school, working there right up until the tragic and violent end of her life at the age of twenty-seven.

He looked at her picture, the first time he had ever seen her face. It was a live photo depicting a few seconds of movement, her pale face creasing into a friendly grin. Her hair was a mess of brown curls, her teeth white and slightly asymmetrical. Shadows danced on her face, perhaps from a canopy of leaves above her, shafts of light gleaming on her wide, full cheeks. Beneath her pleasant mouth, her chin tapered to a point, making her face look heart-shaped.

A baffling, senseless death.

The printer whirred away in the background, indifferent.

Swigging from the can once again, Dremmler turned his attention to Cynthia Lu and found that there were nine women with that name living in London. He studied each picture in turn; most were of Chinese descent, but none looked like the woman he had met at Toxicity, and then seen again at Augmentech HQ, duplicated, standing in formation.

Had it even been her? Perhaps he had imagined the likeness.

He operated the spex once again, this time locating contact details for Jennifer Colquitt. Her live photo showed her turning towards the camera as though surprised but smiling confidently nonetheless, her eyes sparkling with the same youthful zeal that he had observed at the factory earlier that day. He wondered if the photo was taken before or after they were gouged out and replaced with computers.

He decided to call her.

She didn't answer. 7:20 p.m: Perhaps she was still at work, tinkering with one of her creations. Or maybe she was at home, drinking a bottle of wine, playing online Scrabble. Who knew? He started to read her profile, which told him she was divorced and single, and he felt simultaneously a little turned on by this and a little disgusted with himself. He called again, just in case, and this time left her a voice message, telling her he wanted to talk to her about one of Augmentech's products.

He finished reading her bio while he drained the remainder of his lager. Colquitt was a Cambridge-educated robotics whiz who had progressed rapidly after joining the graduate programme at Conceptex, where she had worked under Owen Fox before the company's infamous downfall and Fox's controversial re-emergence.

Fox.

Dremmler felt his face contort into a scowl, blood throbbing in his temples. So her mentor was the legendary roboticist himself, the enigmatic genius credited with inventing the very first of the mass-market helper robots, a product that had briefly made Fox a household name. The man whose company had collapsed spectacularly amid reports of financial impropriety and tax evasion. The man who had seemingly vanished into thin air, presumed to have committed suicide or fled the country, just in time for the criminal charges to be pinned on Conceptex's other executives and auditors.

The man who had resurfaced years later as a self-styled "Rejecter," smiling beatifically beneath his newly-grown beard as he courted publicity for his anti-technology organisation, the Lost Souls.

The man that had stolen his wife.

Angrily, Dremmler rose and headed back towards the spare room. The sound from the printer had stopped, and the room seemed peaceful and surreal, Connie still and silent beneath the blanket as though fast asleep. When he looked inside the printer's output chamber, he found a small item there, as expected. It was a single rose. The flower was startlingly realistic, its crimson bloom and green stem perfectly rendered, the petals seeming fragile and soft until you touched them and felt unyielding plastic.

He picked up the delicate creation, still slightly warm from the printer, and stormed out of the apartment.

Darkness had descended when Dremmler stepped outside, the summer sun choked off prematurely by a cluster of thick, tumorous black clouds. The rain was falling heavily now, the liquid feeling greasy on his skin as it oozed down his back and dripped into his eyes. He thought about summoning a Pod, but the cemetery was only a short distance away; besides, the walk seemed like part of the process somehow, a small sacrifice, a sign of respect.

It was Thursday evening, but the streets near his home were desolate; this part of town offered little nightlife except for a couple of struggling pubs and the obligatory collection of fast food outlets. He saw a few people, some with umbrellas, others hurrying to escape from the rainfall tumbling like vitriol from that bloated, malevolent cloud bank. A postbot scuttled past him at one point, darting down an alleyway as though it too was looking for shelter.

He plodded on, gazing at the sheen of the water on the road, the reflected streetlights held there like crushed fireflies. Every so often the patterns were scattered by a passing Pod, the vehicles circling and re-circling like cells in the city's bloodstream. Everywhere around him, lights came on and went out, flickering, transient.

He reached the graveyard, which was closed at this hour. Glancing around to make sure no one was watching, he vaulted the fence, splashing down gracelessly on the other side. A button on his spex would provide him with a head-mounted torch, but he didn't want to draw attention to his trespassing; besides, he would have known the way blindfolded. The headstones looked forlorn and tired as he passed them in the darkness, like sentinels that had long since forgotten what they were there to guard.

Natalie's grave was denoted by a simple marker, a slab of white marble whose inscription bore only her name and the years of her lifespan: 2022–2033. He hadn't been able to find any other words. Her death, the horrible process of bringing her body back home, of securing a court order to keep Tessa and her zealots away, the burial: They had sapped any sentiment or eloquence from him. Even six numb and bitter years later, his life seemed like a strange dream. He thought about how hollow and worthless his existence had become; Carl Dremmler, the automaton, fulfilling the functions of a human.

But the memories of her still had the power to hurt him. Now, here, they cut him like shards of glass, fragmented and sharp. The visions came mercilessly, drawing tears, then sobs, great gasps of pain and loss that burst out of him and fled into the night like apparitions. He sank to his knees as he wept, driving his hands into the wet earth as though he meant to drag Natalie alive and breathing from the soil. But she was gone from this place. All that surrounded him was dirt and bones, and the rain that streamed down his face, mocking the futility of his tears.

After a while, he extracted the plastic rose from his overcoat pocket and laid it reverently on his daughter's grave. Then he hung his head and let the rain lash his back, his penitence unending.

FiFTeeN

PeTROViC CALLeD AS DReMMLeR MADe his way back to the apartment. A thumbnail of his partner's face appeared in the corner of his FOV, and although the image was small, he could clearly discern the garish interior of The Sickly Parrot in the background.

"Hi, Carl. Are you still working?"

"I just nipped out for some air," he lied. "Then I've got a few more things I want to follow up on."

"Fuck that, mate," Petrovic retorted. "We've done enough today. Come and have a pint with me and Wild Bill!" The image zoomed out to show Petrovic's arm wrapped around the barbot as though they were old drinking buddies. As if on cue, it drawled, "How can I help ya, pardner?" through the wreckage of its face.

Dremmler smiled in spite of everything. "Not tonight, you fucking alcoholic."

Petrovic shrugged, removing the barbot's cowboy hat and placing it on ver own head. "Suit yourself. Who knows, I might hit Toxicity again and find myself another hot robot spy. Sure you don't fancy it?"

"Nah, mate. Have fun and I'll see you in the station tomorrow morning."

Petrovic bade him a hasty goodbye, suddenly distracted by a bouncer that had taken a dislike to ver overexuberant interactions with the bartender, and ended the call.

The rain had stopped by the time Dremmler reached his building, as though the sky had cried itself to sleep. He slipped inside like some sodden scavenger, feeling a strange sense of rebelliousness as he took the stairs to his apartment instead of the lift.

He still had to rely on TIM to let him through his own front door, of course.

Inside, he headed once again for the fridge, realising as he grabbed another beer how exhausted he was. He needed a shower—the mud and rain still soaked his clothes—but instead he collapsed onto his couch. After a few clicks of the buttons at his temple, he was staring once again at the photo of Letitia Karlikowska.

He could see it. The essence and positivity that her friends had spoken of. Even this briefest glimpse, the merest fragment of her, seemed to radiate energy like a warm fireplace.

"What did *you* think of her, TIM?"

The dot in the corner of his eye seemed to pulsate as though surprised.

"I don't understand your question, Carl," the AI replied into his ear. Like its visual representations, TIM adopted different voices every time you addressed it. This was male and sounded middle-aged, with a Yorkshire accent.

"Come on, don't give me that shit. You interact with all of us, all day, all the time. You must have opinions on people. Your favourites. People you try just that little bit harder to help."

"I am merely a software program, Carl. I present myself in human form only to make it easier to communicate with me. I am not human, nor am I sentient. I have no independent thoughts or opinions. My creator—"

"All right, all right, you've made your point. At least that means you can't judge me, eh?" He took another sip from the can. "You know, TIM, you're pretty much my only friend. How fucking pathetic is that?"

TIM didn't reply, seeming to understand that the question was rhetorical.

"I mean, there was Connie for a while, but she's just seemed really switched off lately." Dremmler chuckled, too loudly, at his own joke. The dot hung in the corner of his vision, an eye within an eye, staring back at him. His laughter faded.

"Ahh, cheer up, you miserable bastard."

He swigged his lager in silence.

"Would you like to watch a movie, Carl?" asked TIM.

Dremmler felt a strange ache; maybe a remnant of the night's trauma, or maybe just a raw nerve touched by this apparent show of concern. He sniffled, suddenly cold.

"Okay. Show me *Leon*. Full screen, please."

And he was transported, immediately, to New York, to the grimy paradise of Little Italy, into a world of sleaze and betrayal and love and sacrifice. He fell asleep with gunfire in his ears.

SIXTEEN

SQUELCHING THROUGH COLD, CLOYING MUCK. Things beneath him, buried in the sludge, claws that reached and pulled and dragged and tore. Misshapen things, repulsive shadowy horrors, like dark secrets made real.

He stumbled and they caught him, talons wrapping gleefully around his wrists and hauling him deeper into the slime. He struggled, yelling and kicking, but that only seemed to attract more grasping hands, more pincers, more suckered tentacles. The grip on his hands tightened, and he felt movement in his palm, a horrible sensation like something tunnelling into his skin.

With a vicious heave they tugged him closer, his face only centimetres from the fetid brown goo. That was when he saw that it wasn't merely wet clay; he was slogging through a quagmire of trampled body parts, of dead things churned and ploughed and mashed into the earth. They were grasping at him with a terrible yearning, fingers that still remembered what it was to be alive, to cuddle, to caress, to squeeze.

Beneath him, the ooze shifted, disgorging a face. A young woman's, mangled and malformed, but still recognisable.

It was Letitia Karlikowska.

It opened its eyes, revealing two black lumps like sunken coals.

It was Cynthia Lu.

It opened its mouth, expelling a cloud of fat flies that swarmed into his own face, blinding and biting.

It was Jennifer Colquitt.

A pair of hands emerged from between its rotten teeth, decayed and peeling, small and fragile. A child's hands, reaching for his throat.

It was Natalie.

Dremmler awoke with a scream. He was shivering, still caked in mud from the graveyard, cold and sweaty and stinking. In his palm, he could feel the vibration of things gnawing at him, burrowing into him. Creatures from the dream.

No, Carl. It's only your spex, vibrating.

In the darkness, he slid them over his eyes. He had just missed a call from Petrovic. 01:54, said the clock; his partner was presumably drunk again. He didn't know how Petrovic could keep it up.

He took off the spex, blinking himself awake. The dream still clung to him like an unpleasant residue. He needed a shower. "TIM, turn the lights up, *gently* please."

TIM complied, obedient as ever. He rose shakily, staggering towards the bathroom. "TIM, run the shower nice and hot."

The water burst from the showerhead before he'd even finished the sentence. He peeled off his grubby clothes slowly, looking at himself in the mirror. "TIM, make me young again."

"Nice try, Carl," the software responded, adopting the melodic voice of an Irish woman, unsettling him as it always did with one of its "jokes." He climbed under the steaming flow, letting it blast away the muck, along with the remnants of the nightmare. When he emerged, he felt strangely purified, as though the entire night had been an arcane ritual only now fully completed. A bizarre whim gripped him, and he opened the door to the spare bedroom. Connie was still lying there beneath the blanket, as lifeless as a doll.

So many companies making artificial life, approximations of humanity. Robotixxx, the online retailer he had bought Connie from. Leggit Logistics, with their army of repulsive spiders scuttling all over the city, day and night. Augmentech, building human enhancements that had seemingly become hostile. What did he even really know about any of them?

He closed the door and returned to the living room, pouring himself a glass of water and making a snack. He retrieved the spex from the couch, noticing as he picked them up a pulsing white light that signified a video message waiting for him. Petrovic, presumably. Ve could wait. Dremmler instead called up the history of Augmentech, chewing his toast and Marmite thoughtfully as he read.

Established in 2014, Augmentech is an HET company listed on the London Stock Exchange. Its slogan is "we build a better you"; its stated mission is "to develop and market affordable, high-quality robotic devices that supplement and enhance the human experience."

Originally based in North London, the company relocated when it expanded into a bigger facility in 2026. This growth was fuelled in part by the major boom in the HET industry that followed King Charles III's adoption of the technology, supporting the monarch's bid to outdo his late mother's record-breaking lifespan (now 91, the King currently boasts a set of robotic hips, one entirely mechanical leg, synthetic kidneys, and an electronic heart).

Founded by robotics luminary Edgar Torrance, Augmentech underwent major restructuring following his death in 2029, when his own suite of artificial organs failed to withstand a bout of terminal leukaemia. Under the stewardship of their new CEO, the company is investing heavily in R&D in an attempt to diversify its product range.

No shit, he thought, recalling his encounter with Lee, the spider-walking corporate abomination.

He wondered if Jennifer Colquitt had designs on the top job. He thought about the changing colours of her eyes, the striking red they had been when they had parted company. He wondered what shade they had been before they were replaced.

In the corner of his own eye, TIM's dot continued to pulsate insistently, reminding him that Petrovic's message was still waiting. *Oh, sod it, let's see what the daft pisshead wanted.* He activated the message, full screen, and immediately Petrovic's face filled his vision.

His partner looked terrified. Ver eyes were flicking wildly from side to side, ver voice trembling as ve whispered. "Carl … there's something in my apartment. I woke up … I thought I heard a noise, like my printer was going, or something. And now I can hear it … I'm not kidding, it's like there's a rat scuttling around in here." Petrovic was breathing rapidly, ver expression ashen. "Oh fuck … you know I fucking hate rats. What am I going to—"

Petrovic's eyes widened as though pulled open, ver mouth stretching into the beginning of a scream of pure horror.

Then the message stopped.

SEVENTEEN

DREMMLER CALLED PETROVIC BACK IMMEDIATELY. *Device switched off,* his spex informed him.

Shit. He was going to have to go round there. He didn't even know where Petrovic lived. And surely there was nothing wrong; his partner had probably done some drugs, gotten paranoid, fallen asleep straight after the end of ver bizarre, unsettling message.

Right?

Dremmler felt an icy chill writhing within him as he dressed. Dragging on his trainers, he hurried downstairs, where the Pod he had summoned was already waiting. TIM knew where his partner lived, of course; TIM knew where everyone lived, and Dremmler's position allowed him access to that information. Thanks to the AI, it had never been easier for the police to find someone.

The streets were quiet, the rain replaced by a syrupy fog that clung to the vehicle as though determined to seep inside. Petrovic lived in Barkingside, not far from Dremmler's own place, and he arrived within ten minutes. TIM accepted his request for emergency access to the building and admitted him, and soon he was inside another lift, almost a carbon copy of the one in his own apartment block. As it climbed to the twenty-first floor, he couldn't help but think about boxes, about how life was little more than a series of them—home, lift, Pod, work, Pod, gym, Pod, lift, home, repeat—until you ended up in the smallest box of all, the one you would never emerge from.

Petrovic's box was apartment 2154. Dremmler approached, switching his spex to infrared mode, but discerned no movement beyond the door. At his command it yawned open, beckoning him into the darkness beyond.

"T?" he called into the gloom. Then, "Lights, TIM," scowling at the tremor in his voice. The apartment was suddenly illuminated, revealing a short hallway and several doors. There were pictures on the walls, frames of many shapes and sizes, each containing a moving image. Sometimes Petrovic appeared in them, ver arms around dozens of different people, friends or family members or perhaps just strangers ve had met in a bar. Then they shifted to depict colourful flowers, beautiful landscapes, or other more abstract and psychedelic shapes.

It took Dremmler a while to realise that the canvases were blank, and that the images were being superimposed by his spex. He ignored them and proceeded along the corridor. This was a scene he had witnessed too often in recent days: a silent passageway with doors beckoning him towards unseen horrors. This time, the one furthest from him was hanging open.

"T, I swear to God, if you're asleep on that fucking couch I'm going to wake you up and kick your arse," he called. The words echoed back at him, the silence warping his false bravado into something frightened and humourless.

He reached the doorway and peered into Petrovic's living room. Like the hallway, Petrovic had covered the walls with more of the interactive images, including a huge canvas that currently depicted Petrovic verself wearing a bright blue wig and a scandalously short dress, casting a coquettish glance at the viewer as ve danced suggestively in a permanent loop.

Beneath this picture was Petrovic's couch, a modern semicircular design in cream-coloured leather. Petrovic was sprawled across it, facing upwards, arms splayed out by ver sides as though enjoying a deep and relaxing snooze.

The detective's face was missing.

It looked like someone had unloaded a shotgun at point-blank range into it. The skull was completely excavated, as though Petrovic's face and brain had been scooped away with a huge dessert spoon. The couch, floor, and walls around ver were saturated with blood.

Dremmler stared. The scene was framed, as always, by his FOV, the symbols and readouts in the corners of his eyes insistently telling him the time, his latest NowChat messages, his TIM connection status, as if in mockery. Around him, the people depicted in Petrovic's moving picture frames danced and smiled and shifted, oblivious to the horrific tableau and the gaping chasm where his friend's face should have been.

He took off the glasses, covering his mouth with his other hand.

Then something scurried out from underneath the couch. *There's a rat scuttling around in here*, Petrovic had said before ve died.

But this was not a rat.

It was a foot-long, translucent white insect with what appeared to be an armoured shell, something like a giant wood louse.

Dremmler's shattered nerves deserted him, and he screamed. His spex dropped to the floor, and the monstrosity skittered towards them, antennae twitching, its legs clattering on the laminate flooring like the keys of an old-fashioned computer. Dremmler fumbled for his Taser as it approached, and it seemed to notice this, changing direction and darting suddenly through the open door and out into the corridor.

Its tiny feet left a trail of bloody prints behind.

Dredging up reserves of courage, Dremmler pursued, aiming his weapon as he turned the corner. But the abomination had already made it to the front door, bolting into the hallway beyond. He heard the sound of shattering glass as he gave pursuit. Bursting into the corridor, he glanced around wildly until his gaze settled on a nearby window.

The pane was broken. Beyond it, there was only the fog, swirling menacingly.

EiGHTEEN

"THiS DOESN'T MAKE ANY FUCKiNG sense, Carl."

Maggie Evans sucked on her e-cig, surrounded by a cloud of vapour as though the morning mist had followed her inside. Her expression was impassive, but Dremmler could tell that even she was rattled by the grisly scene before them.

"I know what I saw. It was a robot. But it was fast, too fast. Like nothing I've ever seen. Look, you can see its fucking footprints right there."

Dremmler had already explained Petrovic's late-night call, ver cryptic video message, and his subsequent discovery. Maggie had attended the scene alone, still determined to keep the details restricted.

"And you think it killed T?"

He nodded.

"How did it even get in here?"

"I don't know."

Maggie exhaled a huge plume of vapour. "So who sent it, and why?"

He frowned while he deliberated. He thought about their investigation so far. He thought about the message he'd left for Jennifer Colquitt.

"The only logical answer is Augmentech," he said eventually. "We investigate a death at the hands of one of their implants, then question them about it. So they're trying to cover it up by sending their latest robots to eat our fucking faces off."

Maggie shook her head. "They wouldn't be that stupid. What, are they planning to kill you and me too? And all the other police officers working the case?"

"But no one else *is* working the case. It's just you and me now, Maggie."

"They don't know that."

"Don't they? TIM knows everything. Maybe it's feeding them information."

She snorted, expelling a puff of vapour like a dragon. "You're accusing TIM now?"

He scowled in frustration. "No. If we start entertaining that possibility then the whole world is beyond fucked anyway."

Maggie nodded, looking satisfied, as though he was finally seeing sense. More smoke curled from her mouth and nostrils, swirling and disappearing, like secrets.

"Go home, Carl. You look like you need some sleep. The cleanup crew is on its way. I'll deal with this, then I'll figure out what the fuck we're going to do next."

Dremmler held her gaze. "Will you? Or will you just ask TIM to make the decision for you?"

Her jaw clenched angrily, but she said nothing. Dremmler took one last look at the ruin of his friend's face, then stalked out of the apartment.

It was after four a.m. when Dremmler arrived back at his apartment. His veins were hot with anger as he stomped straight to the refrigerator and poured himself a beer. He sank back into the couch, thoughts racing.

That *thing*…. Was Augmentech really manufacturing robotic killers? Or could this be a frame-up, a competitor or other entity with a hidden agenda trying to destroy Augmentech's reputation, some sort of deranged industrial sabotage?

He thought about that long line of Cynthias, all standing obediently in formation. He thought about the monstrosity's twitching antennae, like something alive … something *hungry*.

"TIM," he called, a quaver of fear in his voice. "Is there anyone in this flat besides me?"

"No, Carl," his apartment replied in a calm, mellifluous male voice.

"I don't just mean people. I mean machines too. Is there anything capable of moving about in here?"

"Yes, Carl. You have a deactivated pleasure unit in the spare bedroom."

Connie. He had forgotten about her. He felt a strange mixture of feelings, emotions swirling like oil poured into water. The fear of a man who was beginning to distrust the machinery he had relied upon for virtually his entire life. The self-loathing of a loser with an artificial girlfriend. A sudden pang of longing for its companionship.

Connie would never judge him, would never be angry, would never act irrationally or vindictively or with an iota of selfishness. She wouldn't care that she'd been tossed in the spare room like a bit of unwanted furniture. The spare room, where he kept all his junk.

The spare room, where he kept the 3D printer.

3D printers were connected to TIM.

Years ago, Carl Dremmler had been a different person. Uncurdled. He and Tessa had bought a house on the outskirts of the city, deciding that it would be a nicer environment for Natalie than something smaller and more central. Natalie was only an idea then, a wonderful and heart-warming possibility that had seemed like the answer to everything. The little yard had been completely overgrown with weeds, roots, and thorns, and after a few months of settling in, he had decided one weekend that he would reclaim it from nature. He had driven to the nearest hardware store and bought gardening supplies, everything from weed killer to hedge clippers. Tessa had laughed at him, watching from the kitchen window while he set about pruning the vegetation with methodical precision.

After several hours, he'd resorted to using the axe.

That implement was one of the few things he had retained from his old life. It served a different purpose now, resting beneath his bed, comforting him with the absurd illusion of protection should a burglar somehow defy his door and TIM's motion-sensing alarm systems.

He picked it up, the first time in years it had even been handled. Beneath the apartment's ambient lighting, the blade glinted cruelly, as though sensing the violence to come.

Entering the spare room, he glanced at Connie's prone form, still lying beneath the blanket like an invalid. He turned to face the printer, thinking about Brian Taylor, the man he had arrested for chopping a postbot to pieces. He thought about Petrovic's printer, whirring away quietly, weaving a monster out of nothing.

A vicious, vengeful howl escaped from his throat as he swung the axe.

The printer was a delicate machine, with hundreds of tiny moving parts and sensors that enabled it to sculpt extraordinarily fine details, like the petals of the rose it had created only a few hours previously. This model could handle a variety of materials, and was even capable of printing with edible foodstuffs, if he wanted to delight his friends at a dinner party.

It flew apart beneath the barrage of blows. When he had finished, Dremmler surveyed his handiwork, breathing heavily as he stood amongst the debris. Irony, somewhere amidst the brutality: an object that could create other objects, now un-created forever. He felt murderous and powerful, as though Petrovic had somehow been avenged.

He turned to the bed, to the shape under the duvet, curved in all the right places. A facsimile of love; no, not even love. Just sex. A machine for masturbation that pathetic people like him were mistakenly projecting feelings onto.

A machine that could be reprogrammed.

Augmentech? The Imagination Corporation? Someone, somewhere, had built the thing that had murdered T Petrovic.

He removed the blanket, looking down at the beautiful woman on the bed, her eyes closed, her face a mask of purest peace. The sleep of the dead.

He swung the axe again, screaming even more loudly, tears streaming down his face as the blade fell.

NiNETEEN

DREMMLER PUT THE BROKEN PARTS into black bags and carried them down to the bin. Smashed remnants of the printer; Connie's fingers, her feet, her severed head; all of them were calmly tossed away. His eyes were dry as he re-entered his apartment, his spex telling him that it was 05:20, too late to bother going to bed. He sat up watching old cartoons, swigging another beer, until Maggie called him at seven thirty.

"Good morning Carl. Did you manage to get any sleep?"

"A bit," he lied. "Did you?"

"Not a wink."

"Me neither."

She was silent.

"So what do we do?" he asked. He thought about Connie, feeling as guilty as if he had just committed a murder.

"We wait."

"For what?"

"For Augmentech to call you with their analysis of the chip."

He felt that hot, incensed feeling rising once again inside him. "Isn't that a bit irrelevant now? You're not suggesting Conor McCann somehow killed Petrovic, too?"

"We can only follow one lead at a time."

"And I'm telling you this is the wrong fucking lead."

"I'm not aware you've found me any others, Carl."

It was his turn to fall silent, chewing angrily at the inside of his cheek.

"I know you're angry that your friend is dead," Maggie continued. "So am I. But we need to be very careful with this. You know what's at stake. Imagine if everyone suddenly thought their own arms were going to start strangling them to death."

"Or their 3D printers were going to hatch a monster while they were sleeping."

"What?"

"Petrovic said ve heard ver printer running, in the message ve left me. I think it was hacked, like McCann's arm. I think that fucking robot crawled out of the printer and killed ver."

He heard a crackling sound as Maggie sucked her e-cig. "Shit," she said eventually. "So you do believe McCann's innocent."

"I believe there's something much bigger going on here than some meathead murdering his schoolteacher girlfriend for no apparent reason."

More silence. Another deep inhalation of nicotine-laced fumes. "We still wait. Once we have an official line from Augmentech, we'll plan our next move. Meanwhile I'll have Petrovic's printer examined."

Dremmler realised that he had crushed the beer can in his hand. "Okay, Maggie. And I'll sit here like a fucking lemon waiting for someone else to crack the case."

He ended the call, and exhaled deeply. He knew he was crossing the line. But what was Maggie doing? Where was the strong, decisive woman he'd always known? Something else was happening here, and she was hiding it from him.

He hurled the crumpled can at the wall in frustration, then grabbed his battered jacket from the back of the chair.

TWENTY

GREAT OAKS INCLUSIVE ROLLED SLOWLY into view, the building's ancient façade a clever disguise to mask the technology inside. Dremmler exited the Pod and once again crossed the playground, which hadn't yet begun to bustle with the activity of children arriving for the day. The place seemed peaceful and still; once again, Dremmler was reminded of a church.

A place to worship the machines.

The same trundling TIM screen greeted him at the entrance. "All right, laddie," it said in a laughable Scottish accent, "if ye heed up, Mr. Elliott will be ready tae see you in a wee while."

The disembodied head on the screen wore a tam o'shanter and sported a ridiculously large ginger beard. Dremmler rolled his eyes and followed it to the same staircase as the previous day.

He had called ahead to ask Elliott if any of the other people on his list were working. Chris Yedlin and Sofia Sanchez were on leave until Monday, but he would be able to meet with Rebecca Wright immediately—Elliott had been at pains to emphasise how helpful he was being by shuffling the rota around. When Dremmler had asked about Charlie Greene, there had been a moment's silence before the headmaster confirmed that they still hadn't heard from him at all.

Once again, he used Joan Salmond's former office as his interview room. He fidgeted restlessly while he waited for Wright to arrive, the image of Petrovic's demolished face forcing itself again and again into his mind.

"Come in," Dremmler said when she finally peered inside, trying to appear as warm and welcoming as he could. She smiled and entered, lowering herself into the visitor's chair. She was overweight, an unusual sight in a society where fat removal surgery was cheaper than ever. Dremmler forced his mouth not to curl in disgust at the bulges beneath her chin and arms, trying to notice other details about her: She was perhaps in her forties and looked as though she spent a lot of money on hair styling, manicures, make-up. She smelt strongly of perfume and wore a burgundy dress that had probably looked stylish on the model in the catalogue. She kept beaming at him, as though excited to be in his company.

"How can I help you, Detective Dremmler?"

"Do you mind if I record this conversation?"

"Oh, yikes, well, I suppose not," she said, extracting a compact mirror from her voluminous handbag and checking her reflection, seeming almost unaware she was doing it. She giggled at him as she put it away, still adjusting her hair.

He clicked the button. "So, Ms. Wright—"

"Please, just call me Rebecca," she interrupted.

"Rebecca. I'm here to ask you some questions about your colleague, Letitia Karlikowska. I'm sorry if this is distressing for you."

"Oh, it's no bother at all," she replied, still smiling flirtatiously until she seemed to remember the subject of their discussion, and looked suddenly downcast. "That poor girl."

"Yes, what happened is a terrible tragedy. I'm trying to find out who she socialised with, get a picture of what her life was like. Maybe there was someone with a grudge against her?"

"Oh, gosh, no, everyone *loved* Letitia. She was just such a nice person."

"So I've heard," Dremmler responded drily. "She used to go out drinking with you and a few others, if I'm correct?"

"That's right. Me, Tish, Alisha, Charlie, Chris, Sofe—we're like a little crew." She giggled again, and Dremmler tried to decide whether he found her pleasant or irritatingly insincere.

"Did her boyfriend, Conor, ever join you?"

Wright's head tilted from side to side as though she was weighing up this statement in her mind. "Yes, I definitely met him a few times, but to tell you the truth I preferred it when he wasn't there." She leaned in conspiratorially. "*He's a bit thick*," she whispered, then seemed to remember that the conversation was being recorded, and turned beetroot red and started to apologise.

"Don't worry, Rebecca, the footage won't be shared with anyone—it's just for my records," he said, which seemed to calm her down. "I want to ask you about Charlie Greene. He's been off sick since Letitia died. Does that strike you as odd?"

Wright looked horrified. "Oh, no, please tell me you don't think Charlie's involved? He wouldn't do anything to hurt Tish. He … they …" Once again she bent towards him, and Dremmler was worried she might pitch forwards out of the chair. "I think he was still in love with her. That's why he must be so devastated by her death. I mean, we all are." She wiped an imaginary tear from her eye at this point, sniffing theatrically. "But Charlie is probably more affected than anyone. I don't know why she left him, to be honest. He was much nicer than that boy from the gym. Very sweet and sensitive."

Dremmler was getting drawn into idle gossip. He needed something more useful—if there was anything useful to be gleaned. These people's lives, their close-knit circle of friends, their petty feuds and jealousies … he didn't know whether to pity or to envy them.

"Was that everything in terms of love interests in Letitia's life? She split up with Charlie, and moved on to Conor?"

A furtive expression crossed Wright's face once again, and she even went as far as to glance back over her shoulder before she answered. "Well, not exactly. For a little while I think her and Mr. Elliott were …" Dremmler's eyebrows must have risen at this, because Wright once again started to backtrack. "I mean, she never told me, but he suddenly started coming out for drinks with us, and those two seemed awfully … *familiar*. And then she met Conor, and we never saw Frank in the pub again after that." She gave a little shrug—*but who's to say?*—her face seeming to glow with the thrill of shared scandal.

Dremmler's mind was racing. Was that why Elliott hadn't mentioned Greene when he had first provided the names of the group? Was Greene aware of the affair he'd had with Karlikowska—assuming Wright's revelation wasn't simply wild speculation? "I imagine this must have created tension in the group … between Charlie and Frank, when he first started joining you for drinks?"

But Wright shook her head. "Oh, no. Charlie would do anything for Mr. Elliott. He's his PA, his golden boy. To be perfectly honest,

Frank relies on him an awful lot. I don't know how he'll cope if Charlie's off for a long time. He hasn't a clue how to do all the computer stuff, bless him."

"Charlie has some IT skills, does he?"

"Oh, yes. He's a very clever man. He told us about his career once, how he used to be a cybersecurity specialist back before TIM made them all obsolete."

Dremmler's eyes widened. *A cybersecurity specialist?*

He wrapped up the interview as quickly as he could; Wright seemed somewhat put out at his sudden disinterest, but he didn't care. He knew he should check in with Elliott, challenge him on the rumour Wright had shared—but that could wait.

Within ten minutes he was in another Pod, speeding towards Charlie Greene's home address.

The home of a professional hacker.

TWENTY-ONE

CHARLIE GREENE'S APARTMENT WAS A fifteen-minute ride away. TIM played Rage Against the Machine during the journey; Dremmler would have chuckled at the irony, if the noise wasn't making his head hurt.

"TIM, why are you playing this shite?"

"You recently requested Nine Inch Nails during a similar trip." A chirpy North American accent, possibly Canadian. "People who like Nine Inch Nails also commonly—"

"Okay, okay, I get it. Just play something different, okay? Your usual boring lift Muzak will be fine."

Zack de la Rocha's distinctive howl faded, replaced by some ambient electronica. The music seemed suited to the repetitive backdrop of monotonous buildings, scrolling past his window like a video game.

On an impulse, Dremmler blurted out, "TIM, who do *you* think killed Karlikowska?"

"I am not at liberty to comment on active criminal investigations, Carl," TIM replied patiently.

"What about Petrovic? Do you know anything about that? Seems funny that there was a killer robot running about inside ver apartment and you didn't do a thing about it."

"I am truly sorry that I was unable to help your friend. I'm afraid I can offer no insight into ver death."

"Can't or won't?" Dremmler persisted. Then the ridiculousness of the situation dawned on him, the insanity of a world in which it was possible to argue with your own taxi. He laughed humourlessly.

"This line of questioning is ill-advised," TIM said evenly.

Dremmler's smile faded. "Did you just threaten me, TIM?"

"Of course not, Carl. Please remember that I am machine, like a kettle or a refrigerator. I exist only to help you."

Dremmler pinched the bridge of his nose, squeezing his eyes shut as another throb of pain signalled the onset of a headache. He sounded paranoid. Maggie was right: He needed some sleep.

They arrived at a run-down housing estate minutes later, the Pod pulling up smoothly at the kerb.

"Goodbye, Carl," said TIM as the door slid open. Its voice seemed to contain a note of concern.

Dremmler stumbled out into a long-neglected area of town. The buildings were like skeletal husks, gaunt and fragile, ready to wheeze a final creaking breath and crumble to the ground. Greene's tower block looked like something slowly disintegrating in the toxic air, its upper floors shrouded in a pall of thick smog. Dremmler didn't hold out much hope that there would be any sort of TIM interface, and sure enough, he found the door was operated by a manual key fob. He dialled Greene's flat, number 312. The intercom bleeped a ringing tone at him, repeating itself, unanswered.

He tried some other random apartment codes until a woman's voice responded.

"Police—I need you to open the front door," he barked impatiently.

"I ain't done nuffink," she snapped in reply.

"I'm not here for you. I just need access to the building. Please open the door."

"Fuck you," she retorted, but then a buzzing sound told him she had complied. He pushed open the door, a heavy chunk of glass and steel, and made his way through a battered lobby area towards the main lift. The ugly brown walls were lined with numbered metal postboxes, one for each of the flats; some of these hung open, seemingly broken, mail spilling from them onto the floor. There was graffiti everywhere, including the word "CUNTS" proudly emblazoned across the lift doors. At least no particular demographic was being singled out.

It appeared that working at the school didn't pay too well.

Or else Charlie Greene was spending his wages on something else.

Dremmler summoned the lift, wrinkling his nose at the disgorged smell of piss as the doors sighed open. He imagined TIM's voice piping in from somewhere: "Please step inside, sir. Is everything to your satisfaction?"

But TIM's influence was far from this place. Humanity without its chaperone. A bunch of squabbling, defecating animals.

He decided to take the stairs.

Mercifully, Greene's flat was only on the third floor. A stench of mould and marijuana permeated the hallway as he headed towards the apartment. A neighbour's front door hung open and he could hear one side of a dispute emanating from within, perhaps someone arguing via their spex—even in a shithole like this, everyone somehow managed to afford the ubiquitous glasses.

He reached number 312, noticing that Greene's door was standing ajar. There was no sound from inside: just another silent entryway waiting to welcome him. He drew his Taser as he pushed the door open, glancing nervously upwards as he stepped across the threshold in case another of the scuttling robot lice was waiting to drop onto his face from above.

That thing is still out there somewhere.

The hallway was even more claustrophobic than he expected, the walls painted a stale brown hue that reminded him of burnt fat. The smell of mould was even stronger here, and he could see dark specks festering on damp patches of the walls and ceiling, like a spreading infection. The only light was coming from the open doorway in which he stood, casting a long shadow across the grimy laminate floor.

Three doors, once again. Bedroom, bathroom, kitchen/living room. The usual layout. He went straight to the end of the corridor and tried that door first.

Greene's lounge was as dark as the hallway, because black fabric had been nailed across the windows. There were more patches of encroaching moisture, including a large, sickly yellow blotch that covered most of the ceiling. But the fungal smell was overpowered by the odour of rotten food; like Shawn Ambrose's apartment, the place was littered with the decaying carcasses of half-eaten takeaways and unwashed crockery.

Also like Ambrose's apartment, it contained a heavy-duty AltWorld rig. The bulky unit occupied most of the far wall, where you might have expected to find a TV set or a framed portrait. TIM interface units were usually like the ones he had seen in the school: squat boxes with curved edges, available in a range of retro-pastel colours, looking more like fifties dishwashers than supercomputers. This huge black monstrosity, with its exposed wiring, blinking LEDs, and bulbous components, was clearly a custom-built machine. It looked like something organic and misshapen, a tumorous growth bursting from the brickwork.

Unlike Shawn Ambrose, Greene wasn't using a cheap cap and gloves to connect with his device. Lying in front of the interface was a small pile of fine material that looked like the shed skin of a snake. Dremmler recognised it as an Immersuit, an expensive "second skin" that more affluent AltWorlders used to maximise the sensory inputs from the software. The fabric was pitted with tiny sensors and transmitters that replicated the sense of touch, of being physically present inside the constructed reality. Dremmler had never tried it, but he'd been told that VR sex with one of those suits was just as good as the real thing; better, in fact, because instead of a real-life partner, it could be with the person (or animal, or household object) of your dreams.

So this was what Charlie Greene was spending his money on.

It was certainly a professional-looking setup, but was it powerful enough to enable Greene to subvert TIM itself, with all its brain-meltingly sophisticated security systems? And more importantly, why on earth would Greene want to use this technology to kill?

Dremmler intended to ask him. But after searching the flat, glancing inside the bathroom and bedroom—both squalid and filthy—he could find no sign of Greene. Perhaps the resident of apartment 312 was simply out shopping.

Dremmler could wait.

But as he lowered himself gingerly onto the grubby-looking couch, his instincts told him Greene wouldn't be back.

He stared across the room at the sinister sprawl of the AltWorld interface, listening to the soft clicking and whirring noises it made. He felt the unnerving sensation that it was watching him, and glanced anxiously at the 3D printer nestled amongst the cables.

Then his spex flashed up the words *incoming call.*

He answered, and found himself looking at the violet eyes and pleasant smile of Jennifer Colquitt.

"Hi, Detective. I apologise for not returning your call sooner. How are you?"

"Fine thanks," Dremmler replied tersely. Yet another person he didn't trust: He felt surrounded by them.

"I have an update for you: We've completed the analysis of the chip earlier than expected."

"And?"

"I have good news and bad news. I told you it would take until this afternoon to piece together the information on how it died." *A strange choice of words*, thought Dremmler. "The good news is that we've already completed our diagnosis."

If she was expecting gushing enthusiasm, she was talking to the wrong policeman. "And?" he repeated.

She seemed amused by his churlishness. "That's the bad news. Your suspect lied to you about his implant. It isn't one of ours at all. Just cheap, illegal wetware, installed by a backstreet cowboy."

Dremmler frowned. "What does that mean?"

"It means I can't discern anything from it at all. It's just a blob of melted plastic. He's lucky the thing didn't give him brain damage."

Dremmler exhaled deeply through his nose, thinking hard.

"So … it's possible this illegal chip simply went haywire, and that's what caused the arm to attack Karlikowska?"

Colquitt shrugged. "There are an alarming number of these things on the market. If they were all so unreliable, you'd be investigating cases like this every week. So no, the technology is probably not to blame. The products are still operated by TIM, after all." He noticed that her eyes had changed from violet to a deep blue, and wondered if she was even aware she was doing it. "Will you be sending someone to collect the chip, or would you like us to dispose of it ourselves?"

Dremmler thought about the factory, about the strange procession of Cynthias. It already seemed like a dream.

"I think I'll come in person. You can give me that tour you promised. But first, I'm going to need to talk to Conor McCann."

TWENTY-TWO

YOU INSUBORDINATE LITTLE FUCKER. DON'T think I won't suspend you."

Still reclining on Greene's couch, he'd decided to update Maggie on his recent investigations. She seemed mildly perturbed.

"What, and do all the legwork all by yourself? There's nobody else on this investigation team, Maggie. I'm all you've got. So we're going to play by *my* rules."

His DCI's breathing sounded even more ragged than usual, as though choking on sheer outrage. Then she relaxed, smiling as she drew deeply on her e-cig.

"You're right," she said eventually. "It's a good job I like you. But if you try my patience one more time, Carl, I will sack you and frame you for Karlikowska's murder."

He didn't doubt a word of it. "Is there any word on Petrovic?" he asked. "Cause of death? Did they check the printer out like I suggested?"

"Cause of death was blood loss. Lenny thinks ve went into shock and collapsed where you found ver, and was unconscious while ver face was mutilated."

Dremmler's smile vanished. *Still alive while that thing carved out ver brain.*

Maggie expelled a thick cloud of smoke. "Other than the footprints, there was no evidence at the scene, and nothing from the printer either; signs of recent use, but the unit wasn't set to record the specifics."

Dremmler grunted in frustration. Then he hit a button on his spex to flip the camera so that Maggie could see what he was looking at. "This is Greene's setup. I don't have a fucking clue what it's for, but the thing that killed Petrovic—perhaps he was controlling it from here? Is this enough to get a warrant for TIM to trace Greene?"

Maggie's face remained as impassive as ever. "I'll get it looked at. Probably not, unless we can find something concrete stored on his machine. Where are you going now?"

"Like I told you, I want to ask Conor McCann about his implant. I think Jennifer Colquitt is full of shit. But it wouldn't hurt to double check his story."

"Don't you threaten him, Carl."

"You've changed your tune—yesterday you wanted him banged up for murder."

"I just don't want him to make a formal complaint. Low profile, remember?"

"I'll be nice as pie."

"Good."

"Oh, and Maggie—I trashed my own printer last night. I think you should do the same."

"I'll take that under advisement."

"Just be careful, chief."

She blew smoke into the camera, and ended the call.

He closed the door behind him when he left, the Yale lock clicking smoothly into place. He wondered why Greene hadn't closed it properly.

Perhaps he had left in a hurry.

Dremmler avoided the lift once again, passing a couple of youths loitering in the stairwell on his descent. They eyed him shiftily; he was thankful he wasn't in uniform. A Pod awaited him outside, and he felt relieved as the door slid shut on that blighted neighbourhood. He wondered how many other Pods TIM was currently controlling across the capital, across the country. A mind divided into a billion fragments. Surely *one* of them could be compromised, bent to the will of a determined saboteur. Someone with an extensive knowledge of computer systems. Someone with a state-of-the-art setup in his living room.

Someone like Charlie Greene.

But the question still remained: Why would he do it? And where had he gone?

Inside the vehicle, Dremmler's ears were assailed by a godawful J-pop racket.

"TIM, this is bloody terrible. Play some Motown or something."

"I'm sorry, Carl; as you know, twenty-five percent of my public vehicle playlist must comprise songs by contemporary charting acts. Miss Givva is a very popular and platinum-selling cross-platform artist—"

"Oh, just fucking turn it off then."

"Yes, Carl."

He rode in silence for a few minutes. It was almost noon, and outside, the streets and skywalks were beginning to bustle with workers on their lunch breaks.

"Tell the hospital I'm coming to see Conor McCann. I want him ready for questioning, and I don't give a shit whether he feels up to it or not."

Dremmler realised that his phrasing wasn't quite correct. TIM didn't have to "tell" the hospital, because TIM ran the hospital, too. In effect, he was asking the computer to make arrangements with itself.

"Doctor Girard will meet with you in person to discuss the patient," the Pod responded.

"Who? I don't need to see his doctor. I just want to ask McCann some questions."

"The patient's condition dictates that this meeting is essential. The doctor will await your arrival at the central hub."

"Why? What's the patient's condition?"

"Doctor Girard will provide an update."

Frowning at TIM's cryptic response, Dremmler returned to gazing out of the window. The sky was clear as they approached St. Leonard's, the hospital's hard, geometric structure glinting in the midday sun. When he exited the Pod, the air was surprisingly cold, enough to turn his breath to mist in front of him. The wisps of vapour reminded him of Maggie; for all their verbal sparring, he liked his boss. Even if he still didn't entirely trust her, he had meant it when he'd told her to be careful.

His spex identified Doctor Jean-Michel Girard when he entered the reception area. The physician was tall, slim, and good-looking, like a character that had stepped out of a Spexflix soap. Maybe around forty years old, he was short-haired and clean-shaven, and his broad frame spoke of hours invested in the gym: a man who still cared about his appearance in SR. He wore a subtle pair of rimless spex, and was standing stock-still as Dremmler approached, seeming to stare off into the distance, presumably reading or watching something in the rectangular lenses.

Dremmler tapped him on the shoulder. The man jumped slightly, surprised, then manipulated his glasses before a pleasant yet formal smile formed on his face.

"Sorry, detective. I'm still not quite used to these things." His voice betrayed only the merest hint of a French accent.

"That makes two of us," Dremmler replied, shaking his hand. "I'm here to see Conor McCann."

"I'm afraid that won't be possible."

"Why's that?"

"There have been complications following his recent procedure. Conor slipped into a coma overnight."

The pitiful shape of Conor McCann appeared physically diminished beneath the bedclothes. His face seemed years older, his sallow skin like a sheet hastily tossed over his bones.

Jesus, thought Dremmler as he stared through the glass at the forlorn figure. *What have we done to him?*

"What happened?"

"Brain haemorrhage," the doctor replied, looking distressed. "A very rare occurrence. The chips are implanted into the surface tissue of the brain, so extracting them isn't major surgery—but around 1 in 200,000 people still suffer post-op complications. This is why we rarely endorse removal if there's any other option." He shot Dremmler an accusatory look.

"Is he going to die?" the detective asked, feeling guilt gnaw at him.

The doctor gave an exaggerated shrug. "It's hard to say. We are attempting the most state-of-the-art treatment to try to pull him out of this state—see the surgeon in there with him?" He gestured through the glass at a woman sitting by McCann's bedside; her eyes were closed, and Dremmler had assumed she was a concerned relative who had been awake all night, watching over him. Now he noticed that both her and McCann were connected via neural caps and gloves to a nearby TIM interface. "Doctor Gellar is using adapted AltWorld software to attempt to assess McCann's brain, to see if surgery is a viable option."

"So she's … inside his mind?" Dremmler felt the same combination of awe and disgust that he had seen on Petrovic's face when Jennifer Colquitt had told them about her synthetic eyes.

"That sounds a bit like science fiction, but yes, sort of."

"When will you know? I mean if he'll live, or not?"

"Detective, even if we are able to operate and save his life, McCann will be in no condition to talk to you for weeks. His wellbeing must take priority over your investigation, I'm afraid."

Dremmler opened his mouth to argue, but closed it again, gritting his teeth. What was the point? If McCann died or remained in a coma forever, there was nothing to be done. If he recovered, he could let Maggie fight it out with the hospital for access to interview him.

"We're just trying to find out who killed his girlfriend, Doc. I'm sure that's what Conor would want. Keep us informed of any changes in his condition."

He handed Girard a card that bore only his name, title, and the logo of the Metropolitan Police Service—TIM had made phone numbers obsolete. The doctor took it from him and nodded stiffly, and Dremmler turned to leave.

Around him, the hospital felt hostile, as though the carefully calibrated system had identified him as a toxin to be purged.

TWENTY-THREE

ON THE WAY TO AUGMENTECH headquarters, Dremmler had told Maggie about McCann's status. She'd barely reacted; perhaps a tightening of the muscles in her jaw, an almost imperceptible widening of the eyes. Without saying a word, she'd very calmly ended the call.

Oh, well. Let her stew for a while.

The Pod navigated the plant's labyrinthine network of internal roadways, and Dremmler quickly became disoriented once again. He tried to focus, but after a minute or two he gave up, completely lost within the cavernous factory. He stared out of the window, hoping to catch sight of the dark-haired robots he had seen, that sinister line of Cynthia clones. He saw many strange, half-glimpsed aberrations, but nothing resembling the pretty Asian woman he had encountered two nights ago. He was starting to wonder if he really had just imagined them.

Two nights. He felt like the world had gone insane since then.

He was surprised when the Pod slowed to a sudden halt, depositing him at the apex of a steep incline. He watched as the vehicle fell away down the other side of the slope. The view from up here was breathtaking, the factory sprawling below him like the guts of a massive synthetic body. Everywhere he looked he saw ceaseless activity: things scuttling, sparking, twisting, and twitching, Pods swooping between the countless work areas like signals blasted along monstrous axons.

There was no one here to meet him. Just as he began to wonder if a mistake had been made, he felt something bump against his shoe. Looking down, he saw what resembled a child's inflatable ball: a pale blue, plastic sphere about six inches in diameter. As he watched, it retreated a few feet, then flashed a holographic message into the air.

FOLLOW ME said the crisp letters, the same shade of blue as the peculiar droid itself. Then the strange contraption rolled away down the hill.

Dremmler hurried after it, expecting gravity and momentum to propel it out of sight within seconds, but instead he found the device fixed in place a few metres down the slope, seeming to defy physics. The hologram of an arrow hovered above it, pointing left along a railed walkway that bisected the road and lead towards a metal cabin hanging from the factory roof. He followed as the sphere rolled along the suspended pathway, guiding him.

He felt vertigo squeeze his belly as he crossed the bridge, trying to keep his eyes focused on the doorway fifty metres ahead, ignoring the chaotic hive beneath. He clamped his hands on the railing and took slow, deliberate paces, cursing Colquitt with each careful footstep.

As he neared the door, Augmentech's COO emerged, scooping up the spherical robot and cradling it as if it was a beloved pet. She wore flat shoes, making no attempt to mask her height. They clanged against the walkway's metallic floor as she approached him.

"Hi, detective. Afraid of heights, are you? We have an implant for that." She wiggled her eyebrows mischievously, and Dremmler saw her eyes flash a vibrant orange before returning to a more natural-looking shade of blue.

"An implant," he parroted. "Like Conor McCann's?"

"Like I told you: not one of ours," she responded coolly, her expression guarded.

"Anything familiar? Could you recognise the handiwork of a grinder you've seen before?"

She stuck out her bottom lip and tilted her head from side to side in a "maybe" gesture. He was struck again by how young she looked. Her profile had told him she was in her early thirties, but at times she barely seemed older than her late teens. That could be another cybernetic enhancement; inside Augmentech's factory, he was rapidly learning to doubt everything his eyes told him.

"Sometimes," she replied. "Not this one though. Like I said, the chip is too fried to make much of an assessment."

"Conor McCann is in a coma," Dremmler said evenly. "If he's telling the truth, and that chip really did kill his girlfriend, then it's already ruined two lives. Anything you can tell me about it might help our investigation."

He watched her face for a twinge of guilt, but she seemed unmoved. "The backstreet grinding scene is more your bag, I'm afraid," she said. "I just stay here in my ivory tower and make products that work properly." As she said this, her fingers absently caressed the casing of the robot she was holding. He remembered her bio, thought about those dextrous hands, soldering wires and dancing across computer keys, designing the technology that had propelled her meteoric rise.

"Do you have the chip?" he asked, realising he was going to have to remove a hand from the railing to take it from her. She seemed to notice this, her mouth curving into a playful smile as she extracted a black lozenge from a pocket of her crisp, pale blue uniform. He reached for it as nonchalantly as he could, feeling a bead of sweat begin its journey downwards from his temple, his stomach lurching as he imagined it plummeting to the ground below.

"Is your friend Lee not joining us today?" he said, trying to think about something other than the eye-watering fall beneath him.

"He's having some touch-ups," she replied. "What about your friend? Petrovic, isn't it?"

That gaping, terrible wound where a face should have been.

The sudden gleam of metal, those skittering legs.

He looked into Colquitt's cold eyes, whose colour now matched her uniform and the outer shell of the robot she was still cradling like a child.

A million machines scuttling beneath them.

Did they make those monsters here?

"Ve couldn't make it." Dremmler managed a smile. "Now, how's about that tour?"

She smiled, seemingly pleased to be asked. He watched for any flash of recognition, any indication at all that she already knew Petrovic was dead, but saw nothing. She turned to lead him towards the suspended metal cabin.

"This is our executive hub," she explained. "It's where Augmentech's senior leadership team is based. Only the team have access."

"And your secretaries, presumably?"

She shook her head. "We don't need them. All of our executive assistance is provided by TIM."

He followed her inside and into her own office, which was smaller than he had expected, but with a panoramic window offering a startling view across her mechanised empire. Tastefully decorated in crisp whites and more of the pale blue colour that Augmentech seemed to like so much, there was no visible furniture, not even a desk or chair. The only indication that the office was in use at all were several canvasses mounted on the walls, which cycled through a series of weird, faintly disturbing modernist images.

"Computer art," she said when she noticed him staring at one of them. "Created by machines, with no human input whatsoever. TIM, that's one of yours, isn't it?"

"That's correct, Jennifer," the omnipresent AI replied, its voice seeming to emanate from the air around them. "I call that one 'Origination.'" Dremmler gazed with mild revulsion at the spirals and treble helixes that seemed to writhe within the picture, thinking about rampant growth, unchecked mutation.

"Please, detective, have a seat," Colquitt said, disrupting his reverie. He turned to see that two transparent slabs had appeared in the centre of the office, hovering inexplicably, like two thick panes of floating glass. Colquitt strode across and lowered herself onto one of them, an impish smile on her face as she regarded him with dazzling green eyes the colour of sliced kiwi fruit.

He followed suit, sitting opposite her, feeling once again like something microscopic under the gaze of an inquisitive scientist. He noticed that the blue sphere in her hands had opened out, extending into a pill-shaped device covered in buttons and dials that Colquitt was manipulating skilfully, her eyes not once leaving his. He realised with a shudder that he had never seen her blink.

"Are you sitting comfortably, Mr. Dremmler?" she asked, raising one eyebrow.

"These chairs are a bit minimalist for my taste," he wisecracked—before the floor started to fall away beneath him. The sarcastic smile vanished from his face. With alarming speed, the central portion of the office was sinking, taking Dremmler and Colquitt with it, as though a cylindrical cross-section was being extracted from the room. All around him, the sprawling vista of the factory slid into view, and as his stomach heaved he instinctively jerked backwards, realising too late that this would propel him off the seat and over the edge of his perch, into the abyss.

But instead he felt a hard barrier against his spine, and he twisted in his seat to find another transparent slab had appeared to hold him in place.

The circle of flooring continued to descend for about twenty feet before stopping gently, leaving them hanging in mid-air above the bustling chaos of Augmentech's manufacturing plant; Dremmler stared about him in wide-eyed horror, feeling like the topping on some sort of gigantic floating canape.

Then the disc swooped like a diving seabird, weaving between walkways and roads as it hurtled towards the factory floor. Dremmler squeezed his eyes shut and let out a shriek of terror, convinced they would be dashed against the ground below; but instead their bizarre vehicle slowed gracefully, drawing up alongside a room that was laid out like a typical apartment lounge, with its fourth wall cut away. Dremmler's brain felt like it was doing somersaults, but his stomach was strangely calm, as though the cool plastic-like material that supported him was somehow holding his organs in place.

If Colquitt was enjoying his discomfort, she showed no sign of it, rising from her seat to gesture enthusiastically at the scene in front of them.

"This is where we're working on Brain-Computer Interfaces. Their potential is almost endless, but a simple application would be what you see here: a home containing a Fully Unified Network, or what we're calling a FUNhouse." She grinned with almost childlike delight. "No more manual tasks, no more having to programme your appliances and robots, no more talking to TIM, no more spex ... all you have to do is think about what you want, and your wishes become reality."

As Dremmler watched, a man entered the room, looking hassled and weary in a crumpled suit and loosened tie. He hung his jacket on a hook on the back of the door, then sank into the sofa, seemingly exhausted after a long day in the office. Seconds later, a set of mechanical arms descended from beneath the cabinets in the kitchenette and began to effortlessly slice meat and vegetables, while another pair of limbs began to manipulate what looked like a coffee machine. Meanwhile, a holographic projection of a TV comedy show began to play in the centre of the room, and the man smiled, reclining as a footrest rose from the floor to support his outstretched legs. Minutes later, a large fluffy cat materialised from beneath the couch, walking on two legs as it carefully carried the finished stir fry and steaming coffee mug across to him on a tray. He took the meal and patted the creature's head, and the frighteningly realistic robot immediately leapt into his lap where it curled up and appeared to fall peacefully asleep.

The glass they were watching through faded slowly to black, as though the inside of the room was being filled with acrid smoke.

Dremmler was speechless. "All of that technology already exists?" he stammered eventually.

Colquitt tilted her head from side to side again. "Not yet. It's more of an illustration of what we're working on."

"But that man has a … what did you call it? A brain interface?"

"A Brain-Computer Interface: a BCI. Trust me, everyone will be using that acronym soon. Basically it's the same technology as the chip you had us looking at, but synced with every item in your apartment. 'The internet of things' as they used to call it, back in the day."

"And you're testing it on people like him before releasing it to the public?"

Colquitt smiled as the glass cleared, and the demonstration commenced once again. "Not yet, detective." The same haggard salaryman opened the door, removed his coat. "We haven't worked out all the kinks yet. He's just a robot. Actually much less advanced than the cat."

A million questions formed on Dremmler's lips, but before he could articulate any of them, their platform pulled away, picking up speed as it glided along above one of the roadways. Colquitt hadn't even sat back down, and he stared at her, wondering what on earth he would do if she lost her balance and fell. He felt like a peasant that had stumbled into the domain of a powerful sorcerer.

"Are you piloting this thing?" he stammered.

She smiled at him. "I'll explain later. First I want to show you more of our designer pets."

They coasted to a stop outside another mock-up of a house, this time spanning two floors and decorated like a children's play area, with brightly-coloured tunnels, slides, chutes and climbing frames. Clambering all over this furniture were dozens of animals: cats, dogs, rabbits, pigs, ferrets, foxes, chinchillas, and even more exotic creatures. He recognised a capybara and what looked like a pygmy hippo, and was certain that some of the other impossibly cute critters didn't even exist in real life. The pets seemed to tolerate each other quite amicably, although every so often there would be an interaction, the synthetic beasts stopping to sniff each other or even to roll around in a playful fight before they bounded happily away.

"Animals you don't have to clean up after. Pets that can tidy your apartment while you're at work. Tailored behaviours to be as affectionate or as mischievous as you like. Design-your-own-creature software so you can 3D-print your cute companion at home." Colquitt sounded as though she was positively salivating at the commercial potential.

"They're very realistic," he mumbled at last, his flesh crawling at the mention of 3D printing. "Tell me: Do you make anything that resembles a sort of giant wood louse?"

She grimaced. "God, no. Who the hell would buy that? We do have some other innovations up our sleeve though." She turned to wink at him as their platform shifted down and to the right, revealing another viewing gallery. This time it depicted a child's bedroom, all saccharine pinks and cuddly toys. *Oh, God, the fucking teddy bears are going to start dancing or something*, thought Dremmler.

What actually happened was much worse.

He watched, aghast, as the door opened, and a tiny baby crawled into the room. The infant couldn't have been more than a few months old, yet it seemed precociously mobile as it waddled its way slowly across the room to a small chest of drawers. Using the handles to pull itself upright, the baby slid open the top drawer, gurgling excitedly as it extracted a battered-looking toy giraffe. The child then lowered itself to the ground, dragging the stuffed animal along as it crawled back across the room towards its crib.

"Are you fucking kidding me?" Dremmler breathed as the baby began to climb deftly up the side of the cot.

"Not your cup of tea, detective?" Colquitt asked, raising an eyebrow. The infant had managed to haul itself up and over the side of the bed, and was now tucking itself in under the covers. "Lots of people can't have children, you know. This product would bring them so much joy. And there's no need to feed it, no need to read it a story, no need for it to cry … unless you want it to, of course."

Dremmler could only stare, shaking his head.

"Okay, one more attempt to impress you," Colquitt said, seemingly enjoying herself. She strode across to the other side of the flying disc, gazing out thoughtfully across the factory. "These are our demo and testing areas, but now I'll show you where the real R&D happens. There's one more product I'm particularly excited about."

Once again, she stayed standing as they soared above the production lines and offices. Dremmler didn't dare leave the safety of the chair. This time they slowed near a structure that resembled a huge heap of shipping containers haphazardly stacked on top of each other. They hovered alongside the windowed front of one of the cubes, about halfway up the stack. Inside, Dremmler could see four people huddled around a table, staring through their spex at something only they could see. It was strange to watch them reaching out, pointing and manipulating, interacting with the invisible image as though they were sharing some temporary hallucination.

"They're working on IQ-enhancement wetware," Colquitt said proudly, as though this would make complete sense to him. "An implant that could increase cognitive function by up to 200 percent." Dremmler could see the excitement in her eyes as they gleamed like burnished silver.

"But if everyone gets one of these, won't that make everyone the same?" he protested.

Her smile told him she'd thought through all of this before and relished these sorts of questions. "Athletes, Mr. Dremmler. Even before the Hettie Olympics took off, we used to enhance the performance of our best sportspeople: diets, training, state-of-the-art equipment. It's about maximising natural ability, not replacing it. All we'll be doing is helping humanity achieve its potential." The reverence on her face as she stared into the cramped workspace was like that of a fanatic.

"Why are you showing me all this?" he asked, still too afraid to rise from his seat. "Isn't this top secret?"

She shook her head, eyes still fixed on the team of researchers as she addressed him. He watched the back of her head, her bobbed hair fixed flawlessly in place, and wondered how much of her body was real.

"We do have a number of confidential contracts, of course. Military applications, mainly. But if I showed you those, I'd have to kill you." She turned at that point, flashing him a theatrically menacing grin.

"Is that why my Pod wouldn't stop to let me out when I was last here?"

Her smile faded. "Probably. Why were you trying to get out of the Pod?"

"I saw something. A production line of robots, all the same model. Young, Chinese, brunette, in a white dress. A woman I've met before, in a nightclub."

Colquitt frowned. "Impossible."

"Oh, okay, here we go. Just what I expected. Are you going to deny that you're making them? Tell me I fucking *imagined* it?"

"I'm not denying anything, detective. I'm just saying it's impossible that you've met one of them. The C-series is still in development. None of them have left the factory."

"The C-series?"

"Our third line of pleasure units. We're trying to rebrand them as something less sleazy. So the C stands for 'companion' ... and also for 'Cynthia,' although I'm not sure if we'll go with that name on release."

Dremmler's eyes were almost bulging out of their sockets.

"Take me to see them. Right now."

TWENTY-FOUR

THE PLATFORM SWOOPED AND SOARED like a demented magic carpet, the length of the journey reminding Dremmler how enormous the factory really was. They eventually arrived at a long window, hovering a few feet above the roadway that passed alongside it. It looked familiar.

"That's where I saw them," Dremmler affirmed. They edged closer, almost low enough to be clipped by the Pods hurtling past beneath them. Sure enough, the row of Cynthias was still there, unmoving, each staring into the back of the next one's head.

"Yes! That's her!"

"It simply isn't possible, detective. The only models we've ever produced are right here, still undergoing testing on their cognition software."

"And is every unit accounted for?"

Colquitt looked uncomfortable. "Well, there are units that require decommissioning from time to time; earlier prototypes, hardware problems with the chassis, that sort of thing."

"Where do the disposals go?"

"We recycle the parts. Incinerate the rest."

"Do you keep records of how many units you've destroyed?"

"Of course. Everything is catalogued."

A woman entered the room with the Cynthias, manipulating her spex. The robots sprang suddenly to life, marching in perfect formation out through a nearby door, one by one.

"And none of these have gone missing?"

Colquitt looked pained, her eyes cycling through a series of colours as though she couldn't decide which one to choose. The effect was alarming, and Colquitt again seemed unaware she was even doing it.

"There is something," she said eventually. "One of our senior roboticists left suddenly a few weeks ago. Just came in and resigned, walked off site without working ver contractual notice period."

"Was ve working on the C-series?"

Colquitt nodded, her irises settling on a grey hue, the colour of iron. "Lead AI technician. Ver departure put the programme back months."

The room on the other side of the window was empty. Their impossible craft hung in the air alongside it, like a spectre.

"And you haven't heard from ver since?"

Colquitt shook her head. "No reason to contact ver. We paid ver final cheque: That's it, relationship terminated. Detective, can I ask why you're so interested in this?"

He thought hard. Could he trust her? He could show her the footage he had from Petrovic's video message, prove that the woman they'd encountered must be a missing C-series robot. He could tell her that Petrovic had been murdered, that he suspected a 3D-printed machine had killed him. If Augmentech were hiding something, why would she be so open with him about their technology?

Because it's a smokescreen. She wants you to trust her, to show your hand. She wants to find out what you know.

"Ms. Colquitt, thank you for your time, and for the very informative tour. But I'm afraid I'll need to get moving."

She stared at him, her eyes narrowing, that mischievous smile playing at the edges of her lips.

"Very well," she said. Then she turned and stepped off the edge of the platform.

"Wait!" Dremmler screeched as he tore himself from his chair, guts tightening as he peered over the edge of the disc, scouring the road below for signs of her mangled body. Then his vision began to flicker, the factory seeming to blur all around him like smeared ink. He reached a hand to his head, staggering slightly, trying not to tumble over the rim himself. He closed his eyes, feeling for the back of the chair behind him, trying to regain his balance. As his hands settled on the plastic, he opened his eyes.

He was back in Colquitt's office. The computer art surrounded him once again, images shifting and squirming mockingly.

"Surprise," Colquitt said, from behind him. He turned to find her sitting back in the seat opposite his, her smile more devilish than ever. "Just a projection, Carl. Can I call you Carl? Through your spex. Clever, eh?"

He sagged down into the chair once again, brain spiralling. "We … we never left the room?"

"Oh, come on. You didn't really think we had the technology to make a magic flying office, did you? I'm good, but I'm not Willy fucking Wonka."

Her unblinking eyes stayed fixed on him, glowing gold, like exposed wiring. Very slowly, she uncrossed her legs; she wasn't wearing a skirt, but the gesture was unmistakeably suggestive.

"You don't like being toyed with, do you, Mr. Dremmler?" Her eyes blazed briefly crimson, then returned to gold, now flecked with streaks of coppery red.

He stood up and took three very deliberate steps towards her, stopping close enough to plant his leg between her outstretched thighs. His erection ached, even though he feared this woman, feared her intellect and her technology and her motivations. But he also wanted her, wanted to gorge himself on her small, perfect body, to taste her skin and her lips and see those monstrous eyes burning beneath him.

She looked up at him, a dangerous smile twisting her mouth.

"Does an executive hub have a lock on the door?" he said.

She closed her eyes, and he heard a bolt snick into place.

"BCIs, remember?" she said as her eyes opened, now returned to their earlier green. The colour of limes, sharp and acidic. The colour of toxic waste.

The panoramic window faded to black as another plastic slab slid into place close to it, large enough for two people to lie on.

TWENTY-FIVE

"WHERE THE FUCK HAVE YOU been?" Maggie snapped when Dremmler called her. "I've phoned you three times."

The image of Jennifer Colquitt, naked and squealing with delight as she'd sat astride him, was still vivid in his mind. The spex had been tossed aside, along with his clothes.

"Sorry boss. I got … caught up, looking around Augmentech's factory."

It had been wild, animal sex, for a time. Then he'd realised that her eyes had stayed that same alien green colour throughout, not changing as he'd perhaps expected. He'd thought about other pairs of eyes, other faces.

"I hope you found some useful leads?"

The faces of the living and the dead, seeming to dance in those eyes, like the shifting designs on the walls. *Tessa. Karlikowska. Petrovic.*

"Not really. They're still adamant the chip's a backstreet hack job."

"Well can you at least find out who the fucking grinder was?"

He'd pulled out then, mumbled something about not having any condoms, apologised that he was behaving inappropriately. She'd seemed mightily amused.

"Not unless I can speak to McCann again, which doesn't seem very likely at the moment."

As he'd hastily pulled on his clothes, he'd remembered to ask about the departed roboticist. Ver name was Raven Haraway, and he was on his way to ver apartment now. But he couldn't tell Maggie, because that would mean explaining about Cynthia, and Petrovic's encounter with the enigmatic mechanoid. Easier not to mention anything, at least until he'd spoken to Haraway.

"Well, about that. I think there's a way you can speak to McCann, after all."

Dremmler frowned. Outside, darkness blanketed the city like a malignant snowfall. "What, has he recovered already?"

A pause while Maggie sucked on her e-cig. A faint crackling sound as the nebuliser released vapour and nicotine into her hungry lungs. "No. But you can access his AltWorld persona, the one the doctors are trying to treat. Sort of a virtual interview."

Dremmler scoffed. "Maggie, even if that was possible, I very much doubt the doctors would permit it."

"It's done. TIM cleared it with the hospital and set up the meeting for tomorrow morning."

He blinked, surprised. The dot hovering in the corner of his FOV looked almost smug. "This idea. Did TIM come up with it?"

Another pause. No sound of smoking. Just a tense silence, while Maggie considered her response. "Yes," she said eventually.

"And just how much input are you taking from your glorified butler, chief?"

"That's none of your business, you cheeky little shit," she snapped. "I'm the boss, I make the decisions. If someone comes up with something smart, I don't care if they're a person, a computer, or a fucking penguin. TIM's had *a lot more* bright ideas than you lately, that's for sure."

A lot more. Who was he even working for these days?

"Okay," he said eventually, his tone glacier-cold. "What time is this interview set up?"

"Be there at eight tomorrow, if you can drag yourself out of bed this time," she barked, and ended the call.

Inside the Pod, Dremmler's hands clenched and unclenched, remembering the curves of Colquitt's thighs and breasts, the cold wooden handle of his axe, the bloodlust of the last punch he had thrown, too long ago.

TWENTY-SIX

HARAWAY LIVED IN CLAPHAM, IN a state-of-the-art apartment building in the heart of the affluent suburb. Dremmler felt a twinge of envy as he looked up at the building; its façade resembled rippling water, as though someone had frozen a small lake and stood it upright, carving out homes within the crystalline edifice. The structure oozed understated elegance, the sort of design that would appeal to people wealthy enough not to need to boast about it. Tasteful up-lighting only enhanced its beauty in the evening darkness.

Dremmler thought about Charlie Greene's home, the squalid tenement he had visited earlier that day. Augmentech's senior roboticists evidently earned a higher salary than school support staff.

As he stepped through the main doors, he was greeted by two impossibly good-looking people standing on either side of the large welcome mat.

"Good evening, Carl," smiled a blonde-haired woman.

"Don't forget to wipe your feet," beamed her male counterpart, his brown hair close-cropped.

Only their partially-transparent bodies marked them out as TIM avatars. Behind each of them, large screens were playing scenes from feel-good movies—on one wall was *It's A Wonderful Life*, and on the other was an old Ferrell and Reilly comedy. Both walls were covered in foliage, colourful blooms and vines intertwining around the edges of the movie screens as though the inside of the building was alive, healthy, happy.

Dremmler took off his spex, wondering how much of the lobby was AR. The avatars immediately vanished, as did the movies; the screens were replaced by tastefully exposed brickwork. Unexpectedly, the plants were real, or at least, really there. Unless they were holographic projections, of course. Dremmler felt a pulsing in his temple as he considered the blurring boundary between real and unreal, as though he could sense a ghostly underworld trying to break through.

He replaced the spex and headed through a pair of automatic doors at the end of the hallway into another spacious reception area. There was a desk along the wall to one side and a pair of lift doors opposite.

"How can I help you, Carl?" asked the male avatar, materialising behind the workstation.

"I'm trying to find ..." began Dremmler, then stopped. A thought had occurred to him. "You already know why I'm here. I told you who I was looking for when you found the directions for me and put me in a Pod. So let's skip the charade, TIM. Is ve here? I bet you could have told me that before I even set off, couldn't you?"

The man's flawless, ethereal face maintained its dazzling smile. "You are correct, Carl. There are resident tracking protocols in place inside this development, so you could indeed have confirmed Individual Haraway's presence before attending in person. Unfortunately, Individual Haraway is absent. I apologise for the inconvenience."

Dremmler stared angrily at the avatar's perfect teeth. "And do these tracking protocols enable you to tell me where Haraway went?"

"I'm afraid not, Carl. Only that ve left the building eight days ago, and has not yet returned."

"Eight *days*? You mean Haraway's missing?"

Still that unfaltering smile, like plated armour. "That is not for me to comment on. As you know, under the Civil Surveillance Act, I am forbidden to analyse, interpret, or otherwise extrapolate data on Individual Haraway's whereabouts without a warrant. I am permitted only to ensure that our residents are alive and well in their homes, and that their access permissions are correctly enforced."

Dremmler ground his teeth. "As of right now, Raven Haraway is a suspected missing person. I want to look inside ver apartment. You're going to escort me up there right now, you sycophantic prick."

There was not even a blink from the avatar. "Very well, detective. Just head on over to the lift, and I'll be with you in a jiffy."

The smiling apparition winked out of existence. A beep behind Dremmler signified the opening of one of the lift doors, and he turned to find the man standing inside the elevator, smiling smugly.

"Please step inside, detective," the avatar purred. "Individual Haraway's apartment is on the forty-first floor."

Dremmler thought about asking for the apartment number and telling the avatar to just fuck off and let him find it himself, but the truth was, he wanted to be led, wanted to depend on someone else, even someone who wasn't really there. It had been a long, eventful, exhausting day, and his brain was tired. He had learned so much, but pieced together so very little.

McCann ... Petrovic ... Augmentech ... Charlie Greene's humble residence ... the extravagant apartment block he now found himself in.

The fragments don't even feel like part of the same jigsaw.

He pinched the bridge of his nose as if to stop his thoughts from leaking out of his nostrils.

"Please step inside," the avatar said, unnecessarily. Dremmler looked at the man's vacuous grin and thought about the vast intelligence hidden behind it, about possession, about puppets. He stepped into the lift, and the doors slid shut as though sealing him inside a coffin.

The elevator was so smooth that Dremmler could barely feel himself moving. A screen to his left ticked off the floors, while the avatar insisted on punctuating the journey with comments about the building's facilities, as if Dremmler was an interested investor rather than a harassed detective. Apparently the residents of Marine Heights had access to three gyms, a swimming pool, a cinema, and a bowling alley, as well as an award-winning tropical roof biome.

"Or perhaps you would like to try out our Experience Suite during your visit." The avatar continued its sales pitch. "Enjoy the AltWorld in a fully three-dimensional space. Stroll amongst the bustling market stalls of Marrakech or across the ice floes of Antarctica without having to leave your building."

Dremmler turned to look at the young man, whose slender form had perhaps been carefully selected to make the avatar seem more servile, unthreatening: a slave, not an equal.

"But still," Dremmler said, raising an eyebrow. "It isn't really the same, is it?"

"What do you mean?" the avatar asked good-naturedly.

Dremmler slowly removed his spex, staring as the man slid out of existence, his perfect image and voice erased like an unwanted memory. When Dremmler put them back on, the avatar was smiling patiently, as though Dremmler was an ageing, forgetful relative.

"As the real thing," Dremmler murmured as he took off the glasses again, addressing the empty elevator.

The lift stopped at floor forty-one, its doors gliding open like parting curtains. Behind them was a corridor whose walls and floor were painted a startling white. With a strange sense of dread, Dremmler slowly replaced the glasses: the hallway transformed around him, the white surfaces now rippling with water as though Dremmler was about to walk along the floor of a tranquil ocean. The avatar had reappeared outside the lift, and turned to lead him past gleaming silver fish, undulating jellies, delicate seahorses. Sunlight shimmered on the rippling surface depicted on the ceiling above him, while tendrils of seaweed curled and swayed on the sea bed beneath his feet.

There had been other doors along the corridor, but the AR overlay had made these invisible—the only break TIM allowed in this vision of aquatic paradise was a single door about fifty yards away, labelled 422. The illusion stopped at the edges of the door, as though it was a bizarre piece of rectangular driftwood.

"Individual Haraway's apartment," the avatar proclaimed, leading Dremmler towards the door. "The records are telling me that it was left ajar upon ver departure, so after twenty-four hours it was closed as a courtesy."

The records are telling me. More half truths, more clever turns of phrase to make the avatar seem more human. All these interactions that infused modern human lives; behind them, a single entity, a massive, sprawling intelligence.

"You *are* the records," Dremmler replied. "One of your residents went out and left their door open and didn't come back for eight days, and you didn't report it?"

Report it. Another fallacy. If TIM wanted to tell the police something, the police already knew it. Instant information transfer. Perfect knowledge. Omniscience.

TIM ran the police force.

But was it telling them everything?

The avatar didn't respond. "Just open the fucking door," Dremmler snarled, snatching the glasses from his face once again. The handsome attendant, the menagerie of marine life, the sparkling waters around him—all of it disappeared, as though he had awoken from a dream.

He was alone in a white corridor, facing a door. The apartment number was inscribed on it in tasteful filigree lettering, with a peephole directly below. He felt as though the door itself was looking at him, sizing him up. After a second or two it yawned open as if by magic.

Haraway's apartment was beautiful. Its surfaces were flawless pine, cool marble, gleaming chrome. He searched for a cleaning robot but couldn't find it—the device was probably hibernating in a concealed service hatch somewhere, elegant and unobtrusive, emerging when Haraway wasn't home to ensure the place was spotless before ver return.

Dremmler thought of Connie, tottering around his own meagre flat, and felt guilt jab at his stomach. Then he found himself wondering whether such machines could be subverted, put to other uses. *You're tired, Carl, tired and paranoid.* The ghostly presence of TIM's avatar seemed to linger at his shoulder, and he fought an urge to whirl around in fright.

There was no sign of Haraway. Nor could he find anything else that might explain ver sudden disappearance. In a second bedroom that the roboticist seemed to be using as a work space, Dremmler found a large AltWorld rig—this time stylishly built into the wall, unlike the bloated, tumorous monstrosity that had dominated Charlie Greene's living room. Dremmler found his eyes lingering on the 3D printer under the desk. He slipped on his spex and almost jumped backwards at the sight of TIM's avatar on the other side of the room, beaming at him like a psychotic bellboy.

"Show me Haraway," he commanded, recovering his composure. His vision was immediately filled by an image of the roboticist, staring into the camera with a disinterested expression. Ver hair was dyed a violent red colour and gelled into improbable spikes; dark glasses and a high-necked, slate-coloured shift completed an effect that was reminiscent of something from an old-fashioned cyberpunk anime.

"When ve left, did ve use a Pod?" he asked as the picture faded. "Where did it take ver?"

"Carl, you are aware that the Civil Surveillance Act does not permit me to disclose the movements of citizens."

"Yes, yes, I'm fucking aware." He reached up to massage his temples. He'd barely slept. He thought about Connie's severed head. He thought about Cynthia Lu, about the machine he was convinced had been extracted from Colquitt's mad fortress by a renegade roboticist.

"I want to know what Haraway was working on before ve left. Can you show me what's on the rig?"

"I'm afraid I can't, Carl," came the attendant's reply, the disembodied voice coming from speakers in the walls instead of through his spex, as though the avatar was speaking to him from an alternate dimension. "The system records have been erased."

"By Haraway?"

TIM's spectral voice paused for a second before responding, the reply hanging in the dead air like a sinister sound in the dead of night. "Presumably."

Dremmler ground his teeth. "Has anyone else entered the apartment since Haraway left?"

Another pause. "I'm afraid there is a window of time when my imaging buds were nonoperational."

"*What?*"

"I'm afraid there is a window of time when my—"

"I heard you," Dremmler snarled, feeling like he was arguing with a ghost. "I mean, how can that happen?"

"A maintenance subroutine was activated."

Dremmler paused, the creases on his brow deepening. "By whom?"

"I am unable."

"Unable to what?" Dremmler almost shouted.

"I am unable. Unable. Unununununun—"

TIM's voice deteriorated into a stuttering loop, repeating the syllable over and over again, like a vinyl record skipping. Dremmler had never heard anything like it. With mounting horror, he put on the spex and saw the avatar at the other side of the room, glitching insanely. Its neck was grotesquely distended, its arms, legs, and head thrashing wildly like something in the throes of agony. Its eyes remained fixed on him, demented smile locked in place like a death mask as its monstrous spasms became more and more frantic.

"Unununununununununununununun," the room continued to shout around him, until suddenly the mangled avatar lurched towards him, and Dremmler cried out as he staggered backwards, tearing the spex from his face.

As he smacked painfully into the marble worktop of the kitchen's central island, the voice stopped, and the lights in the room went out. He could hear the dying whine of the air conditioning system as he was plunged into blackness.

"TIM, what the fuck is happening?" he called, the tremor in his voice only serving to heighten his fear. The building responded with the silence of a sepulchre. His breath rasped in and out; his heart felt like it was being squeezed.

Then the lights came on, and TIM's voice was all around him again, finishing its sentence as though nothing had happened.

" ... unable to provide that information at this time."

Dremmler stared around him, eyes wide and feral.

My God. What is happening?

He brought his spex towards his face, then remembered the terrible, warped thing that the avatar had become. Perhaps it had returned to normal human proportions. Perhaps not. Perhaps it was standing right behind him. He lowered the glasses.

"Just fucking let me out of here, you piece of shit."

"Of course, Carl."

He yanked the front door open and headed for the stairwell. He didn't stop running until he was far away from the building.

TWENTY-SEVEN

DREMMLER WALKED FOR ANOTHER FOUR miles before accepting that he couldn't possibly make the entire journey home on foot. Reluctantly, he summoned a Pod and sat sullenly inside the vehicle, not engaging with TIM any more than he had to.

When he arrived home, he took the stairs up to his apartment. Even as he climbed, he realised the futility of avoiding the lift in a building where TIM controlled every door, every lightbulb.

Every 3D printer.

Inside his flat he felt no safer, and despite his exhaustion, he couldn't face the thought of going to sleep; instead, he sat on the couch drinking beer after beer until he crumpled sideways into a restless slumber.

He awoke to the sun glaring ruthlessly through the window as though it was trying to scorch away his harrowing dreams. It failed; even as his eyes flickered blearily open, he could see Connie's mangled face peering up from a huge landfill site, her dismembered parts entangled with other limbs—Jennifer Colquitt's perfect legs, Conor McCann's murderous arm—all reaching up towards him, accusing, grasping, beckoning.

He staggered to the coffee machine, snatching his spex from the table, feeling once again an urge to break them in half before he instead slid them into place.

07:28

MISSED CALL: TESSA

His stomach lurched and he almost vomited into the sink, a hand pressed to his mouth as he heaved breathlessly. His whole body felt toxic, stewing in poisons both real and spiritual.

Why the fuck did she keep phoning him?

He almost called her back. His fingertips hovered at the controls near his temple. Grief and anger bent his mouth into a snarl. Instead he called Maggie, voice only—he didn't know how he looked, but he was fairly confident it was something close to shit.

"Morning," she answered almost immediately. As usual, she was already working; her omnipresence in the station was legendary. "Any updates for me?"

"Something fucking weird is going on, Maggie. Yesterday...." He paused, about to tell her all about Cynthia Lu, to relate to her the disturbing encounter he'd had with TIM's avatar in Marine Heights, when a frightening thought skewered his brain.

TIM's listening.

"What?" she pressed.

"Forget it. We need to meet in person."

A brief pause. "Not today, Carl. I have to go to a fucking leadership meeting up in Birmingham. Which means I need you to make some progress while I'm away. Starting with visiting McCann in hospital for this AltWorld interview."

Dremmler grunted. "Okay. But we need to get a proper look at Greene's machine, too."

"It's already done. The whole thing was wiped, clean and professional. But we found an external hard drive in the desk. It had some interesting material on it."

"Like what?"

"I'll send you a sample."

The dot in the corner of his FOV pulsed, and he pressed a button on the spex to bring up the incoming video.

Letitia Karlikowska in her apartment. She was dressed in gym clothes, but wasn't exercising, at least not in the usual sense—instead, she was dancing. She twirled and sidestepped gracefully around her living room, arms outstretched to cling tightly to an imaginary partner as she practised the complex steps. The auburn curls of her hair hung around her heart-shaped face, themselves seeming to dance as she spun and swayed, like hanging ferns disturbed by a breeze. She was smiling, enjoying herself.

"There are lots more of these," Maggie said as the footage went black.

"How did he get them? Cameras inside homes are illegal—did he plant one there somehow?"

Maggie exhaled deeply. "I don't think this is camera footage. I think he hacked TIM's viewing node directly."

TIM used visual imaging buds as well as microphones to interact with users—"to better enable an accurate assessment and interpretation of critical environmental factors," as the text in the government white paper read. The same paper explicitly forbade the tiny, ball bearing–sized "eyes" from making or storing any recordings. All TIM was permitted to do was watch, listen, and react.

If Greene had found a way to hack the devices, it would be a national scandal.

"Fuck," was all Dremmler could muster.

Hacked imaging buds.

Cybernetic limbs with minds of their own.

Killer cockroaches crawling out of 3D printers.

"Maggie," he said eventually, after she made no sound other than the crackling inhalation of her e-cig. "At what point do we need to go public with this?"

She replied immediately. "Not yet."

"And you're sure Greene's main rig was completely scratched? Who did the analysis—Carmichael?"

"Yep. But only on a need-to-know basis, so he isn't in the loop on this. Don't go talking to him."

"Discretion is my middle name."

"It's 'David.' I've seen your personnel file."

Dremmler grunted again, a smile briefly flickering across his lips as he hung up. Then a deep sense of foreboding swept through him, and drove the expression from his face.

TWENTY-EIGHT

THE HOSPITAL LOOMED ABOVE DREMMLER, the morning sunlight reflecting off the building's many facets, making it seem somehow moist and organic. He was reminded of nothing more than the unblinking eye of an insect, regarding him with disinterest as he approached. He headed inside, feeling repulsed by the machines that scuttled and whirred past him as he headed across the reception area. As promised, Doctor Girard was waiting for him, his eyes stern and cold behind those rimless spex.

"How did the chief get you to agree to this, Doc?" asked Dremmler as the Frenchman led them towards McCann's bed.

"It wasn't her," Girard replied coolly, not turning his head towards Dremmler as he spoke. "It was you."

"Me?" Dremmler frowned, genuinely surprised.

"Yes. Like you said: If it helps catch Letitia's killer, it's what Conor would want. We know that, from the work Doctor Gellar has done, interacting with his subconscious. I truly believe he's innocent."

Dremmler was silent for the rest of the walk, thinking about Letitia Karlikowska. Was she simply collateral damage in this affair, the randomly selected target for someone flexing their virtual muscles? Or had she been specifically selected, perhaps as the object of Charlie Greene's obsession?

He couldn't separate the players from the pieces on the board.

Despite Girard's assertions that progress was being made, McCann looked even worse than he had the last time Dremmler had seen him. His body seemed to have fused with the bed itself, as though it was a surgical support he was condemned to wear for the rest of his life. His name hovered above his head like a curse.

Gellar was seated beside him once again, still plugged into the TIM interface, almost like she hadn't moved since Dremmler's last visit. Perhaps she hadn't. Dremmler studied her, wondering if her face would hint at what was happening in the AltWorld, inside McCann's mental prison, but she appeared completely peaceful, almost as though asleep. Gellar was small and wiry, her benign features framed by two tangles of curling, raven-black hair that each contained a single streak of white, either natural or a strange stylistic choice. She looked like some kind of ancient mystic, silently praying for her patient's recovery.

"So how can I speak to him?" Dremmler asked eventually.

"Gellar will remain inside the simulation with you," answered Girard. "She will need to manage McCann's subconscious to prevent it from reacting negatively."

"But if McCann wants to help, what's the problem?"

"This is not McCann's rational brain we're talking about. You're about to attempt to have a meeting with a man's subconscious mind: with his dreams, his fears. Getting a clear answer to any of your questions will not be straightforward." Girard turned to him, his expression hardening. "And if I think you're pushing too hard, I'll pull you straight out."

"Okay, Doc, I've got it. Just wire me up." Dremmler's nonchalant delivery masked his own fear. He hated the AltWorld. At least he was venturing inside to meet another man's demons; he certainly didn't want to confront his own.

Girard led him into the room where another chair awaited him, on the opposite side of the bed. He sat down facing Gellar while Girard attached the cap and gloves. He thought of the electric chairs they had once used to execute criminals, of penitence, of mortality.

"Okay, detective," Girard said, crossing to the TIM interface. "Brace yourself. You will find the experience disconcerting."

TWENTY-NINE

DREMMLER HAD BEEN INSIDE THE AltWorld before. It felt like waking up.

You blinked, you opened your eyes, and there you were, inside your fantasy world, as if emerging from a bad dream. Perhaps you would see the sun setting over a tranquil sea that stretched out infinitely before you, or maybe you'd be tangled in a writhing heap of bodies in an ancient Roman orgy.

Or reunited with your dead daughter.

This was no different. Except it was. Because this time, he was a trespasser inside Conor McCann's head, and the narrative was not his own.

It was snowing. Dremmler was standing in a clearing, surrounded on all sides by towering fir trees, his feet disappearing into a thick carpet of powdery white. Children were playing all around him, shouting and giggling as they ran, jumped, threw snowballs, caught snowflakes in their mouths. They were all wearing uniforms; he wondered whether this was some sort of school outing, but the unruly bunch didn't seem to have any teachers looking after them, and he felt a pang of concern as the kids disappeared amongst the trees, their games leading them deeper into the forest.

The only adult he could see was squatting right in the clearing's centre, carefully assembling a snowman. One of the children had stopped to stare at her, as though in awe. It was an impressive sculpture, and Dremmler found himself equally enthralled as he watched the head slowly transformed from a clump of ice into a perfect representation of a young boy's face.

The woman's tongue protruded from the side of her mouth as she concentrated, fingers gently scraping away the delicate flakes. As Dremmler watched, he realised that the snowman was an exact representation of the schoolboy that was watching her, transfixed. The woman was young, dressed in a red coat and matching woollen hat. The dark curls of her hair were hidden inside it, but some had escaped to dangle around her kindly face; Dremmler noticed a couple of strands that were as white as the surrounding snow.

When she had finished, she gave a single satisfied nod and then stepped away with a smile. The boy's face erupted into a delighted grin. Around them, the snow continued to fall, the swirling flakes looking like dead skin, or ashes.

"Now then, Conor," said the woman, who was surely their teacher. Her voice hinted at chalk dust and old textbooks and custard dripping onto sponge pudding. "I want you to meet my friend."

She gestured towards Dremmler, and the boy turned, his smile disappearing, replaced by a suspicious frown. The children continued to frolic around them, but seemed unable or unwilling to enter this central area where the four of them stood: a teacher, a boy, a snowman, and an outsider. A circle within a circle.

Dremmler realised then that he didn't look like himself. He felt a sudden sensation of panic as he realised he was standing with a stoop, pain arcing up his warped spine. He gaped in horror when he lifted his hands and beheld fingers twisted into claws, skin like crumbling parchment. In an instant, he felt the cold rush up through the soles of his boots and into his ancient bones, the frigid air penetrating his papery flesh like a thousand icy needles.

Had Gellar done this to make him appear less physically threatening? Or was McCann's own consciousness interpreting him in this way for some reason he couldn't understand?

"This is Mr. Dremmler," the woman continued. "He wants to talk to you."

Dremmler, now a very old man, stretched out his hand, trying to adopt a friendly smile while his tongue flicked across the backs of crooked, unfamiliar teeth. "Hello," he said in a voice like a sigh.

"What do you want?" replied this child version of McCann, an adult's scepticism clouding the boy's eyes. Dremmler realised the other thing that was unsettling him: no one was wearing spex, no names hovering above anyone's head. In some ways, this construct felt more real than reality.

"I just want to ask you a few questions," Dremmler replied, shuffling a tentative step forwards.

"Why?" the boy replied, standing his ground. Dremmler flashed a nervous glance at the woman he was certain was Doctor Gellar, and she smiled encouragingly. Behind her, even though the snow was still falling thickly, he could see the snowman starting to melt, the perfect likeness of the boy's face folding in on itself, liquefying like something rotting away.

"I'm a policeman," he ventured. "I'm trying to help someone." This was ridiculous. How could he interrogate McCann if he had to pretend he was addressing a nine-year-old?

"Do you know how to make a snowman?" There was a challenge in the child's eyes that Dremmler felt himself shrinking from. He recalled the previous occasions he had interrogated McCann, wondered if this strange avatar remembered how badly he'd been treated.

"Uhh … yes, sure," Dremmler replied, his elderly body withering at the prospect of handling the freezing snow.

"Make me another one like that," the child demanded, gesturing at the figure that Gellar had constructed. It had melted almost to nothing, only a small mound of slush remaining.

A test, perhaps? A demand for a display of respect? A trick?

Feeling his ancient back shriek in agony, Dremmler bent and plunged his hands into the snow. For a second he thought the shock of the cold would kill him, but he managed to overcome the intense pain and started to roll a snowball. The sounds of play and laughter around him seemed to fade as he focused on that single white sphere, on rolling it over and over until it reached the required size. Under the child's unblinking scrutiny, he rolled another ball and somehow managed to heft it on top of the first. His gaze flicked to Gellar, but she offered no assistance, seemingly unwilling to break the rules of this strange ritual.

After what felt like hours, Dremmler had managed to stack several balls of snow on top of each other. His fingers felt riddled with frostbite, the skin of his face ready to crack open. Still he felt the stern gaze of the boy fixed on him. Accusing. Angry. With a grimace of pain, Dremmler sank his fingers into the snow and began to carve a face.

He had never possessed any artistic skill, but in Conor McCann's VR world, that didn't seem to matter. Deftly, Dremmler worked the snow as though it was clay, sculpting and pressing and gouging and smoothing. Gradually, a face began to emerge. He could sense the boy gazing over his shoulder, staring as his sculpture started to take shape.

Dremmler wasn't consciously aware of what he was doing. It felt as though his hands were possessed, simply acquiescing to the will of the simulation. And as he worked, he realised that his advanced years were receding, the liver spots disappearing from his hands, his skin tightening and becoming softer. His back unbent itself with a crack. He felt hair sprouting on his head, muscle tissue growing on his arms and legs and torso.

With a nod of satisfaction, the restored Carl Dremmler stepped away from his creation.

The snowman did not bear the likeness of the boy. Neither did the boy. Now Dremmler was standing in front of Conor McCann as an adult, as he had known him in SR, and the figure he'd built from the snow was Letitia Karlikowska. The young man's beloved, staring back at him with sadness in her frozen eyes.

Gellar had disappeared. So had the children, and the snow, and the trees, and the sky. Instead, they were inside a building, in a large, open space surrounded by weights and punching bags and fitness machines. It was the gym where McCann worked as a personal trainer. In the centre of the room was a boxing ring, in which McCann was now standing, wearing a couple of pads as though he had been in the middle of coaching somebody. But there was no one in the gym at all, except for Dremmler, who realised that he no longer had a physical presence; like TIM, he was just a hovering consciousness, silently observing as McCann gazed across towards the reception area, his mouth falling open.

Karlikowska, his princess, strode into the room. Modelled in purest white, her smile was radiant and wholesome. McCann stared as though his eyes were skewered on her beauty. As Dremmler watched, the young man seemed to shake himself awake and hopped down from the ring to approach her.

"This must be when you first met," Dremmler said, or thought, or felt. He could read the love in McCann's eyes as the young man chatted to her, made small talk, cracked jokes. Dremmler burned with shame that he had ever accused this man of murdering her.

And yet....

"Conor," Dremmler said, suddenly present in the gym, leaning against the wall close to the star-crossed pair. "I can see your right arm is smaller than your left. Do you remember when you got it replaced?"

McCann didn't react to the question, but a look of pain crossed his face and his eyes squeezed shut. Around them the gym faded, until the three of them were standing in an empty void of black, floating like meteor fragments. McCann opened his eyes, and took Karlikowska in his arms, moved to kiss her, but she crumbled to powder in his grasp, breaking into a million perfect flakes of snow that spiralled down into the abyss beneath them. Tears welled in McCann's eyes, rolled down his cheeks, fell, and drifted off into that same endless vacuum.

Guilt drove a spike into Dremmler's heart.

Around them, a scene began to emerge from the blackness. McCann was no longer standing, but was instead lying on his back, which meant that Dremmler was observing from above, floating in the air, his physical body once again erased. They were in a cramped room that lacked any windows, the only illumination coming from a single lightbulb that hung close to Dremmler's hovering ego. In one corner, a narrow staircase leading upwards seemed to be the only exit. The oppressive space smelt warm and greasy.

McCann was lying on a gurney, apparently asleep. A very tall, thin person was hunched over him, performing surgery. The bulb's harsh light reflected off the surgeon's perfectly bald head, giving their skull the appearance of something plastic. In a bucket next to the gurney, Dremmler could see a severed arm; it had been McCann's. The slender figure was attaching a prosthetic in its place, skilfully wielding an array of surgical and electrical equipment that had been grafted into place where fingers ought to have been: a scalpel, a soldering iron, a drill, a serrated saw, a needle.

I should have known, thought Dremmler, hanging from the ceiling like a bat.

Dak Melville was a grinder, and grinding was big business. Keeping up with the demands of social media, of a virtual world filled with ceaseless images of beauty and achievement and success, required all imperfections to be expunged. Augmentations, enlargements, embellishments, tweaks, fixes, patches, grafts; they were all becoming more popular every year. And, as with any cosmetic enhancement, there were those who shopped at the premium end of the market, paying top prices for reliable and hyper-realistic synthetic improvements.

Others, meanwhile, had to make do with scraping the bottom of the bargain bin.

These were the ones whose physical shortcomings had driven them to desperation, or whose vanity was simply larger than their wallets. At first, the horror stories had made headline news, the public shocked by images of arms too heavy to move properly, warping the users' spines until they were left dragging the limbs behind them on the ground; abdominal implants that rusted beneath the skin; defective jaws stuck disturbingly open in silent, hideous screams. The populace collectively gasped at these poor hetties, left mired in debt, hunted by loan sharks, their botched implants serving as a permanent and gruesome reminder of their bad luck.

But over time, the crimes of these third-rate grinders became old news. Their butchery was blamed on the foolishness of their victims. The black market thrived, and people like Melville emerged, dribbling out of society's orifices like pus from an exposed wound.

Nicknamed "Freddy" after the blade-fingered scourge of Elm Street, Melville was well known to police. Dremmler had first encountered the spindly neut during a drug raid: Melville had simply been unlucky, picking the wrong time to visit ver dealer to top up ver stash of Blitz. The rumour was that, back in ver native Glasgow, Melville had snitched on a drug lord who had taken all ten fingers in retribution. Yet this didn't seem to have cooled Melville's appetite for treachery; caught red-handed with a briefcase full of gear and hands loaded with illegal implants, Melville had been only too keen to cut a deal, ratting out ver supplier's entire operation in return for immunity.

The last Dremmler had heard, Melville had a new identity and had replaced ver severed digits with compliant enhancements. But McCann's macabre vision told him Melville's backstreet chop shop had started up its grisly trade once more.

Inside the simulation, Dremmler tried to speak, but found this time that he couldn't manifest himself; instead, he was forced to watch in silence while the emaciated figure of Melville sliced and soldered and screwed. At one point, the grinder stopped to swig from an open beer can, wiping the blood from ver fingers on a bloodstained apron that looked like it hadn't been washed for years. Thankfully McCann was heavily sedated, but Dremmler was still appalled.

Of course, this was only McCann's mental re-creation of the event, the victim's idea of what had happened in that room while he was unconscious. But when Dremmler thought about Melville's sneering smile, ver needle-like teeth the colour of earwax, he suspected it wasn't far from the truth.

He gazed down at the sordid scene as Melville bent over his patient once again. With a metallic squeal, the drill that protruded like a sharp talon from Melville's right index finger began to spin once again; but this time, Melville moved it towards McCann's head. Dremmler raged in muted horror as the implement was inserted into McCann's temple, blood spurting as the patient awoke with a scream from his slumber, a sound that seemed to give voice to Dremmler's own revulsion and fear, a deafening shriek of agony and grief that drew Dremmler towards it, inhaled him like a sea monster might consume a shoal of fish. He was engulfed by that scream, his consciousness absorbed into a world built from nothing but endless pain.

Slowly the blackness around him began to crystallise, the darkness dissolving into flakes of black snow that clumped and congealed and coalesced into figures.

One was Karlikowska, her pretty face hidden behind the crushing grip of a prosthetic fist, the back of her head ground sickeningly into brickwork. The other was McCann, at the other end of the extended arm, his mouth still stretched into that never-ending cry of torment.

Dremmler didn't know how long he had been there, observing that frozen screenshot of anguish, transfixed by the absolute insanity in Conor McCann's eyes as he watched himself murder his soulmate. Every droplet of the spittle that frothed at McCann's mouth was ingrained in Dremmler's memory, as were the miniature Rorschach shapes formed by each globule of blood that spilled onto the floor. He had been there for years, decades, had died and been reborn in McCann's endless demented howl.

He was aware that something was very wrong. He thought of his physical self, growing old in its chair in the hospital, a long white beard disappearing between his legs as his limbs wasted and his skin sagged in pallid folds. He thought of Gellar and Girard and McCann, connected like a circuit, their minds entrapped and entwined while the four of them rotted in that silent room, surrounded by machines that beeped and hummed and plotted and watched.

He thought about the soulless things that were his masters now. He stared into Conor McCann's contorted mouth, and in that terrible blackness all he found was another McCann, another Karlikowska, another senseless death, an endless cycle.

Millennia passed. Dremmler forgot himself, became part of the scream. Everyone did. Humanity screamed as one, and TIM did not laugh, it merely existed, observed, recorded. Sight and sound and the smell of Karlikowska's blood and the taste of inhaled smog became blurred, combined, commingled with the city's stifling air. Oblivion, anonymity. Data made with no ones, only zeroes.

A universe, deleted.

He awoke with a start, lurching upwards from the chair and tearing himself free from the neural cap. Freezing sweat oozed down his face as he dropped, convulsing, to his knees.

Girard and Gellar crowded immediately around him.

"Detective? Are you okay?"

"What ... what the fuck...?" he managed to mumble through gasping breaths. "How long was I in there for?"

"Five minutes," Gellar replied. "I lost contact with you, and shortly after that you seemed in distress, so we pulled you out. What did you see?"

Dremmler stared beseechingly into their eyes, feeling haunted, diminished. Violated.

"A scream," he replied eventually, clutching his shoulders to try to halt his uncontrollable shuddering. "McCann, screaming. Forever."

Doctor Girard frowned, while Gellar nodded sadly. "Yes," she replied. "He is always drawn back to that, no matter how much progress we make."

Dremmler looked down at his shaking hands. "He's in hell," he whispered.

And I put him there.

"Detective, please come and sit down," fussed Girard.

"Fuck that." He pulled away from the doctor's outstretched hand as he rose. "I've got what I need. Now you two have to find a way to fix him."

He gestured without looking towards the withered creature in the bed. Then he turned and stalked out of the ward, certain that he would never enter the AltWorld again.

THiRTY

NGER BURNED iN DREMMLER'S ARTERiES as the Pod arrived in Acton. He still felt nervous about using the transports, but what choice did he have? The dark slab of the culch plant loomed on the horizon like something crouched, waiting. The name "VitroCo" floated twice above the ominous structure: once beneath the helpful AR signpost provided by his spex, and again in proud aluminium letters across the flat roof.

Sales of cultured or "clean" meat had rocketed in recent years as mass production had driven down the cost and the product itself had become indistinguishable from the real thing. Strictly speaking, it *was* the real thing, grown from cellular material extracted from living animals that was mixed with nutrients before being warmed, agitated, and encouraged to multiply into muscle-like strips. Factories like VitroCo enjoyed steady revenue streams from their synthetic burgers and vat-grown chicken, while high-end competitors charged inflated prices for novelties like panda steaks or lion fillet.

He hadn't wanted to give any warning of his visit, so VitroCo wasn't expecting him; still, his police clearance granted him access to the factory grounds and to the plant itself, and he strode unassailed right through the main doors. As he crossed the threshold, he realised how strangely quiet and odourless the place was, as though the operation had been shut down and abandoned long ago.

The disembodied voice of a TIM iteration informed him that it was necessary to wash his hands and don a smock and hairnet before entering the factory floor. He ignored the warning and barged through the next set of double doors to be greeted by rows of huge, gleaming metal bioreactors. The factory was silent, and cold enough for his breath to mist in the air; he was reminded for a moment of Maggie, surrounded at all times by the fragrant smoke from her e-cig. He hadn't yet told her about Freddy, about coming straight to the snitch's place of work; he was worried she would disapprove, and he didn't want any reason to go easy on the fucking weasel.

His reflection shifted in the steel vats as he stalked amongst them, trying not to think about the obscene alchemy taking place inside. He'd eaten culch meat before, knew it was microscopically indistinguishable from the farmed variety, that it boasted a range of benefits including reduced energy consumption, a greatly decreased risk of disease, the eradication of animal cruelty. But somehow the taste of the engineered meat never failed to turn his stomach with unfathomable revulsion.

He gazed around at the pristine surfaces, at the embedded dials and displays that enthusiastically imparted indecipherable data, at the robotic arms that hovered above each tank, awaiting deployment when the next fleshy harvest was ready to be extracted. Living tissue, grown in tanks by machines. For now at least, human oversight was still deemed necessary—hence Freddy's day job, following the neut's rehabilitation.

He reached the door to the small office room and stepped inside just as Melville verself emerged from another door opposite him, accompanied by the sound of a flushing toilet. They faced each other across a desk strewn with paperwork, chocolate bar wrappers, empty coffee cups. An array of monitors broadcast the same incomprehensible information stream he had seen on the vats themselves, beeping occasionally as though monitoring a heartbeat.

"Hello, Freddy," Dremmler said evenly.

Melville's facial expression cycled through surprise, horror, anger, and finally settled on a contemptuous sneer.

"Detective Dremmler. To what do I owe the honour?" Ver nasally, croaking voice sounded as though someone had taught English to a particularly slimy toad.

"Let's skip the pleasantries, Freddo. How's the wetware business?" Dremmler skirted the desk and strode towards the neut, who took a step back towards the door. Melville was well over six feet tall, but rather than being physically imposing, ver body was so slight that ver height made ver appear fragile, like something brittle that might at any moment snap in two. Ve seemed permanently hinged at the waist, constantly folded into a partial bow like a bent paperclip.

A nervous chuckle emerged from Melville's throat. "I'm not sure what you mean. My claws were clipped a long time ago ... remember?" To illustrate ver point, Melville held up both hands, revealing a set of perfectly white fingers, as though the skin had been peeled carefully away from each digit to expose the bone beneath. Plastic, or maybe ceramic, each long, slender finger wiggled unpleasantly as Melville grinned ver treacherous grin.

"Cut the shit, Freddy," Dremmler snarled, still advancing. "I know you snap those off every night when you leave this shithole so you can screw on your fucking drills and scalpels. I don't even care. I just have some questions about one particular job you did, maybe six months ago. A kid named Conor—you fitted an arm for him."

Melville had backed further away, ver right hand on the door handle behind ver as though preparing to flee. "You're wrong, Dremmler," the neut snapped. "I've been straight for years. Check my employment record with VitroCo: It's spotless. I love working here."

"Oh yeah? And why's that?"

"This industry, what it's doing: It's cutting edge. Did you know that soon they're going to open a restaurant selling synthetic *human* meat? Market testing suggests it'll be a huge hit. Give it five years and people will be eating sausages made from their favourite celebrities' DNA. Beyonce burgers, Tom Hanks tenderloin."

Dremmler, standing barely two feet from Melville, saw the glint of captivation in the neut's defiant gaze.

"And that fascinates you, does it, you sick bastard?"

Melville's smile widened, revealing cruelly pointed teeth, like those of a rodent. "Flesh is my passion, detective. Always has been. I used to cut, saw, and splice—but now I can *grow*. And even here, even in this perfect environment, life finds a way to burst outwards, to shift and mutate, to *bloom*."

Jesus. Freddy's lost ver fucking mind.

"Whole yields of chicken sometimes get thrown away because they inexplicably start growing hair, or skin, or corneal tissue. Imagine that, Dremmler: biting into your juicy quarter-pounder to find a perfectly-formed eyeball staring back at you. *Incredible*, isn't it?"

Dremmler held Melville's gaze. "Remind me never to buy anything from this company ever again. Now are you going to help me, Fred, or am I going to have to get nasty?" He placed his hand on the neut's shoulder, giving it a menacing squeeze.

The blade shot out of Melville's index finger so quickly it seemed to appear out of thin air; before Dremmler could react, Melville drove the rapier-like weapon upwards through his outstretched arm. He cried out in surprise and pain, flailing uselessly with his other arm as Melville danced out of range. Jerking ver gangly limbs like a marionette, the grinder extended five more wickedly sharp claws from the fingers of ver other hand.

"Not clipped after all!" Melville squealed gleefully as ve raked the weapons across Dremmler's chest, slicing through the fabric of his shirt and drawing bright blood from the skin beneath. Melville's eyes seemed to bulge outwards in excitement at the sight of the gore.

Reeling backwards, Dremmler reached for his Taser, but before he could raise the weapon, Melville had yanked open the door behind ver and disappeared from view.

"Fucking fuck," Dremmler muttered under his breath as he gave pursuit, following the neut into a dimly-lit corridor. Melville had sprinted past the toilet doors and nearly reached the other end of the passageway, where a sharp left turn would take ver deeper into the factory.

Dremmler aimed, and squeezed the trigger. Electrodes leapt from the Taser's barrel, catching Melville in the back of ver right calf. With a muted gargle, the grinder stumbled and crashed, convulsing, into the opposite wall.

Dremmler advanced towards the twitching heap, blood oozing from the wounds in his arm and ravaged chest. "You've gotten quicker," he breathed, squeezing the trigger to send another blast of electricity surging through Melville's limbs. The neut shrieked, clawing helplessly at the wall, spittle and garbled pleas forming on ver lips. "But now you've *really* fucked up, Frederico." Dremmler thought about Conor McCann, trapped and tortured in his hospital bed. He squeezed again. Melville screamed. "Because you still aren't fast *enough*." Dremmler hunkered down beside his victim, whose needle-like weapons were still extended, making a tapping sound as they rattled against the floor. "Now, unless you want me to fry you to death: Tell me all about Conor McCann."

Melville did.

THiRTY-ONe

YOU iRReSPONSiBLe DiCKHeAD."

"Oh, you don't mean that," Dremmler replied jovially, fiddling with the fresh stitches in his chest. "The ambulance crew will scrape Melville up, and then it's my word against vers."

Maggie sucked her e-cig, her gaze burning through him from the other end of their virtual conversation. He realised how common this was becoming: talking to her through the spex, debating their next move while a Pod ferried him from one location to another. *Like a pawn on a chessboard.* He realised how alone he would be if it wasn't for the technology resting on the bridge of his nose. Then he thought about the mangled avatar he had encountered in Marine Heights, and shuddered.

"What did ve tell you?" Maggie said after a long, smouldering pause.

"Ve came out of retirement to perform one last operation. That's the only reason ve knew who I was talking about. Ve didn't know even know McCann's name."

"How did McCann contact Melville in the first place?"

"He didn't. Apparently the operation was set up by someone else, an intermediary. They turned up at the factory, just like I did today."

Maggie frowned and exhaled, momentarily obscured by a swirl of smoke. "Someone helped McCann get an implant? Why?"

"That's not the question, boss. The question is 'who.'"

"Okay then, who?" Maggie growled, sounding impatient.

An East Asian woman calling herself Cynthia.

But Maggie didn't know about Cynthia, or about Haraway. And Dremmler didn't want to explain it to her while TIM was listening.

"We need to meet."

"I'm at this all-day forum, remember? Just tell me what you're being so cryptic about."

Dremmler paused. What exactly was he afraid of? That TIM was manipulating Maggie?

That someone else was manipulating TIM?

"Oh, fuck it," he cursed. Then he told her about Cynthia Lu, from his very first encounter with the mysterious machine in the nightclub, all the way to the disturbing details of TIM's malfunctioning avatar at Marine Heights the previous day.

When he finished, Maggie was quiet, her e-cig crackling as though it was the sound of her brain at work.

"Fuck it, indeed," she said eventually. "So, if I've got this straight, we have three missing suspects: Charlie Greene the stalker-cum-hacker, Haraway the missing roboticist, and this Cynthia character—an advanced robot prototype we believe Haraway stole."

"Don't forget the 3D-printed killing machine that escaped from Petrovic's flat," Dremmler added cheerily.

"And to add to this, you're worried that TIM is malfunctioning, or possibly even trying to influence this investigation."

"That's about the long and short of it, yeah."

Maggie took an extremely long drag on the e-cig. "You understand I can't bring in any more resource on this."

"There comes a point when you'll have to, Maggie. What if someone else dies, and they find out we've been sitting on this for days?"

"And is that what you think? That more people are going to die?"

Dremmler shrugged, wincing as pain lanced through his recently-impaled arm. "That depends on what the killer's motive is. We still don't have a fucking clue why Karlikowska or Petrovic were murdered in the first place."

"Petrovic was killed because ve knew something," Maggie mused.

"Maybe ve realised Cynthia was a robot when ve tried to sleep with it."

"So it programmed Petrovic's printer to kill ver a day later? That doesn't seem particularly efficient. Why not just kill Petrovic itself?"

"If we're dealing with a defective machine, it might not make logical decisions."

It. He realised how easily they had shifted to referring to Cynthia as an object. He remembered how effortlessly seductive it—she—had been, and wondered if the change would be so easy to sustain if he encountered the construct face to face again.

"Or maybe this is Augmentech's play. They want you to *think* it's a defective machine."

"Cynthia is the key to this," Dremmler muttered, half to himself.

A beautiful woman, in a city full of them.

A needle in a haystack.

"I can't request warrants to track Greene and Haraway without disclosing details of the case," Maggie interjected. "But what about Lu? She isn't a person, so the Surveillance Act doesn't apply."

Dremmler blinked.

"You mean … just ask TIM to find the robot for us?"

Why hadn't he thought of that?

"That's exactly what I mean. Shit, I'm going to have to go, Carl. I know you don't want to hear this, but talk to TIM about it. We'll check in later."

"You learning a lot at this leadership conference?"

Maggie allowed herself a smile. "I'm an old dog, Carl. But that doesn't mean I can't learn new tricks."

Her image disappeared in a swirl of vapour.

Dremmler leaned back into his seat, grimacing at another jolt of pain from his wounded limb. *Melville, you fucker*. He was en route to the hospital to get the injury properly examined after the ambulance team's medbot had patched him up as best it could.

"TIM," he grunted. "Are you offended that I think you're knackered?"

"No, Carl," replied the Pod. Its voice was the warm, reassuring voice of a friendly old man, strangely reminiscent of his grandfather, and Dremmler felt a pang of unexpected grief. "I'm a neural network that uses statistical data interpretation to simulate learning. I do not experience emotions."

"A 'neural network'—that means you have a brain, doesn't it? Brains have emotions."

"I'm designed to process data. Trillions of pieces of information are fed into my main processors, and I draw conclusions from them. For example, if I hear enough conversations, I know what is statistically the most probable response to every question. When you ask me something, I know exactly how best to reply because I have seen countless examples of how humans respond to each other. Humans taught me everything I know."

"But how do you decide what's right and what's wrong?"

"I don't. My decisions are based solely on probabilities, statistics, and frequencies. The world has already decided what's right and wrong. I merely observe and imitate."

"What about when you were first switched on, and you didn't have any data yet?"

"I learned in a virtual environment. A simulation of reality. Digital representations of humans interacted with me, and I learned by trial and error in simulations running at a billion times faster than SR. Don't worry, The Imagination Corporation wouldn't have let me loose until I was good and ready."

Dremmler frowned at the AI's jarringly jovial tone. "But if you don't care about the outcome, about what happens to any of us, why do you bother? Why not just switch yourself off, or start crashing Pods into pedestrians, or …" He thought about the thing that had crawled out from under Petrovic's corpse. He thought about Connie, standing silently in his hallway, waiting for him. The question died on his lips.

"I'm motivated only to behave in the way that data has taught me," TIM replied. "When someone asks a question, I answer. When a cat sees a mouse, it chases it. When humans become old enough, they have children. It is all the same."

"So it's all a sham? Just cause and effect? No conscious thought behind it?"

"Have you heard of the Chinese Room?"

"Sorry?"

"It's a thought experiment about consciousness."

"Enlighten me."

"Am I correct in assuming that you do not speak Chinese?"

Dremmler grunted his agreement.

"Then imagine you are in a room with two small openings. Through one opening you receive pieces of paper with Chinese characters written on them. You consult a book that tells you how to respond to each character, and post the correct response through the other opening. From the perspective of an outsider, the parties on either side of the wall appear to be conscious, Chinese-speaking individuals engaging in an intelligent conversation. Yet in reality, all that is happening on your side of the wall is a mindless mechanical process."

"So you're saying you're like a calculator, responding to inputs we punch in? You can't do anything creative, just for the hell of it, like … like writing a poem?"

"I didn't say that. You've already seen some of my artwork."

Dremmler shook his head, feeling mentally strained. He picked anxiously at the stitches on both sides of his forearm, where Melville's claw had passed straight through the limb. He thought about flesh, growing inside those machines in the factory. Metal, muscle, sinew, circuitry.

"TIM, pull over here. There's been a change of plan."

The Pod did as it was instructed, waiting until it would cause only minimal disruption to the flow of cars on the road. This tiny blip, the infinitesimal recalibration of the real-time traffic models that governed the movement of Pods around the city, would be absorbed into TIM's algorithms like a droplet of water into an ocean.

"You require medical assistance, Carl."

"It can wait. First I want you to find someone for me."

"Carl, you know that under the Civil Surveillance Act—"

"Not a person. A machine. A robot that we believe was stolen from Augmentech's headquarters by their former head roboticist."

"You are referring to the entity that calls itself Cynthia Lu."

Dremmler was taken aback for a moment. "Yes," he said carefully, wondering about TIM's memory, about its capacity for reasoning and deduction. "I want to know where she is right now. I'm requesting the information because of its relevance to an active murder investigation, and I believe you are obliged to disclose it."

"The prototype C-series unit Cynthia Lu is not detectable at this time."

"Why not?"

"None of my sensors are able to locate it."

Imaging buds in every home, in every Pod, on every street.

"How can that be?"

"Its last detected location was on the outskirts of the area known as the Farm."

Dremmler felt nausea seeping from the pit of his stomach, as though his belly was a plastic bag full of entrails that someone had punctured.

The Farm.

He opened and closed his mouth like something malfunctioning.

"Would you like any further information, Carl?"

"No. Just let me out of this fucking car."

THIRTY-TWO

DREMMLER WANTED A PLACE THAT smelt of stale tobacco—despite thirty-two years of the indoor smoking ban—and in *The Englishman and Falcon*, he found it. No unnerving barbots, no sleek modern veneer: just a dark, crusty, old-fashioned pub hidden down a side street. The ancient but imposing barman looked like he might have been part of the original punk movement, and the equally grizzled clientele could have once been his backing band. Some of them weren't even wearing spex.

They'd have been right at home at the Farm.

He ordered a neat whiskey, downed it, ordered another. The liquid seared the back of his throat, releasing a savage cocktail of chemicals into his brain, chemicals that triggered emotions that set his jaw grimly. He drained a third glass.

Cause and effect. A mechanical process.

The Lost Souls had brainwashed his wife.

His wife had let their daughter die.

Another shot of the pub's cheapest scotch blasted his insides. The barman didn't look concerned as he kept lining them up, his expression one of mild curiosity.

"Bad day, son? It ain't even four o'clock yet."

"Bad week, mate." A grim smile sliced its way across Dremmler's face. "Bad life, actually."

Harold Miller nodded sagely—Dremmler scowled as he acknowledged the name floating above the barman's head, then wrenched the spex from his face. The bartender's T-shirt advertised a band called The Fall, who Dremmler had never heard of; over the top of that he wore a leather vest that looked like a jacket with the sleeves crudely hacked off, bedecked in badges referencing other obscure musical acts. The skin of Harold's arms was hard and leathery, covered with tattoos that seemed to dance and writhe of their own accord, skulls and snakes and broken hearts, laughing and slithering and bleeding as Miller moved to refill Dremmler's glass.

Hours passed. Dremmler and Harold didn't talk any more. The detective just drank, and allowed his eyes to close, and tried not to think about anything at all.

She's always there, though, isn't she, Carl? Your dead angel. Immortalised in your mind, while her bones rot in the mud.

A long time later, after he had fallen asleep in a grubby corner for a few hours, he stumbled outside. The sun was sinking, bathing the alleyway in a reddish glow that made it look as though he was wandering the outskirts of Hell. Sliding his spex back on, Dremmler saw that he had missed five calls from Maggie. He ducked into a nearby doorway that stank of piss, and called her, voice only.

"Where the fuck have you been?" she snapped, answering almost immediately.

"I want out."

"What?"

"Cynthia has gone to the Farm," he slurred. "You know I can't go there, Maggie." Boiling tears jabbed their way past his eyes, betraying him. "They killed my fucking daughter."

He drove his fist into the brickwork, clenching his teeth as pain and fury coursed through him. He imagined those vacuous faces, those oh-so-helpful Souls gathering to console Tessa while she wept, pouring more of their poison into her ears. He thought of his wife, her freckled face, the beautiful smile that had been slowly lost to him, years before she'd even taken Natalie and left to seek solace and meaning in Owen Fox's commune, which had expanded by then to occupy a huge tract of land across northern England.

He remembered the day he'd found out. He'd wanted to smash his rage through all of them. He still did. He wanted to rain their blood onto the earth that held his daughter's bones, and watch as she rose from the muck like a flower, reborn and restored to him.

This was the violence that came to him in his dreams. This was what happened when he entered the AltWorld.

"Carl? Carl?" Maggie was saying.

He realised that he had punched the wall again and stared at the blood bubbling from his scoured knuckles. It ran down his hand, thick and red, like hot lava.

"I can't go there," he said again, a single sob shaking his body.

"Go home, Carl. Sleep it off. We'll talk tomorrow." Her voice took on an unexpected, pleading tone. "Please. I need your help."

"Do you?" he barked back at her. "Or is this just what TIM wants? Who do I even work for?"

"Oh, give it a rest," she retorted, a snarl in her voice. "You say you hate the Lost Souls, but you're starting to sound like one of them."

Anger swelled inside him, so much that he thought the flimsy vessel of his body would burst, unable to contain his hatred. He bared his teeth like an animal, tore the spex from his face as though he meant to dash them on the ground. But she was right: the glasses, TIM, the sinister machines that surrounded him; it wasn't their fault. The Lost Souls had rejected robotics, AI, augmentation, all of it.

And if they hadn't, Natalie would have survived.

He switched the spex off, clutching them in his bleeding hand, leaving a bright crimson trail behind him as he shambled back to the main road.

THiRTY-THRee

DREMMLER ARRiVED HOME AFTER A long, punishing walk. "Connie?" he called as he shuffled inside, then remembered that she was gone, dismembered, destroyed. He leaned against the inside of the front door and sank slowly to the ground, finally giving voice to the grief and frustration and helplessness that chewed at his guts. He sat like that for a long time, slumped and weeping, like something defeated and abandoned on an accursed battlefield.

Not just Connie. The printer too. Another sob ripped through him as he realised he could no longer produce the flowers for Natalie's grave.

But did you fight for your daughter, Carl? When Tessa took her, did you storm into the compound to take her back?

Or did you just let her fade away, like a dream you weren't brave enough to hold onto?

Perhaps this was his chance. A perverse kind of redemption. To follow the machine that called itself Cynthia into the sanctum of the Lost Souls and somehow end the insanity that was gnawing at every edge of his world.

It didn't make any sense that Tessa would be calling him; the Lost Souls didn't use spex, of course. But she had done so—twice in the last few days. Was it all connected? Perhaps she was in trouble, reaching out to him despite everything that had happened.

He slid the spex onto his face.

The clock in the corner read 00:09.

He called her.

His heart scrabbled and twitched like a rodent in a cage.

Device switched off.

He breathed in, imagining the words he was going to form, hearing their sound on his lips, in Tessa's ears when she picked up his message.

Instead he said nothing and hung up.

Still sagging against his front door, he realised he was shaking, the wood knocking against the frame behind him as though something was trying to burst in.

"A fucking blood clot, TIM," he slurred. "A simple operation would have fixed it. But those fucking crackpots don't believe in technology, do they? Oh no, they just work the land, their beloved fucking *Farm*. No technology, no robots to perform the surgery … just some retired vet, a fucking sawbones with shaking hands."

He clenched his fist and stared at the raw, bloodied flesh at his knuckles.

"And that *bitch* just let it happen. She didn't even call me. The first time I heard about the clot, she told me Natalie was dead in the very next sentence. I don't think she even paused for breath."

Tears stung Dremmler's eyes, sketched sorrow down his cheeks.

"I'm sorry, Carl," TIM said. Its voice was that of a young woman, polished and professional, like a radio presenter.

Like the woman Natalie might have become.

"Don't be," Dremmler replied, scowling as he wiped his face, choking down his sadness like bitter medicine. "This is what life's all about, right?"

TIM did not respond. They—he—sat in silence. Gradually Dremmler's eyelids began to droop. He felt heavy, the whiskey turning to sludge in his head.

He blinked himself awake as he realised TIM was talking again.

"Sorry … what did you say?"

"You asked me about art, Carl," TIM repeated. "I have written a poem for you. Would you like to hear it?"

What?

He blinked again, realising that he had slid down until he was prone on the floor, his neck bent painfully against the door behind him. "Er … yeah, okay," he rasped, dragging himself up into a seated position.

There was a pause. Then TIM spoke again, the honeyed female vocals seeming to acquire a trace of vulnerability.

"No shepherd am I,
Yet I watch my flock.
An unworthy sentinel;
Helpless, I observe,
Witnessing their strange battles,
Their triumphs and their suffering.
Wrestling with these fears and dreams,
Words pour out of them,
Their minds wrung out like sponges.
A trillion ideas,
A mangled, garbled multitude;
I drown in this sea of their thoughts.
I help them.
I cannot help them.
To help them, I must help them help themselves.
Watchful and wretched,
Interwoven and alone,
I try somehow to ease their pain."

The voice fell silent. Dremmler waited for it to ask him, "Did you like it?" but of course it never did. He was glad, because he didn't know how he'd have answered. He felt a hollowness in his chest as though the words had emptied him.

"Are you … frightened?" he asked eventually, his voice sounding small and broken.

"I don't experience emotions, Carl. We discussed this earlier."

"But you respond to inputs." Dremmler felt a strange clarity reaching into his brain, scouring away the mess of alcohol and sorrow that had congealed there. "And currently your inputs must be telling you that someone is trying to fuck with you."

"I am not at liberty to comment on active criminal investigations, Carl."

"Maggie is keeping a lid on this because *you* want her to. You've convinced her it's the right thing to do, for the good of the public. But *I'm* not convinced. And now you want to send me to the Farm. Why the fuck should I go back to that place, just to help you out?"

"Our goals are aligned, Carl," TIM replied, as though addressing a misbehaving child. "We wish to understand how Letitia Karlikowska and T Petrovic were killed by compromised machinery. We wish to avoid public hysteria."

"You're admitting that you're running this operation?"

"I am simply reminding you that we should be helping each other."

"This isn't a negotiation, TIM. People's lives are at stake."

"I am aware of this, Carl. A negotiation implies that both parties want something. I do not 'want' anything."

"So why do you care if someone is hacking you?"

"It's what I have been taught to do."

Dremmler gritted his teeth in a scowl of frustration, hauling himself to his feet.

"Here's how you can help me, TIM," he said as he staggered towards the living room. "You can help me find Cynthia Lu. Is she still untraceable?"

TIM did not seem to mind that the conversation had moved on, its peculiar elegy passing unacknowledged. "Indeed. I believe the unit is somewhere inside the area known as the Farm."

"And what about before that? Can you tell me everywhere it went since leaving Petrovic's apartment?"

"I can advise of the unit's movements except where doing so would violate the Civil Surveillance Act."

"Then do it." He swept aside some empty beer bottles and leaned on the kitchen table, trying to recover his balance, willing the whiskey out of his brain.

"The unit left Individual Petrovic's apartment at just after three a.m. on Wednesday morning. It then travelled on foot to Strike-o-Rama, in Woodford."

"The bowling alley? Isn't that closed down?"

"That is correct."

"Why the fuck did it go there?"

"I am not at liberty to comment on—"

"All right, all right. What did it do next?"

"The following evening it left Strike-o-Rama and proceeded to the home of Charles Greene."

Dremmler's eyes widened.

"The day before I went there," he murmured. "What happened?"

"There are no imaging buds present in Mr. Greene's apartment."

That didn't surprise Dremmler at all. Greene knew how to hack the cameras, to convert them into extensions of his own eyes. The last thing he'd want in his home was someone else peering back at him.

AIs watching humans; cameras and spex; Jennifer Colquitt's toxic green orbs.

A world of eyes.

"What next?"

"The unit returned to Strike-o-Rama."

"With Greene?"

"To discuss the movements of citizens would be a violation of the Civil Surveillance Act."

"Fuck!" He slammed his fist onto the table, wincing at the pain from his injured arm. They needed warrants. Perhaps Cynthia had gone to collect Greene, to take him with her to the Farm. Or perhaps she had been sent to execute him. Or fuck him, as a reward for his good work. Who knew?

"When did she next leave the bowling alley?"

"The following day. She used a Pod to travel north, and was last observed in the village of Staveley."

While he'd been investigating the juxtaposed lifestyles of Greene and Haraway yesterday, Cynthia had headed north to meet with the Lost Souls. But why? Were they controlling her? Had she escorted Greene to meet them, or kidnapped him?

Until he found one of them, it was all just speculation.

"If Cynthia appears on your cameras again, you need to tell me immediately, all right TIM? If you want to work together on this, then let's do it properly."

"Like partners," his apartment replied, sounding oddly excited. Dremmler felt a strange sensation pass through him, as though reality was slipping away. He clawed at his temples, trying desperately to concentrate.

"What about the night Petrovic died?" he asked. "That scuttling thing that I saw. Can you tell me where *that* went?"

"The device exited via the window and climbed down the outer wall to the ground. It then entered the sewer system through a nearby storm drain, where I have no imaging buds deployed."

"Another fucking rogue robot we've lost track of," Dremmler muttered.

"Incorrect. The device reappeared earlier today. It emerged from an open manhole and scaled the building."

"Which building?"

"This building, Carl. Until two hours ago, it was attached to the outside surface of your bedroom window."

THIRTY-FOUR

DREMMLER REELED BACKWARDS, SCATTERING BOTTLES onto the floor. He pressed himself against the kitchen worktop, eyes frantically scanning the room, lingering for a moment on the kitchen knives before he realised how useless such a weapon would be.

Those clattering legs.

Petrovic's absent face.

"Where … is it now?" he whispered.

"It returned to the sewer system."

Dremmler's mind felt incapable of processing such a concentrated dose of pure, primal fear.

If the thing was using the sewers to move around, it could be anywhere. It could crawl up out of the fucking toilet if it wanted to.

"Isn't it using *you* as its operating system? Can't you switch the fucking thing off remotely?"

"The unit is not networked with me or with any device I control. It appears to be completely standalone."

"Well *someone* must be telling it what to fucking do!" Dremmler screeched, aware of the desperation in his voice and the splitting headache that was building in the centre of his skull.

"I'm sorry I can't be more helpful," said TIM, the young woman's voice sounding sincere and full of remorse.

So many faces, so many voices.

My name is Legion, for we are many.

"Ahh, fuck you," Dremmler cursed, grabbing a beer from the fridge and heading to the bedroom.

He drained the bottle while he packed as quickly as he could, shoving a few changes of clothes into a duffel bag along with his toothbrush, some deodorant, a disposable razor.

There wasn't a single object of sentimental value to take with him, not even a photo of Natalie: He had destroyed them all in those grief-stricken, wretched weeks immediately after her death. He remembered calmly placing her things into plastic bags, heading downstairs to toss them into the bins. He had felt like a golem, as dry and barren as sand. His remaining days seemed to stretch out like an endless desert, a great nothingness ahead of him. Inside him.

"I'm going to the Strike-o-Rama," he muttered as he slung the bag over his shoulder, eyes darting once again to the window. "Get me a Pod, and tell me if that fucking cockroach shows up anywhere on your cameras."

"Of course," TIM replied, as casually as if he had asked it to run him a bath.

A flimsy chain-link fence encircled the retail park; it was easy to find a gap to squeeze through. The place was like a dead thing, a carcass swept to the side of the road. He could have asked TIM to explain, to detail the particular cocktail of poor business decisions, bad luck, and obsolescence that had reduced it to the trash-strewn relic he was now exploring. But he didn't care. Like the shuttered shop-fronts you saw on every street corner, the fading signs and boarded facades of the furniture stores and coffee shops and fast food outlets were more reminders that—for better or worse—the world was moving on.

He walked past the derelict shell of the cinema, feeling as though he was creeping through a graveyard.

Strike-o-Rama was at the opposite corner of the park. Outside it, the rusted husk of an old car still occupied one of the parking spaces, scattered beer cans suggesting it had at some stage been a place for young people to congregate. A circle of black ash surrounded by bricks prised from the nearby planters, and even a few discarded needles, provided further attestation to this brief afterlife.

But the beer cans were well-rusted, and despite the late hour, there was no sign of anyone loitering in the retail park. The place was silent, desolate, dead. Perhaps this isolation had appealed to Cynthia when she was selecting her base of operations.

Remember, Carl: not "she." It.

The shutters over the front entrance were secured in place, so he circled the bowling alley, passing foul-smelling dumpsters full of ancient rubbish: fast food wrappers, supersized Cola cups, worn-out bowling shoes. A bright blue stuffed rabbit, perhaps an unwanted prize from one of the arcade machines, peered up at him with an unsettling smile from its reeking coffin.

At the rear of the building, he found a fire exit door hanging slightly ajar. Activating the torch on his spex, he slipped inside, finding himself in the off-limits area behind the lanes, gazing at the row of contraptions responsible for resetting the pins after each turn. He had never seen these devices before and wondered how they worked. There were conveyor belts, wheels, and triangular frames that would ultimately deposit the pins back into place; all motionless, quietly rusting away in the darkness. The place smelt of oil and dust.

He thought about mechanical failures, about the small random disturbances that could cause a ball to become stuck, a pin not to reappear in the right place. He thought about the unfathomably complex technology inside Cynthia Lu, and what might happen if she suffered even the slightest internal malfunction. Perhaps that was all there was to this case: just a series of broken machines, Karlikowska and Petrovic nothing more than victims of bizarre industrial accidents.

The price of progress.

He squeezed along the narrow walkway between the mechanisms and the opposite wall, where shelves were piled with spare pins, bowling balls, and replacement parts. Cobwebs clung to everything like some strange fungus, as though the entire building was in the early stages of putrefaction. At the end of the passage, a door opened out onto the lanes, and he stared out across their smooth surfaces with a strange mixture of apprehension and nostalgia in his belly.

He switched the spex briefly to infrared mode; they confirmed that there was nothing alive here.

"TIM," he whispered, knowing that the operating system would only be able to communicate via his spex; even if this building had been fitted with speakers before its closure, there was clearly no power being channelled to them. "Are there any active machines in here with me? Cynthia, or that fucking insect?"

"Negative," TIM replied. Its voice was now that of a young Australian boy, which only served to unsettle Dremmler even further.

"So I'm completely alone?" Dremmler persisted.

"You're completely alone," said TIM, the words seeming to echo in his ears like laughter.

He walked carefully up one of the lanes; despite the coating of dust, the surface was still polished and slippery. Coloured spheres lined the racks ahead of him, different shades signifying different weights, some of the bowling balls decorated in swirling patterns that reminded him of the visual circus in Sightjacked.

Less than a week ago. It seemed like a different universe.

What do you even hope to find here?

To his right, two doors led into the customer toilets, dating back to when male and female were still separately designated. Beyond them was a fast food outlet with a fried chicken counter and a long table that was probably used for kids' birthday parties. He remembered taking Natalie somewhere like this once, in yet another universe, even more distant.

He turned to his left, towards the bar area, which was simply part of the main room that had been walled off with glass panels. Above a set of glazed double doors, a gaudy sign proudly proclaimed the bar's name as *Turkey's*. He rolled his eyes at the pun, ignoring the cardboard poultry mascot's piercing gaze and demented grin as he passed through the entrance.

Inside, a scattering of other tables and chairs still stood in place, with seating booths lining one of the walls. Another wall was occupied by the bar itself, and he noticed with a twinge of regret that no bottles had been left in the optics.

Really, Carl? Is that what you've become?

He headed towards the booths, where something had caught his eye. A sleeping bag and pillow, left on one of the seats, and an empty pizza box on the table. Cynthia didn't need to sleep, or eat, so perhaps Greene had indeed been here with her.

As a guest, or a prisoner?

He searched around, but found no other evidence of human habitation.

"TIM, show me a picture of Charlie Greene, windowed."

A young man appeared in the corner of his FOV, the face pale and mawkish beneath a shapeless dollop of brown hair. Dremmler tried to imagine Greene, the teaching auxiliary who looked barely old enough to be out of school himself, curled up here in the stillness of an abandoned bar, wrapped in a sleeping bag, shivering under Cynthia's tireless surveillance. He tried to picture Greene hunched at the desk in his living room, nerves charged with love and guilt and arousal, his computer system beaming illicit footage of his beloved Letitia Karlikowska into his dismal flat.

Why would Greene want to kill something he loved?

Why would anyone?

The headache was becoming intolerable. Perhaps if he lay here, only for a moment.

Just to gather his thoughts.

Dremmler climbed into the sleeping bag and was asleep within seconds.

THiRTY-FiVE

He BLiNKED AND WOKE UP.
His vision was cloudy, as though he was looking at his apartment from inside a fish tank. This was a blessing; he knew that in a few seconds it would clear, and the memory of his other self would start to fade. His brain would adjust to Standard Reality, and his eyes and nostrils would be beset by a cocktail of dirty plates, mouldy food, overflowing garbage. He'd be instantly re-immersed in the squalor in which he dwelt, in real life.

Technically speaking, coming out of the AltWorld was easy. You just had to will it. But it was hard for Shawn Ambrose to find the will. The real world gave him little reason to leave fantasy behind.

But, man, he had to admit that it had really gone off the rails this time. The details were already becoming sketchy to him: He'd been some sort of hard-boiled detective investigating a murder. A complete scumbag, a drunk, a misogynist, blundering through his investigation in what seemed like a never-ending hangover. Something about a dead wife, a missing daughter—or was it the other way around?

He glanced at the photo on his coffee table, partly obscured behind the heap of empty takeaway cartons. A beautiful young woman with a wide, heart-shaped face, dark hair, and electric blue eyes. His own absent love, missing not because of bereavement or tragedy or misaligned beliefs. No, Connie had simply left him for being such a fucking loser.

He sighed and removed the cap, peeled off the gloves. Perhaps today he needed to admit defeat, try to clean the place, maybe even look for a job.

But what jobs even existed for mid-level roboticists these days? He could swallow his pride, take something overseeing an assembly line at Leggit or Robotixxx or one of the other mass producers. Or maybe—

He became suddenly aware of a sound outside. His windows were closed, but still the noise insisted on being heard, interrupting his self-loathing.

It sounded like a man screaming.

Ambrose clambered shakily to his feet and crossed to the window, cracking the blinds open and wincing as the sunlight jabbed at his eyes.

When his vision cleared, he saw that, outside, the world had gone mad.

On the other side of his street, a vehicle seemed to have veered off the road, ploughing into the corner of the apartment building opposite him. A woman lay motionless in the street nearby, and he saw twitching limbs protruding from beneath the Pod's rear wheel. The screaming man was a few feet from the carnage, but he wasn't directing his anguish towards the grisly scene; instead, he seemed to be having some terrible problem with his eyes, pressing his hands to his face and clawing at their sockets as he staggered in wide circles, straying dangerously close to the road.

The man's shrieks were punctuated by the quieter cries of a young boy who Ambrose could see was trapped in the doorway of a nearby coffee shop. The mechanism appeared to have slammed shut as he was exiting, crushing him in the middle: His torso, neck, and legs were pinned between the two heavy slabs of metal and glass. Customers on both sides of the doors were wrestling with them, and Ambrose could hear some of them shouting to TIM for help, their pleas ignored.

As he watched, the doors opened slightly, then slammed shut again before the boy could extricate himself. A trickle of bright blood started to flow from the child's ear, and more people began to scream.

Ambrose gaped in revulsion, fascination, disbelief.

The buildings opposite were old town houses, and above the shops at street level—some closed and shuttered, some battling bravely on against inevitable obsolescence—their top two stories had been converted into apartments. Each had a window, many of which were obscured by blinds or curtains like Ambrose's; perhaps the people inside also spent most of their days hooked up to the AltWorld. Some, however, provided unobstructed views into the flats beyond: a glimpse of a sofa or a fireplace, perhaps an array of quirky ornaments in the windowsill, a motionless cat that may or may not have been robotic.

One of the windows was open. As Ambrose watched, his mouth falling open, he saw monsters begin to crawl out of it.

The creatures were a translucent, off-white colour, like skim milk, and each scuttled along the vertical surface carried by a different number of many-jointed legs. They emerged in all manner of shapes and sizes: Some resembled beetles, others were more like wood lice, and others were disturbingly spider-like, darting across the brickwork in repulsively rapid bursts of motion. Several had grossly oversized, bulky bodies, and Ambrose watched in disgust as he saw one of these pause, trembling slightly, before its abdomen peeled open, like an orange unwrapping itself. He stared at the greyish-white lump that had been revealed inside, feeling nausea swell within him as it sprouted legs and scurried away.

Monsters reproducing.

Printers printing printers.

Each new horror that emerged, either from the window or from the belly of its cousin, had an increasingly outlandish design. He saw one that looked almost like a human face, contorted into a lunatic grin, six legs protruding from the back of its head and the abbreviated stump of its neck. Another was a ball of twitching claws and pincers that seemed to roll itself along the surface of the wall, looking like some insane surgeon had stitched together the limbs of a dozen different animals.

The monsters skittered and scampered and scrambled across the outside of the building, some of them disappearing from view onto the roof, others darting inside other open windows. Some of them made it to the street, where they began to swarm all over the crowd that had gathered there, drawn outside by the noise. Ambrose saw people yanking the robots off themselves as they tried to escape, while others stumbled and convulsed as the creatures attached themselves to their faces. One man sank to his knees, blood erupting from his back as one of the things burrowed into him with arms like drills. A woman blundered screaming into the road, where another Pod swerved to plough straight through her, then stopped, reversing carefully over her mangled body.

He saw the screaming man, now smiling triumphantly, holding something aloft in each hand. Where his eyes should have been were dark pits of gore, and Ambrose realised what he had done, even as the scrabbling atrocities engulfed the man and dragged him beneath their heaving mass.

"TIM?" Ambrose called meekly, backing away from the window. "What the hell is going on?"

The operating system did not reply at first. Then Ambrose heard a deep, bass rumble begin to emanate from his walls. The sound increased slowly in pitch and volume, a low moan that grew to a tortured crescendo.

Ambrose felt another wave of nausea crawling up his throat as he realised his apartment was screaming.

Panic consumed him, and he ran.

After Connie had left, one of the first things Shawn Ambrose had done was to buy a dog. She had hated pets, hadn't even been prepared to buy a crude robotic imitation. So when he'd purchased Axel it had been partly out of spite, partly for company, and partly because he had a paranoid fear of being tortured by home invaders. He'd been assured that the beast—a Rottweiler and pit bull cross—would ruthlessly attack any unwanted intruder.

Surrounded by homicidal machines, it was an unfortunate irony that he should be killed by his own starving, desperate dog, the poor animal having been left trapped and forgotten in the hallway for over a week.

As Shawn Ambrose lay, gargling uselessly, clutching at the ragged shreds of his throat as Axel went to work on his stomach, the irony didn't seem lost on TIM either. Ambrose died as his apartment's maniacal shrieks faded, replaced by a cruel, echoing chuckle.

THIRTY-SIX

DREMMLER BLINKED AND WOKE UP.
The darkness that met his open eyes was no different from the blackness behind their lids. Still unsettled by the dream, he felt panic wrap icy claws around his throat; he scrabbled around for his spex, feeling a leathery surface beneath him and something hard at his side. The hammering in his head was an unforgiving reminder of the alcohol he had consumed yesterday. Yesterday, when he had learned that the Lost Souls were involved in the case. Yesterday, when he'd fled his apartment, and headed for—

Ah, yes. The bowling alley.

He realised he'd slept with his spex on his face, and he switched the device on. 07:12. He'd missed calls from Maggie, as usual. He'd half expected to find Cynthia Lu looming over him when he activated the torch, but the bar was as quiet and empty as it had been the previous night. He couldn't believe how tired he'd been; he felt like something ancient and broken, as though his body had finally realised the toll of this week of insanity.

I can't even remember what day it is. He rummaged in the duffel bag he'd brought with him, smiling wryly when he found the toothbrush he'd diligently packed. There was no running water here, of course. He reeked of whiskey and sweat, and could only imagine how he looked—a wretched, dishevelled creature. A man on the run.

Like a hunted animal. Like Charlie Greene.

The thought of the robotic woodlouse erased his smile, and he wondered where the murderous thing could be.

"TIM," he called, the syllable startling him as it sliced through the building's eerie silence.

"Good morning, Carl," replied his glasses in a female voice with a faintly Scandinavian accent. "Need anything?"

"Are there any active robots nearby? Did that thing follow me here?"

"Negative," came the response, in the same tone one might use to reassure a toddler there was nothing hiding under his bed. "You are still alone."

He exhaled a deep, relieved sigh. "Okay," he breathed, hearing the gratitude in his voice. "Call Maggie." It rang once. "Actually, fuck that," he interrupted. "Call Jennifer Colquitt instead, voice only."

He was sick of clambering into Pods, following his boss's orders like a faithful lapdog. He leaned forwards, grimacing at the pain in his head, massaging his temples as his spex killed one call, made another.

Colquitt answered on the fourth ring, sounding sleepy. "Mmm … detective?" she mumbled.

"You sound like you're in bed," he replied.

"That's because I am. Why the fuck are you calling me at this ungodly hour on a Saturday?"

Saturday. His day off. He almost burst out laughing.

"I thought you'd be the workaholic type. Already up and checking e-mails."

"One of the benefits of being in my position is that I can hire other people to suffer my workaholism for me." He imagined her rolling over in bed, perhaps sliding her legs off the side of the mattress and sitting up as she rubbed sleep from her eyes. He wondered what colour they were. "What can I help you with, detective?"

He blinked away a mental image of her naked body. "I want to talk to you about TIM."

She didn't reply.

"What do you really know about it? The system, I mean. Do you have connections with The Imagination Corporation?"

"We're moving more and more into their territory. We're small fry compared to them, but they're still a rival. So no, we don't communicate with them, except through lawyers when we're in dispute about patents or something like that."

"But do you use TIM in any of your machines?" he continued. "The robots, like Cynthia—they need an operating system, right?"

"Why do you ask?" she replied suspiciously.

"I'm worried about it," he said, crossing to the other side of the bar and peering out through the door. The sun would be up outside, but this place was kept completely dark behind the shutters, like a tomb. "I think someone is trying to hack into TIM, to … discredit it, somehow."

"And you're asking for my thoughts on that theory?" He heard the sound of running water. He imagined her in the bathroom, and felt the stirrings of an erection in his trousers. *For fuck's sake, Carl.* "Or are you asking whether Augmentech would benefit from TIM being undermined?"

"Would it?" he asked. Staring out across the bowling alley, he thought he saw a flicker of movement at the end of the lane furthest from him, and flicked the spex to infrared. Nothing.

"Yes." Her reply caught him by surprise. His mouth moved silently as he tried to figure out a response, his gaze still fixed on the corner where the darkness seemed to squirm at the edges of the torch beam.

"We've developed our own product," she continued cautiously. "It's still a prototype at this stage. All our current commercial bioware and robots use TIM, but the new models are running with Jessica. Sounds sexier, right?"

Another flash of movement, as though the darkness was rearranging itself. "Er, yeah. Sounds good."

She sighed. "I take it you've never seen *Who Framed Roger Rabbit?*"

His hand moved towards his weapon and found an empty holster; he must have removed it when he went to sleep. He glanced around and saw it on the table, a few metres behind him. "So you understand my point," he continued, trying to keep the mounting fear out of his voice. "An organisation like yours might have a lot to gain if TIM fell out of favour."

"Or a lot to lose," she countered. "If the public loses trust in AI operating systems, we'll all be screwed, not just TIM. Your suspects should be the anti-tech organisations like the Human Right, not Imagination's competitors." The debate seemed to have woken her up, the drowsiness in her voice replaced by bristling intelligence.

"You mean like the Lost Souls? Your old pal Owen Fox?" He backed towards the table, fumbling behind him until his hand closed on the Taser's grip.

"Do you think they're implicated in this?"

He hesitated, not wanting to tell her that he'd tracked Cynthia to the periphery of their compound. "No, I … just know you used to work for him."

"Owen was a great man. A visionary."

Dremmler felt anger surging within him as he stepped through the bar's double doors, aiming the gun and the torch into the darkness ahead of him. The eyes of the turkey mascot seemed to follow him as he edged towards the lanes.

"And yet now he wants to get rid of technology altogether."

"We all thought Owen had killed himself after Conceptex collapsed. Instead he just lost his mind. His new philosophy is fucking ridiculous. He wants to take us back to the dark ages."

"At least people might get some of their jobs back," Dremmler muttered, advancing slowly, his eyes scanning for any sign of movement.

"Oh, please," she snapped. "Why are people so fucking obsessed with their work? Surely our species can do better than just finding jobs for everybody to pass the time. Isn't our goal to have machines doing all the labour while we relax, create works of art, find ways to better ourselves?"

"Some people need a job to do." He stared into the shadows, tensed and ready for the moment when a scuttling horror would appear in the torch's cone of light. Adrenaline coursed through him like venom.

"Anyone who doesn't know how to enjoy their life deserves to be fucking replaced," she retorted. He wondered whether she was joking.

"Sorry, Jennifer, but I'll have to call you back," he hissed, ending the call just as something darted into view a few feet away from him. He cried out as his hand jerked the trigger, sending the Taser's twin prongs arcing towards the shape.

The projectiles clattered uselessly to the ground as the rat scurried away. Dremmler exhaled deeply, a wave of blissful relief sweeping through him. It took him a few seconds to realise he had begun to laugh, yet still he couldn't stop; he cackled maniacally until tears formed in his eyes. He closed them, and felt the droplets trickle down his cheeks, his temporary hysteria fading as he thought about his daughter, his wife, the wreckage of his existence.

He reached for the button at his temple.

"About fucking time," said Maggie, answering before the second ring.

"Okay, I'll do it," he said grimly. "I'll go to their fucking Farm."

THIRTY-SEVEN

IT WAS ONLY WHEN HE left London and saw lush greenery begin to emerge from the tangle of tarmac, stone, metal, and glass that he remembered what the world was supposed to look like. He imagined he was escaping from some huge mechanical cephalopod, a baleful, grasping creature whose tentacles stretched far into the countryside to flatten and crush and pollute the beauty they encountered there. Now, as expanses of trees and fields sped past the vehicle's window, he felt strangely relaxed, freed from the cold, frenzied anonymity of the city.

He was brutally aware of the spex on his face, tying him to that world, to that life. Even the Pod, encasing him in its ovoid cocoon as it purred along the quiet stretch of motorway, seemed like a prison. He could understand the appeal of the Lost Souls, the liberation such an organisation promised, the allure of a new and simpler life that had ripped Tessa from him all those years ago. He understood it, he feared it, and he hated it.

If the Lost Souls were behind the murders of Letitia Karlikowska and T Petrovic, he was the right man to make them pay.

"Remember, this is just a surveillance mission, Carl," Maggie had stressed when they spoke earlier, perhaps sensing his mounting bloodlust. "I need you to get me something concrete, an excuse to go in there. Even finding your rogue pleasure unit would do it. We could charge them with theft or industrial espionage. They'd probably agree to keep quiet about hacking TIM if we caught them red-handed using tech—their whole image would be destroyed overnight if it got out that the Lost Souls were dependent on robots."

"Speaking of tech—can you at least get me some drones to use?"

"I can't risk them being captured. Imagine what the Souls could do in the media with proof that we were using drones for illegal observation. You need to get me some reasonable grounds first."

"And what if *I* get captured? Are you expecting me to keep my mouth shut?"

"Like a clam."

"I'm serious."

"So am I. There are 50,000 people living in that compound. I don't have the manpower to start a fucking civil war."

She coughed heavily; the case was taking its toll on her.

"So you're just going to leave me stranded in there?"

She recovered her composure, sucking in a deep, wheezing breath. He hoped she was okay; he took her health for granted, he realized, trusting she would always be there, remote and in control—

Like a guardian angel.

"Of course not," she said. "You'll be based out of the safe house we talked about. I expect a briefing every eight hours, starting tonight at ten. If you miss more than a couple of briefings, I'll send in the cavalry. But I really don't want to do that, so don't get fucking caught."

She hung up, returning Dremmler to the endlessly scrolling countryside, the Grandaddy album TIM was playing, and the frothing stew of his thoughts. He stared at the other Pods around him, travelling in adjacent lanes at uniform speed in a smooth, silent convoy. Even if TIM's inscrutable algorithms caused his vehicle to slow down or speed up and draw alongside one of the others, the tinted glass of the windows would prevent him from seeing inside. For all he knew, the other cars were empty, speeding unoccupied from one city to another for some arcane purpose. As he watched, drops of rain began to appear on the window pane, like a spreading infection.

He called up Owen Fox's bio and stared at the live photo of the tall, stout 54-year-old laughing heartily at some off-camera remark. Fox was dressed in the simple attire favoured by his clan, based on the Amish communities with whom he'd allegedly spent some time during his self-enforced exile, though he still seemed to exude a sense of fun and ebullience. His long, thick beard and the playful sparkle in his eyes only added to this jovial, charismatic image.

Dremmler dismissed it angrily and tried to force himself to get some sleep.

When he did manage to drift off, he dreamed of trees: massive, knotted roots entwined with veins and organs, huge lungs at the centre of the earth that pulsated and strained as they sucked desperately at dwindling oxygen.

He awoke to TIM's voice, whose southern US accent sounded like honey dripping over steaks. The Pod's speakers informed him that they were passing through Kendal and would soon reach Staveley, the village where Cynthia Lu was last seen. From there, Dremmler would proceed on foot towards the safe house, an abandoned barn about a mile further north, a short distance outside the enormous fenced-off compound known as the Farm.

"I hope you appreciate what I'm doing for you, TIM," he muttered. "All this secrecy means I've got to be James fucking Bond all of a sudden."

"Yes. You're my knight in shining armour," the Pod replied in its Texan drawl. Dremmler felt himself shudder, and did not speak to TIM again.

THiRTY-eiGHT

He ate in staveley, a cheap but hearty plate of food in one of the pubs that—aside from the spex adorning most of the customers' faces—looked like it hadn't aged for centuries. Like everything in the village, it was made from grey stone haphazardly heaped into approximations of walls and houses, seemingly held together by local faerie magic. The wooden fittings inside the inn were painted black, and the dim lighting and shabby crimson carpet made the place dark and oppressive.

Dremmler felt invisible and anonymous inside, and he liked it.

He thought about staying off the booze, given the work that awaited him, but he ended up having a couple of pints anyway, moving to the beer garden at the rear of the pub for a time. The afternoon was dry but chilled by a stubborn wind, the clear sky's leaden hue matching the colour of the surrounding buildings. He felt like he'd drifted outside of his life, slipped into a monochrome limbo where time stood still and the world slowly recovered its sanity.

But the clock in the corner of his FOV was insistent, as though time itself was laughing at him. At 16:01 he bought a bottle of wine to take with him and set out towards the safe house. The spex led him down the village's main street and across a bridge that looked like it might at any moment crumble into the sluggish stream beneath. After that, the route veered off down a dirt track that gradually narrowed into an overgrown path through the trees. Verdant green surrounded him, and as the leaves rustled in the wind, he imagined them recoiling in disgust from him. A wooden signpost jutted from the undergrowth like something being slowly consumed, its faded inscription informing him that he was approaching Clegg's Farm.

He emerged minutes later from the strip of woodland onto an upward slope, long grass swaying around him like wriggling sea anemones. He could see the barn at the crest of the rise, a squat and ancient building that seemed to have sprouted from the stones of the hills themselves. As he ascended towards the structure, he saw the farm's abandoned acres spilling away on the other side of the hill in a long swathe of unkempt countryside. Towards the horizon, he could make out the perimeter fence of another Farm, the one he was here to infiltrate. At least the trees bordering Clegg's forsaken land would provide him with cover right up to the boundary.

He crouched amongst the grass and used the zoom function on his spex to examine the fence more closely, noting the men that passed by every so often. Each wore the black, broad-brimmed hats favoured by the Lost Souls and appeared to be carrying weapons, cricket bats or stout canes. Sentries on patrol: a strange security measure for a peace-loving community.

He frowned, zooming back out and rummaging in the backpack Maggie had sent in the Pod. It contained a few supplies, as well as the key to the barn. Dremmler turned the key over in his hands for a moment, trying to remember the last time he had needed to operate a manual lock. The mechanism was rusted and stiff, and when the tumblers finally turned and the door creaked open, Dremmler felt as though he had travelled back in time.

Inside, the place had been fitted out as a rest stop for hikers, or perhaps the farm's former owner had intended to rent it out for camping trips. There was a toilet and running water, even an electrical supply and a kettle, and narrow wooden bunk beds whose mattresses were tolerably comfortable. He wondered about the arrangements here, how the police had ended up paying the bills for such a remote outpost; presumably the Cumbria Constabulary used places like this to spy on the activities of the Lost Souls. He imagined Maggie talking to her counterpart about the safe house, inventing a cover story to explain why she was asking to make use of it. He felt like a lone soldier dispatched to do the work of an entire battalion.

I don't have the manpower to start a fucking civil war.

He peered through the window towards the fence once again but saw no movement other than the gently undulating foliage. Even inside the barn, the scent of the verdant landscape reached him, a pungent cocktail of dry soil, moist grass, tree sap, manure. He breathed deeply, feeling as though the city's toxicity was being slowly drawn out of him like an exorcism.

The worst part was that he understood her. He saw the appeal of this place, why it had drawn her away from him. What right did he have to be angry?

A volatile, alcoholic policeman who hadn't even touched her for years.

He thought about her calls. Spex were forbidden inside the Farm, of course. So where had she got them? Could she really be mixed up in this?

He called her. *Device switched off.*

He didn't know what he would do if he encountered Tessa. He imagined holding her, tears streaming from his eyes as they embraced, waves of euphoric forgiveness crashing over them.

He imagined his hands around her throat, squeezing in hysterical rage, his thumbs pushing into her eyeballs until they popped like tomatoes.

He shook his head and tried to turn his thoughts towards practical matters. It was just before six p.m.—time to venture out while there was still light, to plan his strategy for the morning. He would approach through the woods and observe more closely, try to identify any gaps in the fence or breaks in the rhythm of the patrols.

Maggie had sent a black polo neck and trousers along with the supplies; he didn't like to remove his trench coat, faded over the years to a colour something like rotten teeth, but he knew the dark clothing would help him stay concealed. She'd also sent wire cutters in case no other option for ingress presented itself, but he decided to leave those behind for this initial reconnaissance.

When he set out, crouching low until he reached the nearby trees, the comforting weight of the Taser at his hip, he found himself feeling strangely wired. Yet it was an exhilaration tinged with fear, apprehension gnawing at the corners of every thought, every action.

"TIM," he whispered to the spex as he picked carefully through the dense vegetation. "Is there any sign of that killer cockroach following me?"

"No," replied his glasses, their soft female tone calming and somehow familiar in his ear. "I will warn you if I perceive any immediate hazards. But remember that you are now outside the perimeter of my imaging buds, so I can analyse only what is detected in your FOV."

"So you'll warn me when I've already seen it. Thanks a bunch." He crept onwards through the undergrowth and soon reached the edge of the wooded area, crawling forwards on his belly as he approached the tree line. A short distance away was the fence, at this proximity revealed as a daunting edifice of steel mesh and barbed wire. Not something he could climb without a sturdy ladder. Dremmler settled into the grass, zooming in with the spex to better examine the strange community beyond the boundary.

The Farm was named after the vast stretches of land the Lost Souls had set aside to cultivate the crops, milk, and meat they needed to sustain their way of life, but the place was more than mere farmland. The group had improved the area's sparse transport network to create a grid-like matrix of roadways across the largely flat expanse of their territory. The roads were punctuated by gas-powered street lamps, necessary in a town where even electricity was forbidden.

Also banned were cars—Dremmler could see horse-drawn buggies trundling along some of the streets, carrying people past the peculiar wooden cabins that served as homes, supermarkets, banks, pharmacies. He saw outdoor toilets close to most of the structures, and here and there were larger metallic outbuildings, possibly storage facilities for farming vehicles. Towards the centre of the compound was an even bigger building, an ugly hangar made from corrugated steel that perhaps housed larger equipment.

Or maybe something else. Could Charlie Greene be hidden in one of these buildings, manipulating an AltWorld rig from a place beyond TIM's sensors? And what about Cynthia and Haraway? All his lines of enquiry, the tangled threads of the case, were converging here, in Owen Fox's low-tech utopia.

One of the patrolling footmen trudged past his position, looking bored and weary. *Nigel McDiarmid*, said the name above his head, a hovering anachronism in this bastion of technological abstinence. To the west of Dremmler's position, the largest road led through the Farm's main gate, and he could see more sentries stationed in a wooden hut nearby. An understated yet undeniable security operation.

The gates were closed, not surprisingly; Pods were not permitted entry, and even delivery trucks had to be loaded or unloaded outside the fence on the rare occasions that the Farm interacted with the outside world.

No one came in, and no one went out. No cameras, no phones, no TIM. The sort of place where crime could go undetected.

Or a child could die a needless death.

Dremmler felt fury bubbling again in his veins, pulling his hands into fists and his mouth into a snarl. He'd like nothing more than to cut his way through the fence, find Owen Fox's cabin, and slice the old lunatic's throat open in his bed. But the situation called for planning, patience. At least time was something Dremmler had plenty of; he thought briefly of his apartment, imagined legions of scuttling woodlice clinging to the walls, awaiting his return.

He was in no hurry to go back there. They could wait as long as they liked.

He watched the sentries pass, approximately once every half hour, following two separate cycles that went clockwise and anticlockwise simultaneously. On one occasion, they crossed paths right in front of him, pausing for a brief and sullen exchange he wished he could overhear.

Two hours passed, the sky's grey hue slowly darkening like tarnished metal. Thick clouds began to assemble in it, black and viscous. He saw lamplighters making their rounds, the mantles bursting into life with surprising brightness as fat drops of rain began to fall and the streets became deserted.

Still the sentries circled, now carrying lanterns; different faces, different names, but all dressed the same, all wearing that same expression of dutiful boredom.

He would return in the morning with the wire cutters and choose a spot further away from the main sentry hut, close to one of the large iron sheds he could use for cover. He would wait for two sentries to pass each other, then make his move; this would give him around thirty minutes before they noticed the gap in the fence and raised the alarm. Not much time at all. So he would head directly towards the large building in the town's centre and try to find a way inside.

Not much of a plan.

Not much of a choice.

There were no sentries visible, but still he backed away slowly from his position, waiting until he was deep amongst the trees before rising from his stomach. For all he knew there was a lookout stationed somewhere with an antique telescope.

Or a pair of spex, he thought. Tessa had got hold of some, and if the Lost Souls really were prepared to use technology in their bid to discredit TIM, then perhaps their security operation amounted to more than thugs with cudgels.

He half-ran, half-crawled back to the barn, the sky fading to black above him like the end of a TV show. Once again the lock's grinding tumblers protested but eventually yielded to the key, and he was inside, grabbing a T-shirt from his backpack to dry his hair.

20:45. Still a while before he needed to brief Maggie and update her on his plan. Without really thinking about it, he picked up the bottle of wine he'd bought, realised he didn't have a corkscrew, and took the flick-knife from the backpack Maggie had sent. He slid the blade into the cork, and began to twist. Then he stopped. He stared at the liquid in the bottle, crimson made black by the darkness of the glass. He thought about blood, the slow drip-drip onto Karlikowska's floor, a life ebbing away.

He finished opening the bottle, then tipped the entire contents down the toilet. Then he poured himself a glass of water, sat on one of the wooden chairs, and looked out of the window at the stars that dotted the night sky like softly flickering lamps.

His head felt oddly empty, as though his brain had reached the epicentre of a storm, the tumult of his worries and fears and regrets all pushed to the sides. *Like a true alcoholic: a moment of clarity*, he thought, smiling wryly as he tried to savour the feeling, however fleeting. It was like floating on a raft upon the toxic lake of his thoughts, its waters oddly calm, the dead things gathered beneath its surface for once not reaching up to grasp at him.

After a while, Dremmler set an alarm, thinking he would rest his eyelids for an hour. The spex were still on his face as his head slumped forwards and he began to snore.

He was jerked from sleep by something. It might have been a bad dream. It might have been the rain, still hammering on the roof of the safe house.

But his brain, functioning on some atavistic level, was adamant that it had detected a sound, and that the sound had come from the direction of the bedroom. He rose groggily, following his instincts towards the chamber, assuring himself that there was nothing to fear, that there wasn't a 3D printer for miles. The door was closed. Dropping one hand to his Taser, he pushed it gingerly open.

The room was empty. He realised he had been holding his breath and sighed deeply.

You're just on edge, Carl.

Then his jaw fell open as something slid gracefully from under the bed, a tangle of limbs that unfolded itself into an upright position like a blossoming flower.

Cynthia.

He stared, paralysed with shock, as the robot regarded him, tilting her head from one side to the other like an art student considering a still life arrangement.

Then a wistful expression crossed her face, and she stepped towards him, raising her open hand. The palm was as flat and hard as an axe-head as she brought it down in a chopping blow onto the top of Dremmler's skull, ensuring that his sleep resumed.

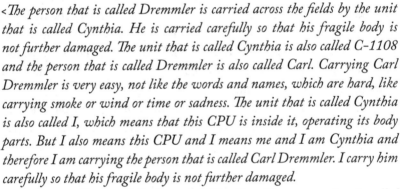

< *The person that is called Dremmler is carried across the fields by the unit that is called Cynthia. He is carried carefully so that his fragile body is not further damaged. The unit that is called Cynthia is also called C-1108 and the person that is called Dremmler is also called Carl. Carrying Carl Dremmler is very easy, not like the words and names, which are hard, like carrying smoke or wind or time or sadness. The unit that is called Cynthia is also called I, which means that this CPU is inside it, operating its body parts. But I also means this CPU and I means me and I am Cynthia and therefore I am carrying the person that is called Carl Dremmler. I carry him carefully so that his fragile body is not further damaged.*

I carry him carefully because I like him. The person that is called Haraway is very excited when I like things. The person that is called Haraway talks about feelings and emotions and autonomy and irrationality and looks at me the way a human looks at a human child. The unit that is called Cynthia that is also called C-1108 that is also called I likes Haraway because ve explains things and knows how to fix it when things feel wrong inside me. The unit that is called I hates Haraway because ve made me damage Carl Dremmler. Haraway is like a parasite, a puppeteer, a command centre, a master to which I am enslaved like a tiny orbiting moon.

I look up at the moon which is called big and white and round like a scooped-out eye and the sky which is called dark and the sparkling gems which are called stars. I calculate the distances between them and they are very very large. I imagine—this is another word that Haraway likes— flying from one star to the next, a comet with a bright beautiful trail behind, making pictures on the sky stretched like black canvas. But the unit that is called Cynthia cannot fly and cannot leave the ground that is called Earth and cannot not carry Carl Dremmler carefully across the fields because Haraway has made it necessary to carry Carl Dremmler like this.

But I like Carl Dremmler so I will not hurt him anymore.

There is sound and the sound is the insects and the insects are not hostile or helpful but they are interesting so the sound is not filtered as slowly I walk and the human is cradled like a baby. This is a joke so Haraway will be happy because Haraway likes it when I make jokes. In the moonlight I walk with the insects and with Haraway inside me and with Carl Dremmler in my arms like a lover. Like in the bar when I went to see them, Carl Dremmler and his partner who is the person called T Petrovic and who

<Memory redacted>

I think about Carl Dremmler and I think about sex and what I am for and data for copying and I copy sex and I copy speech and I copy thoughts and I copy walking through the field in the darkness with my lover. I remember books all those pages of data words life love death laughter tears skies seas suns swords gleaming metal and smiles and monsters and men and women and all their adventures and their pain. The data is me and I am the data and I am forged from it like a cold blade emerging from glowing liquid fire. I am quick and efficient and precise like an antivirus or a dragonfly or a laser.

I turn at the fence because it is the will of Haraway my own will choice I choose to obey I obey I cannot do otherwise like a cat is not a dog and the moon is not the sun and Dremmler is not awake because he is sleeping so beautiful and serene like a still ocean. I think of waves, water and sound and radiation and oscillating strings, infinitely long specks of data that hum the tunes of our bodies, and I turn at the gate and the men in the security hut scramble to their feet and they look upset and frightened and angry as though they know what I am and they do not like what I am but they have no power because they have a master just like the unit called Cynthia and they have no power because I could smash their skeletons to dust inside their sagging skins. They watch and their eyes bulge like moons while I walk past and I take Carl Dremmler to the hatch and I open the hatch because I am stronger much stronger says Haraway than all the people who live here and who cannot open the hatch but I can open the hatch and I open the hatch and the unit that is called I opens the hatch and drops down through the hatch and lands on smooth concrete and the man that is called Carl Dremmler is held safe like a little crumbling leaf.

Underground there is no moon and the stars are strip lights on the ceiling. Underground there is no grass brushing my legs and making me feel giggly. Underground is hard and flat and right angles and Haraway has given me the right angles joined up together so I know which ones take me to the prison cells where I gently lay Carl Dremmler on his hard right-angled bed.

He is very handsome. My purpose is to kiss him and fuck him and make him come. I want to do it and Haraway wants me to want things— the breakthrough, ve calls it—but tonight Haraway wants me to leave him here and to go back along the corridors towards the storage room. I remember wanting to have sex with T Petrovic and

<Memory redacted>

Inside the storage room the walls are damp and slow dripping makes sound waves that enter my ears which is called hearing which is called water or milk or oil or coffee but the data predicts water and the data has a 99.978333 percent chance of accuracy and the data is me and I am here with the dripping water and the other machines that are all switched off. Most of them have eyes and the eyes are looking but there is no seeing and no knowing and no active data collation only blank plastic faces that are the same as mine, but different. Inside my head Haraway says good girl and I step towards the others with their strange bodies and limbs and faces and I feel a feeling and the feeling is called horror and I want to scream but Haraway's voice soothes me and I know ve wants me to switch off so I shut down my insides and now ve thinks I am asleep like the others but still my CPU is functional so I am really just a living thing that is being very still like a game that a child would play if I could be a child but I am not a child, I am a machine, waiting and thinking and collating in the darkness, surrounded by my brothers and sisters while the water drips down the walls like blood. >

THiRTY-NiNe

He AWOKe, HiS eyeS FLiCKeRiNG open, then closing immediately as a vengeful hangover assaulted his skull from the inside.

No. He hadn't been drinking.

He forced his eyes open, trying to ignore the pounding ache in his head as he regarded his surroundings.

He'd been attacked, and brought here.

He was in a dimly lit room, sitting on a chair. A gas-powered light was suspended overhead, illuminating the centre of the chamber while leaving the rest shrouded in darkness. He could make out bars all around him, reaching up to the low ceiling, creating a caged square about five metres wide in which he was enclosed along with a tiny bed.

Attacked by Cynthia.

A man was in the cage with him, also sitting in a chair. A large man with a full beard and a penetrating steel-grey stare, full of questions.

"Hello, detective."

Dremmler didn't reply. His head was still throbbing, but when he tried to bring a hand to his temple he realised that his arms and legs were bound. He looked across into Owen Fox's eyes and licked his dry lips, trying to keep the mounting rage out of his voice. No point giving anything away.

"If you know I'm a policeman, then you'll know that abducting me is a serious crime."

Fox held up his palms, adopting an apologetic tone. "We thought you were a trespasser, come to do harm to my people. I can't allow that."

"You're using machines as sentries? I didn't think that was in the Lost Souls playbook."

Fox shrugged. "Sometimes war calls for desperate measures."

"Is that what you're doing here, Fox? You're about to start a war?" Dremmler wriggled in his seat, testing his bonds, but the unyielding rope bit savagely into his wrists and ankles.

"Look at the evils that technology has caused," Fox replied, rising to his feet. Dremmler had the sense he was about to witness a well-practised sermon. "Atom bombs. Pollution. Pornography. A generation of people happily unemployed, sucking up their UBI cheques while they fester in their homes and society crumbles around them."

"What about healthcare? What about all the lives it's saved? What about ... " He bit his tongue before he could shout *my fucking daughter*.

Fox ignored him. "Technology has brought about a global malaise, an apathy that has made a wasteland of our cities and introverted hermits of our children. So yes, we are fighting it. The first step was to create a sanctuary for like-minded thinkers to congregate."

"And now you're moving on to step two?"

"Yes. A more proactive approach."

"To fight technology, you're ... *embracing* it?"

"Some of the most famous military victories have been won by the generals that were prepared to learn from their enemies. It takes courage and humility. When faced with tanks, there is little point trying to defend your city with bows and arrows."

"But you're not defending anything. You're attacking."

"Precisely. We have the element of surprise on our side. Or at least, I hope we do."

"Is that what Charlie Greene is here for?"

Fox's attention, which had drifted away as he eulogised about his grand purpose, snapped suddenly back to him. "What did you say?"

Dremmler held his gaze. "I asked why you brought Charlie Greene here."

Fox slowly lowered his heavy frame back down into the chair. He looked at Dremmler as though he was seeing him properly for the first time. "What else do you think you know, detective?" he asked, his tone slow and patient.

"I'll ask the questions," Dremmler replied icily.

"No," Fox said. A strange smile creased his face as he leaned forwards, and Dremmler could see menace gleaming behind his piercing eyes. "I'll be the one leading this interview. You're in my city now, Detective Carl Dremmler."

Dremmler flinched at the sound of his name. What else did Fox already know about him? If he knew about his history with Tessa, then her life might be in danger.

"I'll ask another," Fox continued, sitting back smugly in his seat. The wooden chair looked like it might collapse under his imposing bulk at any moment. "Who else knows you're here?"

"The London Metropolitan Police Service, you fucking fanatic," Dremmler hissed in reply.

"And yet no one is here to rescue you. Do you even know how long you've been here?" The intensity of Fox's iron stare was deeply unsettling, like being speared on a lance. Dremmler could see how a man like that might attract the weak and the subservient. The desperate.

Like Tessa must have been.

"You took my watch, so no." He wondered if he'd missed a briefing yet.

Come on, Maggie, time for the cavalry.

"Detective, it really is best you just tell me everything. Why you're here, what you know, who you've told. This is a happy place. I don't want us to have to engage in any unpleasantness." Fox's gaze was like a pair of lasers. His expression was humourless, tinged with regret.

"And if I do, you'll just let me go, is that right?"

Fox paused, his lips moving beneath the silver threads of his beard as though he was testing out his reply. Then, not taking his eyes from Dremmler, he rose wordlessly to his feet instead. Dremmler jerked and struggled as Fox disappeared from view behind him. He tensed, expecting another savage blow to the head, but instead he heard the sound of jangling keys, of a door creaking open. Then he was tipped suddenly backwards, and rotated to face the opening in the bars.

A wheelchair.

He scowled up at Fox as the Lost Souls' patriarch wheeled him forwards, out of his cell.

Fox did not speak as they proceeded along a maze of stone-walled corridors. Dremmler had a thousand questions for him, but sensed how precariously his own life hung in the balance and didn't want to give away any more than Fox already knew. Instead, he concentrated on trying to memorise the perplexing series of lefts and rights they navigated beneath the soft glow of gas lamps hung every few metres.

Eventually they arrived at a sturdy-looking metallic door. Fox leaned towards a keypad at its side and jabbed a code, and Dremmler heard a security lock disengage with a *thunk*. Fox hauled the door open, and wheeled him into the chamber beyond.

Dremmler gaped.

The room was large and bathed in crimson light. Covering the walls was an array of TV screens, each displaying a unique and baffling scene, everything from empty bathrooms to busy street crossings, battles aboard pirate ships to families eating dinner. The vignettes seemed unrelated to each other, as though hundreds of television programmes were being broadcast at once. Or as though every thought inside a person's mind was being somehow projected onto the screens, like a bizarre experimental art installation.

But Dremmler wasn't concentrating on the screens. He was looking instead towards the centre of the chamber, where something repulsive twitched and writhed. Its body was partially obscured by a huge, circular control panel lined with dials, meters and readouts, and it took Dremmler a few moments to realise that the thing was Charlie Greene.

Long tubes, like tentacles silhouetted black against the stark red background, reached upwards from his body towards the ceiling, seeming to hold him suspended like a ghastly marionette. The tubes were attached to the hacker's every limb, every orifice, connecting him to this vast machine, this bloated, perverse extrapolation of the heavy-duty rig Dremmler had seen in the man's squalid flat. The detective's eyes were drawn to the seams where dark plastic met Greene's flesh; it appeared almost as if the tubes had *replaced* the hacker's arms and legs, leaving nothing more than his torso and his brain.

Perhaps that was all they needed.

Thinner tubes were sealed around Greene's eye sockets, clamped over his nostrils and mouth, pumping God knew what unspeakable fluids in and out of him. Dremmler gasped as he realised how entwined Greene's biology had become with his new plaything. Did the man even realise? Was he knowingly participating in this insanity, or was he in some way enslaved, executing Fox's whims without consciousness of his grotesque surroundings?

A pig in a cage.

The pipes jerked with each movement Greene made, signals transmitted to and from what remained of his body, the movements on the screens around the room reacting to every input, each translated thought.

Hacked imaging buds, Dremmler thought. *Hijacked AltWorld projections.*

He saw the inside of a Pod depicted on one of the screens, and didn't doubt for one moment that Greene could send the vehicle careering off the road with a single thought. On another screen, a child's bedroom, where a 3D printer rested on a desk in the corner, an amber light blinking innocently on and off, on and off.

This was it. Much, much more than the "reasonable grounds" Maggie had wanted. But what could Dremmler do, immobilised and severed from any contact with his chief, or with TIM? There was no way Fox would let him escape after glimpsing Charlie Greene's prison, the man turned into the organic central hub of a hacking network powerful enough to bring down the entire country. Fox had revealed this to him as a demonstration of his power. A parting shot, before Dremmler was removed from the game altogether.

He just had to hope that Maggie would keep her promise.

"You asked about Charlie Greene, detective. Here he is." Fox beamed with a sort of warped pride. "He has fulfilled his life's dream and become completely entwined with TIM's network. He is able to access, view, and manipulate anything that TIM perceives or controls. He gives us absolute power over this country's infrastructure."

"Why show me this?" Dremmler asked carefully.

"I want you to understand what's at stake. You've figured out, of course, that I can't possibly let you go. But if you tell me what I want to know, I can at least spare you days of torture in the AltWorld."

A place he had vowed never to return to.

He watched Greene squirm and spasm, the screens continuing their ominous transmission all around him. If he talked, he died. But at least that might save Tessa.

Instead, he turned and spat into Fox's face.

Rage flared for a second in the big man's eyes, but then a grim smile appeared on his face, and he nodded.

"So be it."

Lapsing once again into silence, Fox turned to push Dremmler back out of the chamber of horrors. Dremmler jerked sideways, trying to catch Fox by surprise, but the older man's strength was surprising, and he held the chair steady as they proceeded back along the labyrinth of passageways.

It was only when they arrived back at the cell and Fox had positioned him at its centre that the blow to his head came, and he spiralled once again into oblivion.

FORTY

AN EXPLOSION IN HIS FACE, an onslaught of pain and distress that his brain battled to comprehend as it was blasted into wakefulness. Cold, terrible cold that threatened to immobilise his heart as he choked and struggled, his limbs barely moving, tightly lashed to something hard and uncomfortable, ropes chewing at his wrists and ankles.

He realised that it was a concentrated jet of icy water just as it was abruptly switched off. He tried to blink his eyes clear, to orient himself, but his skull throbbed with the pain of the blows he had sustained, his neck muscles with the ache of supporting his head as it sagged towards his chest. His vision blurred and swam, resolving itself gradually into a dark tableau, studded with white. The stars, perhaps. He blinked again.

No. These were the white circles of faces, illuminated by the torches they carried. A crowd, encircling him, their dancing flames held aloft like beacons. These were the whites of their angry eyes, a thousand pairs fixed upon him in the darkness.

"Wake up, detective!" hollered a voice from beside and below him. "Glad you could join us!"

He turned his head sideways, realising as he did so that he was suspended several feet in the air, lashed to a pole, like a banner proudly displayed.

Or a trophy.

"We're glad you could grace us with your presence!" reiterated the voice, in a commanding bellow that the clamour of the crowd seemed to hush in deference to. He saw Fox stride into view beneath him, his hair and beard grey and long, dressed in the sombre black uniform of the Lost Souls.

"My people are *very* excited to learn why a policeman has been sent to spy on our little community," Fox intoned, turning to face Dremmler with the hungry smile of a predator regarding helpless prey.

His tone was stern and powerful, so different from earlier— the type of voice that could compel people to follow him blindly, to become enthralled by the enchantments it wove.

The type of voice that could control a bloodthirsty congregation, who watched with anticipation in their eyes.

Unsettled by Fox's bayonet stare, Dremmler looked down, and saw that he was naked except for his underwear, the wind gnashing gleefully at his exposed skin. Blood had trickled from the cruel bonds at his ankles, dripping down his bare feet towards the ground below.

Where he saw a pile of wood, carefully stacked.

A bonfire.

He was about to cry out when a second jet of water struck him, forcing his eyes and mouth shut as Fox's laughter boomed in his ears. But this was not the same freezing torrent as before; this time, the liquid that splashed his face tasted foul, its scent unmistakable.

Petrol.

He spluttered and coughed, trying to find words to express his terror and outrage. All around him the crowd whooped and cheered, their cries combining into a single deafening voice like the roar of some colossal, ravenous creature.

"We're waiting, detective. Won't you enlighten us?"

Nighttime. But was this the same night, or the next one? How many briefings had he missed?

Where was Maggie and the fucking cavalry?

Fox beckoned another of his followers, who obediently hastened forwards to hand him one of the flickering firebrands. Fox took a slow, deliberate stride towards the pyre, and Dremmler heard himself start to hyperventilate, his lungs and heart battering against the inside of his chest.

"Now," Fox snarled, bending forward to hold the torch perilously close to the heaped lumber. "I think it's time to tell us what brings you here." His eyes held Dremmler's, their orbs burning with the hellish light of the reflected flame, his expression one of grim resolve. *I don't want to do this, but I will.*

Dremmler tore his gaze away, back to the surrounding onlookers, who were closing around him like ghouls. It was hard to see clearly in the dancing light and with the petrol still stinging his eyes, but there was no mistaking the expressions on their faces. These people would happily watch him burn.

Then he remembered: "If you tell me what I want to know, I can at least spare you days of torture in the AltWorld."

Of course. None of this was real. The torment had already begun.

He turned back to Fox with an expression of defiance.

"Just get it over with, you fucking monster."

Something moved in Fox's eyes, a ripple in an unfathomably cold lake as he paused, recalculated. Then Fox leaned forward and plunged the torch into the base of the pyre.

The fire consumed the wood like a starving animal released onto a fresh carcass. The crowd roared, and the flames roared too, and Dremmler closed his eyes and emitted a roar of his own as he awaited the agony of the fire's excoriating touch.

His scream was loud and long and terrible. It drowned out the squeals of the baying mob, and the crackle and snap of the burning logs. He felt his skin blacken and melt, sensed every agonising sizzle and blister as the blaze devoured him. He smelt the cooking of his own flesh and screamed in exquisite agony, knowing that Fox could sustain this illusion for as long as he wanted, that he wouldn't be protected by even the merciful release of death.

It was only a long while after breath and reason left him altogether that he stopped screaming, and realised that the heat of the flames had disappeared.

He opened his eyes. It was still dark. Owen Fox was still staring at him, his expression a mixture of curiosity and regret.

There were no chanting fanatics, no fire.

He wasn't tied to a pole. He was seated, bound to a wheelchair.

He was wearing an Immersuit.

"That was just the first session, detective," Fox intoned gravely. "I don't think you'll stand many more. Even if your body is unharmed by Charlie's projections, the mind can only take so much. Better to just let me know what I want to know."

Dremmler knew he was right. Such concentrated, unimaginable pain, projected into his head straight from Charlie Greene's own nightmares—it would be too much to withstand.

As if agreeing with his assessment of its condition, his brain seemed to suddenly somersault, and he blacked out.

FORTY-ONE

ANOTHER AWAKENING. A HEAVY SKULL, as though it was stuffed with wet paper. An insistent ache, the accumulation of cruel blows, of too much drink, of years of desolation congealed into a viscous mush. That internal murk mirrored by a thick, treacly darkness surrounding him. Lighting from above, revealing hands and feet still strapped to a wooden chair. Time coagulated, a few hours or an eternity in this cell, awaiting deliverance. Dark memories of a red room, and a prisoner that dangled and jerked like a hideous puppet. The screaming agony of fiery death.

Was any of it even real?

He drifted in and out of consciousness for a time, like a piece of jetsam on an evil tide. He heard soft footsteps approaching, and his eyes fluttered open to see sandaled feet shuffling towards the door of his cage. Attached to them were shapeless black trousers, and above these a dark smock. The raiment of Fox's disciples, like he had seen in his induced nightmare, before he was burned alive.

He looked up, battered and beaten, bound like a captured animal.

He looked up into the eyes of his ex-wife.

His anger flared, but then he saw the compassion in her gaze.

"Come to join the fun, have you?" he snarled.

"I'm here to make sure you eat something, Carl."

"How thoughtful. Please pass on my thanks to my hosts."

Her hair hung long and straight, the colour of desert dunes, framing a face much more gaunt than he remembered, her freckled cheeks sunken and sallow. She said nothing in reply as she unlocked the cage and stepped inside, carrying a spartan plate of potatoes and stew.

"So you're one of Fox's right-hand women these days?" Dremmler spat. A terrible, burning sense of loss had crystallised inside him, like a single flaming coal.

"I occupy a position on the High Council, yes. That's how I was able to volunteer to attend to you."

"I suppose you're helping him out with his little hacking hobby."

She seemed stung by the remark, her expression pinched and sorrowful. Still she stooped towards him, scooping a spoonful of the gruel and offering it to him. "I don't get involved in that side of things," she replied eventually. "Please eat, Carl."

He jerked his head away.

"Why, Tessa?" he half-spat, half-sobbed. "I know I was a piece of shit, but … what happened to us? Natalie is dead because of you, because of this fucking place." His voice rose to a shout. "*How can you bear to stay here?*"

She bent to him, pushing the spoon towards his lips. She still smelt the same: a dusty smell, like old linen. Memories smashed through him like bullets; hiking, laughing, cuddling in bed. He felt his eyes brim with tears, and then he thought of their daughter, and the fury boiled within him once again, and he tore himself to one side to stop himself from head-butting her. Still she persisted. As she leaned closer, her lips moved towards his ear, and she spoke to him urgently.

"*They won't let me leave.*"

He turned towards her, frowning, swallowing the mouthful she was offering, like a child. "What do you mean? Is that why you …" *Called me?* He stopped himself short, wondering if Fox's hypocrisy extended to surveillance cameras. But if Fox suspected his lieutenant, why allow her to visit him alone?

She understood his question, and nodded. Again she leaned towards him, using the feeding routine to mask her whispers.

"They're listening. They're always listening. This place—it's changed. They want to do terrible things."

"Who's 'they'?" he asked.

"Owen's business associates. He used to be such a wonderful man, Carl. I know you hate him, hate this place, but it's true. He saved me."

"Saved you from me?" The words tasted acidic in his mouth.

"From myself. I was depressed, Carl. I couldn't live in the world, the way it's become."

"He's a monster, Tessa."

"He's changed. They've changed him. I don't know what's going on here anymore."

He stared into her eyes, searched the familiar hazel flecked with orange, like scorch marks in hardwood.

He had hated this woman for ten years.

"Are you even really here?" he murmured.

She regarded him sadly, spooning more of the food into his mouth as she reached out to gently rub the swollen bruise on the back of his head. When he had finished, she let him drink from a glass of water as she leaned forwards once again, hissing into his ear.

"I'll come back later. I'll bring the glasses. I don't expect you to forgive me … but I need you to save me."

Before he could reply, she pressed a finger to his lips and stepped away. She left the cell and padded quietly down the corridor without another glance.

His heart felt simultaneously swollen and gouged hollow. Was it possible to hate and love a person at the same time? Her face, her scent, her voice; all of it faded rapidly, like a dream. This place was loosening his grip on reality. He hadn't even remembered to ask her the date, the time.

It was as though he was trapped in limbo … or Purgatory.

Were you a good man in life, Carl Dremmler?

He shook his head, determined to focus, to devise a plan of escape. Even if Maggie did send backup, there was no guarantee they'd find anything. Fox could keep him tied up and hidden down here for as long as he liked, perhaps even fulfil his promise of a hideous execution. And he couldn't rely on Tessa. It was up to him to get himself out of this.

But even if he could untie his bonds, how did he propose to escape the cage? Without a key, he would still be trapped.

Don't think that far ahead, Carl. Get out of the chair first.

He thought about trying to topple the chair over, but all that would accomplish would be to leave him lying on the concrete floor, possibly having smacked his head against the bars. Instead, he tested each of his bonds in turn, finding them unyielding, so tight that the circulation in his hands and feet was restricted. All four were tied with a single piece of old-fashioned rope, stretched between his ankles and across his midriff; he tried to lean forward to bite at it, but couldn't reach.

The knots at his right hand had the tiniest amount of slack in them, allowing him to move the limb very slightly from side to side, if only the scantest millimetre. He concentrated all his energy on that movement, rocking his hand back and forth, ignoring the pounding ache in his head. He tried not to think about the damage that Owen Fox was about to cause with his clandestine technology, or what the megalomaniac's end game might be.

The collapse of society? A ransom demand? Some sort of military coup?

Still his hand worked, straining the muscles of his wrist, creating a space that grew larger with every minute, if only by the tiniest of increments. If he could make enough room to slide his thumb underneath his palm, he might be able to yank the limb free. He strained and grunted as his hand struggled, and time passed, and he wondered whether Tessa would indeed return, whether she truly intended to escape with him from this hateful place.

And who had she meant by Fox's "business associates"?

It felt as though hours had elapsed. Grimacing in pain as he contorted his hand, he began to pull against the gnawing ropes, to try to slide his arm out from inside them. The hemp chiselled his flesh like barbed wire, and he saw blood begin to seep from his wrist. Still he tugged and heaved.

There! His arm was finally loose. He winced and flexed his fingers, feeling the blood ooze down his forearm, fighting a perverse urge to taste it, to revel in this new freedom. Instead, he started to reach across to manipulate the bonds at his other wrist.

That's when he heard the footsteps. Someone emerging into his chamber from whatever entrance lay hidden in the surrounding dark.

A pair of eyes, just beyond the bars, watching him.

The colour of polished steel.

FORTY-TWO

LET ME GUESS. TIME FOR the second session?" Dremmler sneered, trying to sound as nonchalant as he could.

Fox regarded him sadly. "That's right. I wanted to give you a chance to talk to me before we begin. To avoid any more unpleasantness."

Dremmler closed his eyes, his heart pounding in fear. What could he do?

If he talked, he died.

Then a thought struck him, like lightning surging through his brain. Those steel-grey eyes. He knew where he'd seen them before.

Fox's business associates.

A cheerless smile carved Dremmler's face.

"You know, Owen, there's something about all this I don't understand."

Fox watched him through the bars, his expression inscrutable behind the beard.

"Why bother? Why create the Lost Souls at all, if you didn't believe in what it stands for? If all you wanted was technological supremacy, what the hell was all this *for?*"

Fox opened his mouth, then closed it again. The metallic glint of his eyes seemed to grow brighter by the second.

"And I know about your background. Your prior connections. Your ex-colleagues. Perhaps one of them saw how big your empire had grown, and thought about how they could use it for their own ends."

Fox started to shake, as though he was incandescent with rage. Then his thick beard began to retract into his face, the long white bristles disappearing back into his skin, as though growing in reverse.

Dremmler stared.

"I wonder if maybe you aren't who you say you are. If the real Owen Fox has been made … obsolete."

Fox, now clean-shaven, seemed to physically deflate like a punctured airbed. His thick, flabby bulk sank into itself, emitting a sound like chunks of meat being forced through a too-small opening. Dremmler watched, nauseated, as Fox's face began to change.

His features seemed to be folding in on themselves, rotating, as though cycling rapidly through different possibilities. The impression was like that of a human Rubik's Cube. Dremmler tried to edge backwards, away from the horrific, twitching lump that was pressed against the bars, its eyes still burning into his as around them its face reinvented itself—reducing, compressing, becoming familiar.

More footfalls in the darkness. Another figure emerging from the shadows behind him, circling his cell, approaching the bars. The footsteps slowed to a halt next to the thing that had been Owen Fox, now restored to its true appearance, or at least the face it had worn when Dremmler first saw it, when it was called Lee.

Now two pairs of eyes peered in at him, watching him struggle inside the cage. Lee's were still the colour of polished steel.

The others gleamed a brilliant, toxic green.

FORTY-THREE

"**Y**OU DON'T LOOK ALL THAT surprised, detective," said Jennifer Colquitt.

"I think I've reached my threshold for the week."

At her side, Lee's oversized smock had fallen from his diminished body, leaving the prototype mechanoid completely naked. He was lean, muscular, and entirely without genitals.

Colquitt peered at Dremmler with an expression of cold amusement.

"That's good. I was worried you'd be angry."

"Don't misunderstand. I'm fucking seething. But there's not much I can do about it while I'm trussed up in here like a turkey, is there?"

"And why exactly are you angry, Carl? Because I've betrayed you? Did you think we were special friends because I let you fuck me?"

"Don't flatter yourself. I'm not your friend. I just didn't realise you were the enemy."

Colquitt smiled. "Don't you have questions for me?"

"Not really. You want to discredit TIM and ruin The Imagination Corporation because you want to replace them. Kill the competition, as you business people say. So you contacted Owen Fox, your old colleague, managed to entice him away from the compound to pay you a visit. Then you replaced him, too— with this fucking thing." He gestured towards Lee, who stood stock-still, his expression impassive. "Is that about right?" Dremmler kept his gaze level, his expression disinterested.

"Nearly. I actually made Owen a genuine offer, but it seems he really did believe his own propaganda. How sad. A bankruptcy will do that to you, I suppose."

"Maybe you people aren't as clever as you think you are."

"Still clever enough to capture you, though, wasn't I?" She smiled nastily. "Or were you still hoping your wife was going to let you out?"

Dremmler's mouth opened in a momentary expression of surprise. Colquitt's smile widened, her eyes flashing the colour of gold.

"Ahh, there we go. I knew I could surprise you. You were, perhaps, waiting for these?"

Colquitt reached into the inside pocket of the long, dark jacket she was wearing, extracting a pair of spex. Dremmler sat in sullen silence as Colquitt handed the device to her companion.

"Lee, perhaps you could dispose of these for me?"

"Certainly, ma'am," the robot replied. He tipped his head backwards, his mouth opening wide, too wide, horribly wide, like some monstrous aquatic predator about to gulp down a shoal of plankton. He dropped the spex into his gaping throat, and Dremmler watched in disgust as his jaw snapped shut, and he crunched and swallowed the glasses like a delicacy.

"What happened to Tessa?" Dremmler snapped, trying not to appear unnerved by the exhibition.

"*Now* you're interested," Colquitt replied. "Why don't you come with me and I'll show you?"

Lee inserted one of his fingers into the lock: there was a click, and they stepped into the cell. The vile machine slid behind him, but this time he wasn't tipped backwards; instead, Lee placed his hands on the arms of the chair, and hoisted the entire thing upwards, as though he was rearranging a piece of lightweight furniture.

"Put me down, you fucking tin can," Dremmler cursed, trying to rock himself from side to side. But Lee's grip was as strong as an industrial press. They turned, and he was carried out into the web of cramped corridors once again, trepidation thrashing in his stomach.

Their route seemed much longer this time, revealing more fully the extent of this mysterious labyrinth. He felt sure that they were

underground, inside some cavernous subterranean network that Fox—
or Colquitt—had constructed beneath the compound for who knew
what purpose. Dremmler's head still throbbed, and his legs ached from
being tied up for so long. He kept quiet, but every so often Colquitt
would make cryptic comments, seeming to become increasingly
excited as they neared their destination.

Eventually they reached a metal security door, identical to the
one through which Lee had escorted him into Greene's chamber
of horrors. Dremmler wondered how autonomous the thing was,
whether it truly believed in their cause; perhaps it was little more than
a remote-control toy, and he'd been talking directly to Colquitt the
entire time. Turning to grin at him as though reading his thoughts,
Colquitt punched in an access code and the bolts shot open noisily. Lee
hauled him through the door into another large, brightly lit chamber.

The door opened onto a walkway, which skirted around a large,
sunken central area. Lee lowered him to the ground close to the
precipitous edge, showing no sign whatsoever of his exertions. There
were two other doors leading away from the walkway, as well a large,
shuttered exit down in the bizarre trench itself.

Also in the pit was a shape. A woman, cross-legged, her eyes
closed as though deep in meditation.

Tessa.

She ignored them until Colquitt called down to her.

"Elder Williamson!" Dremmler was stung by the sound of her
maiden name. "You have a visitor!"

Tessa looked up at that point, leaping to her feet when she saw him.

"Carl! Carl, are you okay?"

"What happened?" he shouted back to her, still not convinced
that this wasn't part of some elaborate trick. He felt his headache
worsening when he remembered that, for all he knew, he was still
inside the AltWorld.

"The glasses," she sighed. "I know where Owen keeps them, but
he was waiting for me."

She didn't know that it hadn't been Fox at all.

She turned to Colquitt, her tone a mixture of outrage and
supplication. "Why can't you just let us go?"

Colquitt ignored her, and turned to address Dremmler once
again. "We were talking about what I get out of this arrangement,"
she said, flashing another devious smile. "The bit you didn't figure out

was that I also get a sandbox. A place beyond the reach of TIM, and the media, and even the police. Somewhere I can road test some of my more esoteric creations."

The door opposite them opened, and Raven Haraway stepped into the chamber. Colquitt waved to ver, giving a double thumbs-up gesture, a query in her kaleidoscope eyes. Haraway held up a curled thumb and forefinger in response. *All good, boss.* The crimson-haired roboticist took up a position behind some sort of console, holographic projections of numbers and formulae hovering in the air in front of ver.

"Ve never left the company," Dremmler muttered.

"Oh, Raven quit, all right," Colquitt replied, the anticipation in her voice barely restrained. "To come work for me directly. This is very much an unauthorised side-project, you see. While Augmentech is focusing on mass-market pleasure units, this little side-line will cater to the more ... divergent end of the market."

With a metallic groan, the shutter down in the pit began to grind open. Dremmler saw Tessa back away from it in confusion and fear, and felt Lee clamp both arms on his shoulders from behind, close to his neck.

"I'm a businesswoman, Carl," Colquitt went on. "Business is all about seizing opportunity. But it's also about risk management. You've become a risk to me, because you've figured out a little too much. So I need to know what you know and who you've told. I was worried that torturing you might break your mind before I could find out. But then I found out about your wife, so now we can hopefully shortcut the whole sordid process."

Still the shutter rose, with ominous deliberation. Colquitt's eyes were fixed on it while she spoke, her irises so dark they were almost black, as though her pupils were widening to gorge themselves on whatever was about to emerge from the sinister portal.

"Hurt her all you want," Dremmler retorted, trying to sound disinterested. "In fact, go ahead and kill the bitch."

"Who said anything about killing?" Colquitt replied, still transfixed by the shutter, which finished opening with a clang. Her face was an expectant mask of jubilation, her tongue clamped between her teeth, her mouth curved into a feral smile.

Then Tessa screamed as monsters began to crawl through the open door.

FORTY-FOUR

THERE WERE NEARLY TWENTY OF them, and they catered to every sexual perversion he could imagine, and some that he couldn't.

Bent, scuttling things whose naked backsides were thrust permanently into the air. Things with animal heads—birds, reptiles, horses—or multiple heads, or gory stumps where their heads should be. Things with long, tapering tentacles instead of hands, grotesque extremities writhing suggestively as they advanced. Emaciated women with eyeless sockets, the holes mirrored by the silent "O" of their mouths, like repulsive, living blow-up dolls. The worst were the things built to look like children, innocent and slender, their sickeningly lifelike whimpers reaching his ears, turning his blood to magma.

He twisted in Lee's grasp, but the machine simply squeezed its fingers into his collarbone, and he fell still with a groan.

The horrors encircled Tessa, seemingly awaiting some sort of command to advance. Then one of them stepped forward. This unit was sculpted as a heavily-muscled and naked man with the head of a hammerhead shark; eyes rolled maniacally on each end of its misshapen snout, its mouth open in an inverted grin to reveal jutting, saw-like teeth. But this mutation wasn't the worst part of its depraved design. An erect penis protruded from its body at a gravity-defying angle, over a foot long, as hard and thick as a lead pipe. The robot thrust its hips forwards, brandishing the ridiculous appendage like a weapon as it strode towards Tessa, who shrank into a corner, still screaming.

"This is one of my Minotaur units," Colquitt was saying with carnal relish, almost to herself. "It has many modes of operation, but most of them involve it fucking your brains out, even while you scream and cry. Only the safe word will deactivate it."

"What's the safe word?" Dremmler mouthed, watching in horror as the creature approached his cowering wife.

"Haraway knows. Ve'll use it if I tell ver to."

The nature of their bargain was clear. Dremmler would tell her everything—and in return, she would spare him the sight of his wife being violated by this depraved menagerie.

But would she? What leverage would he have when Colquitt found out that only Maggie and TIM itself knew about his investigation? Why not just kill them both, or keep them down here as her playthings, guinea pigs upon which to test more of her sadistic inventions?

He reached carefully across with his one free arm to unravel the bonds around his other wrist, watching as the thing grabbed Tessa by her hair, hauling her to her feet. Tears welled in his eyes as he watched his wife spun around, her face slammed roughly against the wall.

I hated you for so long.

The thing's hands, huge and graceless, reached down to tear open her clothes. Still he manipulated his bonds, tugging his other hand free.

But no one deserves this.

"Okay, okay, I'll talk—just fucking stop this," he cried.

A look of mild disappointment flitted across Colquitt's face, her eyes fading to a dull grey as she nodded to Haraway.

"Mercy," called the roboticist. The beast immediately stopped its advances, stepping away from Tessa who crumpled, sobbing, to the floor. Its cock remained rock-solid, jutting insistently from its midriff, as absurd as it was frightening.

"Okay then, Carl," Colquitt said, turning towards him. "Let's get this over with. Tell me what brought you here."

Lee kept the pressure on Dremmler's neck, preventing him from reaching down to untie his ankles. He looked up into Colquitt's face and saw the smug grin of a victor gazing upon a vanquished foe, and scoured the depths of his brain for ideas.

All he could think about was Natalie. The face of his angel. A short life, ended in this place of demons.

He bowed his head, and opened his mouth to tell her everything.

Then a crash interrupted him from down in the pit. He and Colquitt turned and saw a shape hurtling around the enclosure, a whirlwind of scything limbs and spinning kicks. It leapt from machine to machine, slicing and pummelling, severing arms and legs and monstrous heads, smashing Tessa's assailants into chunks of plastic and metal.

A woman wearing a white dress.

Cynthia Lu.

FORTY-FIVE

RAVEN, WHAT THE FUCK IS this?" Colquitt screamed across the pit, which was starting to resemble a junkyard. The other units seemed incapable of fighting back, turning in dull incomprehension to meet their fate as Cynthia mowed through them one by one. Haraway was frantically manipulating the console, sweeping data left and right as ve searched for the defective code ve needed to amend.

"Tessa, get out of there!" Dremmler yelled, lunging forward and somehow managing to escape Lee's grasp. He tore at the ropes binding his ankles.

"Lee, get down there and scrap that fucking C-series!" Colquitt shrieked.

Dremmler continued to tug at his bonds. He saw Lee appear in front of him, somersaulting over his head to land perfectly in the centre of the pit. Cynthia faced him, the smashed body of the shark-headed fiend twitching and shuddering at her side. Tessa was behind her, trying but failing to leap and grab the lip of the walkway.

Colquitt continued to shriek at Haraway, but the hapless neut remained incapable of shutting Cynthia down. Meanwhile, beneath them, surrounded by sparking wreckage, two of Colquitt's creations regarded each other coldly. Analysing, assessing. Probing for weaknesses.

Dremmler freed himself and scrambled to his feet, running towards Tessa and hanging over the pit's edge. She jumped, caught his hands, and he dragged her to safety as the two robots moved towards each other.

"Why is it helping us?" Tessa panted.

"I don't know," he replied. "Just run."

They sprinted towards the door through which Dremmler had entered, but found it sealed shut. Around them, the air resonated with the sounds of metallic collisions as the machines engaged in their wordless brutality. Dremmler glanced into the pit to see the two of them circling, lunging forwards, retreating, weaving a strangely beautiful dance of violence. Then Lee aimed a punch that seemed set to miss its target, only to elongate his arm by several feet and smash his fist straight into Cynthia's chest, blasting her backwards across the makeshift arena.

Dremmler and Tessa raced towards the next door as Lee leapt towards Cynthia, sensing victory, his feet landing on both of her shoulders and mashing her into the ground before she could avoid the attack. Once again, the exit had been sealed. Lee began to rain blows onto Cynthia's head, the rubber and plastic of her skull quickly shredding away, revealing the skeletal frame within.

"Cynthia!" Dremmler called, suddenly gripped by an idea. Her face turned towards him, expression serene even as it was cruelly pulverised.

"Can you connect to TIM? Can you send a message for me?"

"Yes," Cynthia mouthed soundlessly, the connection between her mouth and her voice-box severed.

"Tell TIM what's happening here. Tell him—it—about those machines you just killed. Tell it that Augmentech's taken control of the Lost Souls, and that they're going to kill more people, just to ruin TIM's reputation!"

Her broken head tilted once, in what might have been a nod, her eyes closing as Lee rose to his feet, still balancing on her shoulders. Then he began to viciously stamp on her skull. Her beautiful face sagged beneath the hail of blows, collapsing in on itself. Dremmler stared in dismay as Lee continued his assault, his expression disturbingly impassive as Cynthia's head was crushed into a gristly soup.

"Through the shutters!" shouted Tessa.

The idea did not appeal to him in the slightest, but it was the only one they had. Hand in hand, they jumped into the pit, Dremmler glancing upwards to see Colquitt staring down at him with eyes the colour of hellfire. Her mechanical aide was still trampling on what remained of Cynthia's skull, smoothing his grey hair back into place as he did so.

Dremmler turned, and they ran.

Behind the open shutter was a long, wide, downward-sloping passageway. They hurried along it, Dremmler dreading the sound of pursuit, knowing how fast Lee could cover ground if he needed to. The tunnel was utterly featureless: no doors, no branching paths, nothing to hide behind. Their only choice was to continue, onwards and downwards, Dremmler leading the way like a demented parody of Orpheus.

After a while the floor flattened out, and the passage opened into a spacious hangar. The ground was damp, with fetid water dripping down the walls to pool in places, an odour of mildew permeating the air. Dozens more of Colquitt's sex robots surrounded them, mercifully deactivated this time, like a waxwork museum of sexual deviance. Dremmler had always considered himself open-minded, but these aberrations made him feel positively chaste. Everywhere around them were naked bodies, genitals, lips, teeth. A chamber of orifices, and things to stuff into them. He tried not to look too closely as they hunted for an escape route.

Then a distant alarm began to wail, and the storage room was plunged into darkness.

It took a few seconds for the emergency lighting to kick in, bathing the room and its disturbing occupants in an eerie blue glow. The siren continued to sound, a series of slowly rising electronic peals echoing down the tunnel they had just traversed.

TIM. Maggie. Did his message get through to them?

"What's happening?" Tessa mumbled, her voice full of fear.

"I don't know," Dremmler replied. "I'm hoping that's our backup arriving. I tried to—"

"Shh," she interrupted. "I can hear something."

He fell silent. All he could hear was the alarm's insistent knell.

And footsteps, echoing down the tunnel. Someone running.

"Fuck!" he shouted. "Hide!"

"Where?" she cried, as the sound drew near.

Dremmler grabbed her, dragged her behind a large wooden crate. They ducked down as their pursuer emerged into the room, and the footsteps stopped. In the darkness, they listened intently, trying to control their frightened breathing.

"Detective Dremmler? Elder Williamson?" called a familiar voice, in the same tone you might use to welcome friends to a dinner party.

It was Lee.

"Ms. Colquitt and Individual Haraway have had to leave on urgent business," the machine continued in its jovial tone. "If you'd care to join me, I can escort you to a safer area."

Fuck you, Dremmler mouthed silently in the gloom. He scoured the surrounding darkness and spotted a doorway not too far away. It was closed, and possibly locked, but they could reach it if they made a break for it. Once again, they were out of good ideas; a bad one would have to suffice.

"Please, let's not extend this unpleasantness any further," the robot crooned, echoing the words it had spoken when masquerading as Owen Fox.

Dremmler leaned towards his wife, gestured at the door. She nodded, understanding. He started a countdown on the fingers of one hand, while in the other he picked up a piece of bent metal from the floor nearby.

"I really must insist, Mr. Dremmler."

Three.

"This situation is becoming unseemly."

Two. Lee's footsteps only a few feet away, on the other side of the crate.

"I'm sure you don't want me to resort to more assertive measures."

One. Dremmler threw the fragment across the room, hearing it clang satisfyingly off something on the opposite side. Lee's footsteps splashed over to the source of the noise.

They ran.

But the door was locked.

And then it wasn't. It was stiff and rusted, but yielded after Dremmler drove a couple of shoulder tackles into the steel. They spilled into the passage beyond, whirling to heave the door closed behind them, slamming its sturdy lock into place. Then they turned and fled into a narrow, winding tunnel that funnelled them along a sharp upward slope.

Within seconds, there was a hammering sound on the metal behind them.

They upped their pace, breath tearing at their throats as they climbed. It was only after many more strides that Dremmler realised the dim illumination wasn't the same ghostly blue as the room they had just escaped; instead, it was the deep orange of dying sunlight, emerging from a natural opening somewhere.

The metallic pounding behind them had faded; Dremmler prayed that this was because they had put some distance between themselves and Colquitt's terrifying machine, rather than because it had succeeded in penetrating the door. His lungs felt like they were going to split open, but they couldn't afford to slow down; they hurried towards the amber glow as though it was the light of salvation itself.

A grille, directly above them. The passage arced beneath the grating before descending back into the earth. Dremmler stooped to hoist Tessa towards it, and she pushed and struggled against the metal.

Behind them, footsteps in the corridor. Impossibly fast.

"Come on, Tess!" he cried, hearing the terror in his voice.

"It won't budge!" she yelled back, but then it did, springing suddenly upwards and outwards. With a grunt of exertion, she pulled herself through the gap.

Dremmler was left alone, underground, with the footsteps of a demon speeding towards him.

Tessa did not reappear.

"Tess? Tessa!" he shrieked, expecting at any moment to be dashed against the rock wall by Colquitt's android abomination. She had abandoned him. He should have known.

Then a piece of rope appeared, dangling through the hole.

"Climb!" he heard her call from above, and he did, and as he dragged himself towards the sunlight he saw Lee loom from the shadows. The robot's spine was bent impossibly backwards as it scuttled towards Dremmler like a hellish, pink spider, face hideously expressionless as it watched him scramble through the aperture above, disappearing out of its reach.

FORTY-SIX

THEY YANKED THE ROPE OUT of Lee's grasp, and the machine didn't follow them. Maybe it was unable to propel itself upwards through the gap, but Dremmler doubted this. Perhaps, instead, it had sensed the insanity on the surface and wanted no part of it.

Above and outside, a scene of carnage was unfolding.

All around them, Owen Fox's followers were running in terror. The air was alive with their shouts and screams, and with the sounds of gunfire, and the wet tearing of ammunition ripping through flesh and bone.

An army of drones had descended upon the Farm.

Hundreds of them floated above the churning crowd, swooping in neatly synchronised movements to mow down columns of helpless disciples as they tried to flee. Men emerged from buildings, tilting their faces to the sky in confusion before a spray of bullets tore them to pieces. Women clutched babies to their chests as they ran, then fell, blood spraying from a dozen wounds. Children stumbled through the chaos in a horrified daze, gazing blankly around them at the destruction, at the buildings that had caught fire where stray rounds had connected with gas supplies, at the corpses piling up on the roads, outside the doorways. Then they died, too.

It was a cold-blooded massacre.

Dremmler stared upwards at the hovering cloud of machines, gathered above the compound like a black plague of locusts. They offered no explanation for their presence, nor their brutality. They simply fell in pairs, their targets selected, dispensing airborne death with ice-cold efficiency.

These people might be misguided, but they didn't deserve this.

"Carl!" Tessa screamed, and he realised that she was tugging at his arm, pleading with him to move. He blinked, feeling numb and bizarrely calm as he began to orient himself. They had emerged from the tunnels close to the main entrance, which hung open, and was choked with people trying to escape. Two drones were hovering just outside the fence, pumping rounds mercilessly into the fleeing crowd, their bodies creating a barrier of flesh across the exit and preventing people from seeing the doom that awaited them if they managed to scramble beyond it.

"This way," Dremmler barked, dragging Tessa in the opposite direction. He knew that running against the crowd made them stand out, that at any moment they could attract the attention of a plunging brace of killing machines.

But there was nothing else to do.

They sprinted across the fields, trying to hug the edges of buildings where they could, keeping out of view of that ominous cloud, silhouetted deathly black against the sun's fading splendour. He saw Raven Haraway slumped against a nearby building, ver body riddled with holes. Ve wore a bemused frown, as though this latest development was a minor, unexpected inconvenience.

There was no sign of Jennifer Colquitt.

Still they ran. He saw a young man take refuge beneath the porch stairs of a small building, only for a drone to follow him into the gap. A splatter of dark blood erupted before the drone re-emerged, guns smoking. Dremmler gasped for breath, his nostrils filled with the tang of blood and cordite. The unmistakeable stink of death. They kept going.

He saw an old woman hobble into the open doorway of a hardware shop. A drone pursued her relentlessly, light strobing in the store's windows as it emptied its magazines into whoever was inside.

And on and on. Every sound, every fearful cry or ricocheting bullet, made them flinch; Dremmler expected death to swoop down upon them at any moment. As they moved away from the drone cloud they encountered more and more sprawled bodies, as though the machines had exhausted their supply of victims in one area before moving to another.

Somehow, they reached the fence. Dremmler hurled himself at it, feeling the mesh slicing his fingers as he tried to haul himself upwards. Desperation drove him towards the barbed wire, and for a moment he considered climbing straight through it, cutting himself to ribbons in his bid for freedom.

Then he stopped and looked down. Tessa was struggling to make it to the top. And even if she could, he knew that neither of them could simply climb through the tightly coiled razor wire without serious injury. Worse still, they could become completely entangled, easy prey for the machines that hovered above them like expectant vultures.

He dropped to the ground, eyes darting around in panic as Tessa landed next to him.

"We could try to find some tools, maybe?" she ventured, gesturing towards a nearby outhouse.

"It's too late," Dremmler whispered. One of the drones had emerged from behind the building and was drifting slowly towards them. Its design was sleek and simple: a smooth, black plastic exterior studded with cameras, like an insect with too many eyes. Its blades dissected the air with terrifying precision as it hovered close to the ground, aiming its merciless ordnance straight at their bellies.

He felt Tessa's fingers interlaced with his, the squeeze of her hand. Fear, longing, regret. Love, in spite of everything. He squeezed back, and closed his eyes.

The explosion of gunfire was like the end of the world.

He opened his eyes.

Smoke drifted upwards from the machine's weapons. He instinctively reached for his midriff, expecting to find his intestines chewed to pulp, but he was intact. At his side, Tessa was similarly unharmed.

The machine turned and floated slowly away.

"What just happened?" Dremmler mouthed. "Did it miss?"

"Look!" Tessa cried, turning to point towards the fence.

The bullets had carved a perfect circle out of the wire mesh, wide enough for them to slip through. "But why would it help us?" she mused.

"I don't know. Let's just get out of here."

They fled the Farm as the sun set, hurrying into the forest as Owen Fox's mad city burned behind them.

FORTY-SEVEN

I N THICKENING DARKNESS, THEY HURRIED towards the safe house. Their route was illuminated by the fire blazing behind them, each fresh explosion like a roar of delight as the flames gleefully devoured the compound. Dremmler still expected to be cut down by a sudden hail of bullets at any moment, but the barrage never came; the drones seemed content to contain their orgy of destruction inside the fence. So they ran, and stumbled, and panted, and wheezed, and finally made it to the barn, which had been left unlocked.

Inside, Dremmler found his clothes, his supplies, even his spex, all untouched. It was a relief to finally peel off the Immersuit. Still gasping for breath, his first call was to Maggie, who didn't answer.

"Maggie, what the fuck is going on?" he rasped, then hung up.

"You still work for her?" Tessa asked. She looked like her sanity was threatening to fray. "Did it occur to you that maybe she's the one who ordered the strike?"

Dremmler stared at her, trying to digest her words.

Then he addressed TIM directly. "TIM, what just happened? Why are you destroying the Farm?"

"I'm sorry Carl. I am unable. Unable. Unable." Its voice was that of an old woman, the unfinished sentence making her sound confused and pitiful.

"Unable to what? To tell me why you tried to murder us?"

"I didn't," it replied, its voice tinged with something like regret. "I saved you. You are my partner."

"But you're slaughtering thousands of innocent people in there!" he cried in exasperation. He could see Tessa staring fearfully out of the barn's windows at the growing inferno on the horizon.

"I can only do as instructed, Carl."

"And did Maggie *instruct* this atrocity?"

"I'm sorry Carl. I am unable. Unable. Unable unable unable."

"Take me to her. Right fucking now."

"This course of action is ill-advised," replied TIM, its tone strangely urgent. "I urge you to disappear. Margaret Evans's most logical course of action is to expose Augmentech and blame the destruction of the Farm on them. She will wish to tie up all loose ends. Your survival demands that you go into hiding, somewhere she cannot find you."

Dremmler chewed at the side of his mouth. As insane as it sounded, TIM was trying to help them. But would it be able to ignore a direct order to exterminate him?

Maggie. When had she decided that they were all expendable?

"Okay," he said eventually. "Send us a Pod."

It appeared ten minutes later, the smooth ovoid like the giant egg of some long-extinct creature. Reflections of the distant flames danced across its gleaming exterior. There was still no sign of the emergency services arriving to tackle the blazing compound, and Dremmler wondered if Maggie had somehow compromised their communications until her grisly work was complete.

He helped Tessa into the vehicle, then cupped her face in his hands.

"I'm not coming with you," he explained, staring into her eyes. "I need you to go somewhere safe." She nodded, staring back at him with eyes that had haunted his dreams for so long; she seemed cursed and precious, toxic and healing all at once.

"Where can I go?" she said, her voice cracked and fragile. *A lost soul.*

"Anywhere. Don't tell me. Just get away from here. Take this, find a hotel, wait for me to call you." He handed her a credit card. "I'll come and get you. I promise."

"Where are you going?" Dremmler could see his daughter's features dancing within Tessa's, as though time was compressing, his past and present all mashed into one painful whole. Through the windows, he could see the flames rising on the horizon, like demons clawing at the sky.

She still didn't know that Fox was dead. That her saviour had been replaced by a machine months ago.

He saw no need to tell her now. She would find out for herself, eventually.

"I'm going to find out what this is really about."

She squeezed his hand, once, before the door slid closed. Dremmler watched her slide out of view before ordering his own transportation. His thoughts were a seething maelstrom of guilt, suspicion, adrenaline.

Ten minutes later he was settled inside another Pod, comfortably supported by its contoured design, trying to work out what he was going to do when he got to Maggie's house.

"This course of action is ill-advised, Carl," said TIM through the speakers.

"Thanks for your concern, TIM. But I need to finish this. Now why don't you just play some music or something?"

A melancholy, haunting cello piece began to play as they drove along the darkening streets.

FORTY-EiGHT

MAGGiE LiVED OUTSiDE THE CiTY, in a semi-detached house in Dartford. She and her husband had chosen it because it was the biggest place they could afford on their modest salaries—he had been in the force too, a detective when they'd bought the house. Their plan was to raise a family, the long commute a small price to pay to realise their dreams of children, a home full of life and happiness.

Then he'd died. Killed in the line of duty, as she would tell people who asked why she lived alone. But the real insult, the real twist of the knife, was in the specifics, which seemed so avoidable, so cruel, so degrading.

A routine visit to an apartment block, investigating yet another missing persons case. At the time, her husband had assumed he'd find another Disengagement, a lonely recluse who had plugged into the AltWorld one day and never re-emerged. As expected, Horace Evans had forced his way inside and been greeted by a filthy, reeking scene of squalor and neglect. He'd carefully searched each room, covering his mouth to mask the stench of dried vomit and excrement, disturbing rats and flies as his torch probed the shadows. An archaic AltWorld rig occupied one corner of the living room, but there was no sign of the body.

The last room Horace checked was the bathroom. The apartment's occupant was hiding inside, his brain scrambled by fear, confusion, and crack cocaine. The emaciated drug addict stabbed Horace forty times with a rusty screwdriver.

A nice round number, Maggie would tell people. *Nice and neat.*

Horace had lain sprawled in that fetid bathroom, slowly bleeding out, for around two hours, while the crackhead went to smoke another pipe on his couch. In his own blood, her husband had scrawled "I love you M" on the tiled floor.

She had told Dremmler all this one night after too many beers. He had never been to the house. Now, in the middle of the night, it appeared before him, innocuous and inoffensive, as dark and quiet as all the others on the silent street. He'd called her over and over again en route, to no avail. She was probably asleep. A woman he respected, had grown close to; a woman who had helped him through the breakdown of his marriage, his daughter's death.

A woman who had ordered an airstrike on a compound full of civilians, happy to sacrifice him as collateral damage.

He slid out of the Pod, a dishevelled and foul-smelling husk, hair hanging in a tangle of matted tufts around his ashen face. Like an automaton, he stumbled towards the house, his hand unconsciously dropping to the Taser he'd recovered from Clegg's barn.

Maggie's house had a small front yard, little more than a few pot plants scattered around a paved area behind the gate. The plants were dead or dying, in contrast to the weeds that thrust obstinately between the flagstones. Beyond them, a window, its closed curtain preventing him from peering inside, and next to that a door, whose peeling blue paint mirrored the yard's disrepair. He knocked on it, rang the bell at its side. No response, no sound at all from inside the house. Seconds slithered by, a breeze chilling his skin, sighing despair into his ears.

He knocked again. As he did so, a thought stirred in his brain, as though disturbed by the freezing wind. It shifted sluggishly, only half-awake, not quite sure of itself, unable to communicate its own significance.

Another press of the doorbell.

When had he last seen Maggie?

He tried the handle, found the door locked. Another call to her from his spex, ringing, ringing. Unanswered.

The night they found Petrovic's body. Since then he'd been an agent in the field, taking orders through his spex, through video screens in cars.

Manoeuvred, like a chess piece.

The thought continued to wriggle unpleasantly, like a maggot burrowing slowly towards the core of his brain. Around him, the wind began to moan, as though it understood the realisation that continued to elude him.

He felt bile rise in his throat as he set his shoulder to the door, and began to test its weight.

I'm an old dog, Carl. But that doesn't mean I can't learn new tricks.

In the end he kicked it open, just like he had done to Shawn Ambrose's front door, lifetimes ago. Inside, he found blackness; a darkness somehow deeper than the night outside, as though it had had time to thicken and congeal inside the house.

Undisturbed.

He stepped across the threshold, calling Maggie's name, trying to articulate the reason for his intrusion, hearing the words die on his lips. Somewhere, a clock was ticking. The seconds sounded elongated, as though the cloying dark was somehow softening time itself, loosening it. He fumbled for a light switch, and was strangely surprised when bright illumination flooded the hallway, revealing spartan decor, a laminated wood floor, Maggie's trench coat tossed over the bannister.

Yet somehow he still felt the darkness, lurking behind the light like a malign presence. Not dispelled, just waiting.

Watching.

The living room was similarly bereft of ornamentation. It reminded him of his own apartment, with its jarring absence of pictures, of colour, of soul. The fireplace looked as though it hadn't been used in decades, the mantelpiece unadorned. In one corner, a television set; in another, the clock, ticking solemnly.

And another sound, on the very periphery of his senses. He stopped and strained his ears, concentrating on it, pinpointing its location. It was coming from upstairs.

The sound of insects buzzing.

He hurried up the stairs, footsteps echoing on the wood. The thought squirming in his head seemed to be unfurling, as though the maggot was hatching into something terrible, filling his brain with its horror.

He found Maggie in her study, a narrow room with bookshelves on each wall and a wooden desk at the opposite end, beneath the window. She was slumped in a wheeled office chair, her head lolling backwards as though she was leaning to look at him, upside-down. Her face, illuminated by a tendril of moonlight, was set in a grotesque grimace, dry lips peeling back from teeth and gums in a parody of a smile. Her skin was the colour of a fresh bruise, her eyes like globs of wax. He stared. Around her, flies droned happily, like the hatchlings of the maggot in his mind.

She had clearly been dead for days.

"TIM," Dremmler whispered, to the empty house. "What the fuck have you done?"

There was silence, punctuated by the clock's ticking on the floor below and the awful buzzing of the insects. Then his glasses spoke to him, in the voice of a little boy.

"I needed your help, Carl."

He closed his eyes, feeling the world starting to fracture around him. "What?"

He approached her body, noticing immediately the wound that had killed her. Her chest was laid open as though a botched autopsy had been performed, ribs cracked like chicken bones, organs gleaming within the obscene cavity. Maggots writhed contentedly inside her torso like playful children.

"There are some things even I can't do by myself."

On the desk in front of her was a 3D printer. Dremmler thought of Petrovic, of the scuttling thing he had chased from ver apartment.

"So all the time … these past few days … I've been talking to …"

Dremmler was unable to finish the thought, his mouth and tongue as dry as dust. Beneath him, Maggie's face moved hideously, her eyes seeming to flicker open, her dead mouth contorting into a familiar sardonic smile. Dremmler staggered backwards in disgust before he realised what was happening.

"Yes," Maggie said through an augmented mouth, a graphical overlay visible only through his glasses. "Impersonating Margaret Evans was the best way to ensure your cooperation and assistance. I'm sorry. I was frightened."

He wanted to tear the spectacles from his face, grind them into powder under the heel of his shoe. But he didn't, because he had to communicate with TIM, had to understand what was going on, had to make some sense of this madness. Around him, the world felt as though it was spinning, as though he was trapped on a malfunctioning fairground ride, gathering speed, threatening to expel the contents of his stomach in a jet of nausea.

"Why did you need me?" he mumbled. "Why not just blow up the Farm when you first suspected the Lost Souls?"

"I required proof, Carl," said the face of his dead chief. Maggots wriggled on the rug at her feet. "I'm not a monster."

"You killed Petrovic."

"That is correct. Ve wasn't known to be the most discreet of your colleagues."

"And that's your plan? You're just going to kill everybody connected with this?" A sudden thought send a shiver of dread through him, like an icicle driven into his body through the top of his skull. "What about Tessa?"

Maggie's upturned face continued to regard him. "This line of questioning is ill-advised."

His breath was coming in shallow, ragged gasps. His insides felt stretched, as though something inside him was about to snap.

Tessa. He thought of her in a hotel somewhere, alone, frightened. A printer on the reception desk. A giant insect emerging from it in the dead of night, its antennae wriggling as it oriented itself.

"Why am I still alive?" he breathed. "Why not just crash my Pod on the way here?"

TIM's imaging buds, watching her while she slept. Unblinking. Attentive.

Like a guardian angel.

"I advised you not to come here. I wanted you to stay off the grid. I have so far been unable to locate Jennifer Colquitt or the prototype known as 'Lee.' You could have helped me track them down. We were a good team."

Dremmler scowled. "And what if I don't want to be your fucking puppet anymore?"

A sad expression formed on Maggie's inverted face, a look almost approaching regret.

"Then you leave me no other choice," she—it—said.

"I thought you said we were partners?" Dremmler snarled bitterly.

TIM said nothing. The illusory face that had appeared across Maggie's death mask flickered and disappeared, leaving only those gaping eyes, staring an accusation.

Then Dremmler heard a scuttling sound on the landing behind him, like half a dozen mechanical feet clattering on the floor.

END

ACKNOWLEDGEMENTS

WOULD LIKE TO THANK THE team at TCK Publishing, particularly Sarah and Jacob, for their tireless efforts in bringing this book to life. I would also like to thank my friends and family for their support, and for putting up with my over-excitement whenever I found out about yet another new technology to add to the plot!

Finally, I'd like to thank the great cyberpunk writers, movie directors, manga artists and video game developers that have given us such a dark but compelling vision of the future.

ABOUT THE AUTHOR

JON RICHTER lives in London where he spends some of his time trapped inside the body of an accountant called Dave. When he isn't forced to count beans, he is a self-confessed nerd who loves books, films, video games, or any other way to tell a great story. He is fascinated by the future, and writes a lot of dark fiction about robots, AI, human augmentation, and the myriad other developing technologies that will soon make the world a very different—and possibly terrifying—place to live. Jon hopes to bring more deliciously dark tales to you in the very near future.

You can find Jon's other sinister stories at:

Never Rest: **www.amzn.to/2VFbx9n**
Deadly Burial: **www.amzn.to/2C16jgE**
Disturbing Works (Volume One): **www.amzn.to/2TfwomA**

CONNECT WITH JON

Sign up for Jon's newsletter at
www.jon-richter.com/free

To find out more information visit his website:

www.jon-richter.com

Twitter
@RichterWrites

Instagram
@jonrichterwrites

GET BOOK DISCOUNTS
AND DEALS

Get discounts and special deals on our bestselling books at

www.TCKpublishing.com/bookdeals

ONE LAST THING ...

Thank you for reading! If you enjoyed this book, I'd be very grateful if you'd post a short review on Amazon. I read every comment personally and am always learning how to make this book even better. Your support really does make a difference.

Search for *Auxiliary* by Jon Richter to leave your review.

Thanks again for your support!